CONTENTS

MORIAH'S BOYS

RUNNING OUT OF TIME

1

Bahati sat at her desk, staring at the letter in disbelief, again. Her hard work had finally paid off. She was being honored by Moriah James-Panton, a bestselling author, publisher, and world renowned influential black woman. A tear threatened to leave her right eye, but she blinked it away. She was being awarded the Lifetime Achievement Award for her work as a women's rights activist for black women, and for her bestselling book, *I'm Black and I'm Loud!*, a book showcasing the struggles black women have gone through that is attributed to the stereotype of them being loud and angry.

The book talks about everything from slavery, rape, torture, and broken homes, to not being treated fairly when it comes to being paid for the same jobs as those who are nonblack. Her organization, *Voices of Hue Women*, was also being honored for its achievements in making sure the voices of black women are heard. Her organization has shown up for those like Sandra Bland and Breonna Taylor, who still have not received justice for their senseless murders.

Bahati sat back and let out a breath. A

knock at the door interrupted her taking it all in. She knew that this award held weight. She glided to the door and opened it to none other than her best friend, Carter Malone.

"Hey sis!" Carter said, pulling Bahati into an embrace. Bahati hugged her back and then turned to walk towards her couch, plopping down, a dreamy gaze plastered on her face.

"The hell are you on?" Carter asked, closing and locking the door behind her. She sat on the couch across from Bahati and waited for a response from her friend.

"Life is just great, Carter. Perfect even."

"Are you having a stroke?" Carter questioned, a hand to her chest.

"No," Bahati choked out through a laugh. She sat up and stared at Carter in her eyes.

"You're scaring me and creeping me out at the same time. Did you get some devil dick or something?" Bahati laughed louder and harder this time.

"I wish! But no, I am being awarded the Lifetime Achievement Award by none other than Moriah James-Panton."

"What?!" Carter gasped, jumping up from her seat, scurrying to sit by her best friend. "What are you going to wear? You have to look like a whole 7 course meal at the award's ceremony. You'll be on national television, and her sons will be there I'm sure."

"Oh, I didn't think about them being

there," Bahati lied. Of course she had thought about that. The James-Panton men were some of the finest, eligible bachelors in the city. She had had her eye on the eldest, Mehki Panton, for quite some time, but the men always seemed to have a different woman on their arms every time they were seen in the news or at an awards show. Being a women's activist for black women, she knew she couldn't be seen with any of them. It would go against everything she stood for.

"Bahati, why wouldn't they be there? They're her sons, and they attend every event she puts on, as well as every event that has anything to do with them. When is the ceremony?"

"This weekend."

"So that means we are going shopping tomorrow to find you a dress. You have to look just as snatched as I will."

"Who said I had extra tickets, or that I would be bringing you?" Carter cut her eyes at Bahati, evoking a fit of laughter from her.

"Don't play with me. I know you have two extra tickets for me and Kamaria."

"Yeah, I do. So we will go shopping tomorrow then. Oh, what did you come by for?" Bahati asked, remembering that she didn't call her to come over.

"Can't I just drop by to see my best friend and check on her?" Bahati looked at her quizzically.

"No."

"The nerve," Carter pretended to pout.

"Really?"

"Okay, okay. You will never guess who I am representing in my next high profile case." Carter was a big time lawyer in Houston. They knew each other since they were kids, growing up in the foster system together, never being adopted, along with Bahati's sister, Kamaria. When they turned 18, they went to Spelman together, and Bahati was old enough to be her sister's legal guardian, so she brought her along. After college, Bahati and Carter moved back to Houston, where Carter then went to Thurgood Marshall School of Law. After passing the bar, she opened her own law firm. She was now a well-paid and well-known lawyer, taking on high profile clients only.

"Mike Jones," Bahati teased. Carter glared at her.

"Can you be serious for once?"

"I can't. Carter I am way too lit about this award and what it means for my organization." Looking at her friend, Bahati knew that this was important to Carter, whoever it was she was talking about. "Okay, okay. Who?"

"Jerome James-Panton!" she squealed.

"As in Moriah and Jeremy Panton's son? As in the son of the woman who is about to honor me with an award, Jerome James-Panton?" Carter sucked her teeth.

"You're really still going to make this

about you?" Bahati laughed and hugged her friend tightly.

"I'm just joking. But I know this is a big deal and I know this means huge money when you win the case."

"Fuck the money. It's Jerome-fucking-James-Panton!"

Jerome was the second born son of the James-Panton men. Bahati had seen him in passing, but never paid him much attention.

"What does Derwin think about all this?" Derwin was Carter's on again off again fiancé. They were currently on, but Bahati only knew how long that would last.

"He thinks it's cool," she answered, shifting her eyes and looking forward, dodging the look she knew Bahati was giving her.

"Liar! He doesn't know, does he?"

"Ok, fine," Carter confessed. "He doesn't know, but it doesn't matter. It's not like I'm dating the guy or cheating." Bahati shook her head.

"You're asking for trouble."

2

Friday morning, Mehki got dressed in some basketball shorts and sneakers for his morning run. He did this every morning at 7 a.m. Recently on his run, he would see this beautiful chocolate goddess that made his soul swell with a feeling he hadn't felt since…he shook the memory from his mind. He didn't want to think about that and drudge up the negative and toxic memories and feelings of the past.

He drove to Emancipation Park, parked and got out. He stuck his AirPods in his ear and began his four mile jog around Third Ward. *I'm So Hood* was blaring against his eardrums as he rounded the corner on Barbee St. and ran smack into Bahati. He caught her before she fell back.

"Watch where you're going!" she spewed. Once she was upright, he removed his ear buds and asked if she was okay.

"I'm f…" she stopped mid-sentence as she stared up at him, recognition spreading across her face as her eyes bulged. He smiled showing his blindingly, pearly white teeth. He got that look a lot, but it felt different coming from her.

"I'm sorry, I wasn't watching where I was

going," she apologized, her tone changing.

"No, it was my fault. Are you sure you're not hurt?"

"I'm fine, really," she laughed nervously. She cursed herself for looking stupid in front of this fine ass man. He was tall, with smooth mocha skin, muscular shoulders, defined abs with sweat dripping down like a chocolate fountain, thick thighs, a wide neck that she pictured wrapping her arms around, and a sly smile across his juicy lips. Despite the Texas heat, a fire from within began to spread to her lady parts, warming a river that threatened to flow.

"Good, I don't want the Lifetime Achievement Award winner to be injured and miss the awards ceremony." His words jolted her from her trance.

"What?"

"You are Bahati Carver, right?"

"Yes, but how'd you...?"

"I make it my business to know everyone who receives an award at my mother's events, especially if I'm presenting the award." Bahati was stunned. She thought that Moriah would be presenting it.

"You're presenting the award?" she inquired.

"Yeah, was that part left off the letter?" he frowned. Bahati hadn't actually read the whole letter. She was still stuck on the fact that she was being presented with it.

"No, I just forgot," she put on to save face.

"Great. Well, I guess I'll see you Saturday night then," he beamed.

"Yeah, see you then," she spoke quickly, running off to get away from the embarrassment she caused herself. Now she really had to make sure she looked good.

Mehki watched after her. The way her ass bounced sent heat to his growing loins. He looked around to make sure no one was looking.

"Pipe down my friend, we can't be thinking about that just yet," he demanded of his erection. He continued his run and thought about what he was going to wear on Saturday. He needed it to be extra suave.

Once he made it back home and showered, he whipped up some protein waffles and a smoothie. He dialed his mom's number.

"Well, if it isn't my first born," she quipped.

"Hi Mother. How are you?"

"I am fine, now that you have called." Mehki looked at the phone, and shook his head. She was up to something.

"What is it Mother?"

"Why must I want something? Can't I just be happy my son called?"

"Yes, you can, but I don't trust that that is the reason for the show you're putting on," he mentioned, taking another bite of his waffle.

"Tuh, and here I was thinking my son would be glad that I'm glad he called." Mehki said nothing.

He knew she was bluffing.

"Well, the awards ceremony is Saturday, and you know the Lifetime Achievement Award is always the highlight of the show. I know you are presenting the award, however, I've made a change." Mehki stopped chewing.

"What kind of change?"

"Oh, just a minor one. Nothing big."

"Ma?" he asserted.

"Okay, okay. I was thinking, the award winners would also win a date with one of my eligible bachelor sons. You being the eldest, Bahati Carver would get a date with you."

"Are you being serious right now?" he demanded.

"What? What's wrong with that?"

"Besides the obvious, this is an awards show, not matchmaker."

"Mehki, you haven't had a girlfriend since that cheating, lying, gold digging whore. What was her name?" Mehki gaped at his mother's words. Despite her being right, he was shocked at her language. His mother was always about uplifting other women, and she was just about to award a black woman activist for black women's rights.

"Amarie, Mother."

"Yes, that ho. Anyway, would you please consider it?"

"No, and that's my final answer."

"Fine," she huffed. "I guess I'll never get grandchildren."

"I love you, Mother."

"Whatever. Anyway, what did you call for?"

"Oh, I was wondering if you needed help with anything."

"No, everything has been taken care of."

"Okay, well I'll see you tonight at dinner."

"I guess." Mehki guffawed heartily at his mother's attempt at pouting.

"I'm glad you find my misery amusing. Bye, boy." She hung up on him and he chuckled. Now that his mother was retired, when she wasn't traveling with his stepfather, she was meddling in his and his brothers' love lives. He finished his breakfast and headed to his office.

3

Mehki's office building was located downtown. He and his brothers had taken over his stepfather's, Jeremy Panton, business, Panton Scaping, after he retired. Mehki legally had his last name changed after his father disappeared without a trace, with nothing so much as a note explaining why. Jeremy was the father of his three younger brothers, and he was a father to him as well, stepping in in place of his biological father.

When Jeremy decided to retire, he made Mehki and Jerome co-CEOs of the company, though Jerome, 33, handled more of the landscaping side of the business. He graduated with his master's from Morehouse College. Mehki, 35, graduated from Dillard University with a master's in architecture and business management. He took over the business side of the company. Their second to youngest brother, Jeremiah, 31, worked in the Urban Planning division. He graduated with his master's from Howard University. The youngest Panton brother was Marlon, 30. He graduated with a master's in finance from Hampton University, so naturally, he handled all the financial aspects of the company, which is why it was booming financially.

The brothers were all well-paid, HBCU educated, and fine ass black men. Moriah and Jeremy were proud of how their sons turned out and how mature, responsible and level-headed they grew up to be.

Mehki parked his candy red Land Rover in his designated parking spot. He saw his brothers were already there. They had a meeting today with the Blackstone brothers, their friendly rivals.

Mehki took the elevator up to the top floor and stepped out, greeting the receptionist and heading to the boardroom. He walked in and greeted each of his brothers with a hug, and then the Blackstone brothers. The room was full of educated, successful black men, in an array of Armani suits with loafers. Jordan Blackstone, Mehki's best friend and former cousin, stood up.

"Now that we are all here, let's talk about the elephant in the room," he grinned, putting his hands in his pockets. "It has been brought to our attention that Blackstone Enterprises is now out of the bid for the contracting of the new sports arena near Reliant Park. Seems you all have stolen it right from under us, and we'd like to know, what the actual fuck?" His grin quickly faded and was replaced with something borderline to rage.

"Well, I don't know where you're getting your information, but we have nothing to do with that," Marlon retorted.

"Bullshit!" Dimitri Blackstone spat, slamming his hands on the table. "The contract for that place is $2.5 million, and the only companies qualified to take that project are in this room."

"Well, I don't know what to tell you," Jeremiah glared. "I don't have any blueprints, emails, or any other correspondence from this company, so it isn't us." Tobias Blackstone looked at each Panton brother and shook his head.

"I really thought y'all were better than this petty ass bullshit, but I see I was wrong," he accused, standing to leave, followed by Jordan and Dimitri. Mehki stood up too.

"Wait. That's it? You're just going to leave and not hear us out?"

"I think we've heard all the lies we need to hear. And to think, we were family Mehki," Jordan sneered. The Blackstone brothers walked out of the room.

"What does he mean by 'we were family'?" Jeremiah asked with air quotes.

"Uncle De'Kari used to be married to his mother. They divorced a year after you were born," Jerome answered.

"You think he's still mad about that?" Marlon asked.

"I don't give a damn either way. We need to figure out who Nu Energy hired out for this project." The brothers went to their respective offices, except for Mehki and Jerome.

"Hey, did ma call you with some bullshit about the award winners getting a date with us?" Jerome requested. Mehki threw his head back in a deep baritone laugh. He nodded his head.

"Yeah, she did, and I declined. The fuck I look like? I can't believe she's trying to pimp us out, just to get some damn grandkids."

"I can believe it. That woman acts like she's going to raise these kids as her own."

"The way she's been after us the past few years, she just might." Mehki's thoughts randomly went back to his run this morning when he bumped into Bahati. Jerome stared at his brother skeptically.

"Ki, where'd you go just now and don't tell me nowhere? I see the shit all over your face."

"Man, chill out. It's nothing."

"I know it's not a thing, it's a woman. Who is she?"

"Bahati Carver." Jerome frowned as he recognized the name.

"The one who is getting Mom's Lifetime Achievement Award? The woman who runs *Voices of Hue Women* and wrote *I'm Black and I'm Loud!*?"

"Yes, yes, and yes."

"I didn't know you were into activists. You normally go for chicks that are high maintenance," Jerome barked.

"Man, fuck you. That's why your bitch ass got cheated out of $1 million by your ex." Jerome immediately stopped laughing and Mehki howled.

"That ain't funny man. You know I loved that girl." Mehki was still snickering and then calmed down.

"I think that's what draws me to Bahati. I mean she's fine as fuck man, she's smart, and graduated from Spelman and she's accomplished so much. She's a woman who can hold her own, has her own, and can buy her own table to match mine."

"I think that's why she's receiving the award, dumbass." Mehki glared at his brother and it was Jerome's turn to howl with laughter.

"You won't be laughing when I get married and give Ma grandkids first."

"Mehki, you're the oldest, tf?" Jerome got up, laughing his way out the door. Mehki shook his head and headed to his office to do some research on how Nu Energy was already under contract.

4

Bahati pulled into a parking spot at The Galleria. She was meeting Carter and Kamaria there to go dress shopping for tomorrow's award ceremony. She still couldn't shake the nervousness she felt about Mehki now being the one presenting her the award.

She walked towards *Nubian Queen* where her sister and best friend were waiting. They hugged each other and went in. *Nubian Queen* was a high-end, black woman owned designer store. A two piece set caught Bahati's eyes and she walked straight for it, Kamaria and Carter followed.

"Don't you think that is a bit over the top?" Kamaria asked.

"Being that Mehki is now presenting me my award, I have to look spectacular," she sighed. Carter's and Kamaria's eyes widened.

"What?!" they shouted in unison.

"When did this happen?" Carter asked.

"I found out this morning when I ran into him on my run. I hadn't actually read the whole letter. He told me this morning and I made a complete fool of myself. How can I be attracted to a man who sleeps with a lot of women?"

"One, you're overreacting, and two, you're not blind," Kamaria responded, rolling her eyes. "Also, aren't you supposed to be this 'black women are superior women and we don't let any man see that they have us enamored chick?" Carter reminded her.

"Don't mock me," Bahati shot back.

"I'm not, but what I'm saying is, I think you need to get off your high horse and remember you're also human, and you have feelings."

"And needs," Kamaria giggled. That set Carter off, and Bahati looked between the two, shaking her head. She grabbed the outfit off the rack and headed to the dressing room. She undressed and tried the halter and skirt on. The skirt was floor length. It was royal blue, with thick gold lines going in a slanted pattern around it. In the gold lines were brown and red designs.

The halter top was the same blue as the skirt. Around the top and bottom, it was lined with gold scribbles. In the middle were two red and gold lines that went all the way around, and between the lines were burnt orange diamonds shaded in gold and a red dot in the middle. It was perfect.

When she stepped out of the dressing room, she saw her sister and Carter in similar outfits in different colors and designs. They all whistled at each other and cracked up. After changing, they paid for their outfits and went to eat at the Rainforest Café.

"Welcome to the Rainforest Café. I am Amarie. How may I serve you?"

The ladies ordered their food and drinks. Amarie walked away, and Carter broke their silence.

"Derwin and I set a date!" Kamaria and Bahati looked at each other with one eyebrow raised. This wasn't the first time that they had heard this.

"Well don't look so happy for me," Carter pouted.

"Carter, it's not that," Kamaria apologized. "We've been through this before."

"Yeah, and each time y'all set a date, he breaks up with you. It's a toxic cycle."

"I'm sorry, but when have either of you bitches ever been engaged? Oh that's right, never, because y'all can never keep a man."

"Carter!" Bahati jerked back.

"No, I'm tired of y'all judging and berating me when it comes to my relationship with Derwin."

"What relationship?" Kamaria asked, her hands shooting to her mouth as soon as she said it.

"Fuck the both of you. Some friends you are." She got up as soon as the waitress came back, then stormed off.

"Will she be back?" Amarie asked.

"No, but you can leave her food, I'll pay for

it," Bahati answered. She ate and talked with her sister about the ceremony and about Kamaria's upcoming fashion show. They chatted for another few hours and then went their separate ways.

That evening, Mehki got ready to go to his parent's house for dinner. Upon pulling into the circular driveway behind his brothers' cars, Jeremy stood at the door smoking a cigar. He knew that only meant one thing: his mom was on a rampage.

"Shit," he said to himself as he exited his car.

"What up Ki?" Jeremy said, pulling Mehki into a hug.

"Hey, Pops. What's wrong?" He could hear his mother inside cursing and yelling.

"The caterer got the order wrong for tomorrow and it's too late to change it. The florist double booked and the flowers won't be ready in time for tomorrow. Oh, and the venue lost their liquor license."

"Fuck," Mehki whistled.

"Yeah, so enter at your own risk," Jeremy chuckled. Mehki smiled and shook his head, walking into the house. His brothers were standing in the foyer, terror written all over their faces.

"Is it that bad?" Mehki whispered.

"I can hear you, Mehki Josiah James-Panton!" Moriah yelled. His brothers snickered, and he flipped them all off. “Get y’all none grandchild giving asses in this damn dining room and sit down! Food will be out in a minute. And wash y’all damn hands before you sit at my table!” Jeremy had just walked in and shook his head at the men. They all went to a bathroom and washed their hands, filing back into the dining room one-by-one and sitting down.

Moriah came in slamming several dishes on the table, and then went back into the kitchen. She did this several more times before everything was on the table. No one said a word.

“Why y’all looking scary?” she demanded.

“Well, Ma, we kind of are scared,” Marlon mumbled.

“Good, because I don’t ever for a second want y’all to think you can get over on me.”

“We wouldn’t even think it, Ma,” Jeremiah responded.

“Shut up and stop trying to kiss my ass,” Moriah sneered, squinting her eyes at him before walking out. The men howled as Jeremiah scolded them.

Moriah finally came back in and sat at the other end of the table from Jeremy. She looked at Jeremy and he began praying over the food. Upon his ending, everyone muttered “Amen.” Moriah began slapping food on her plate as the men watched, afraid to move a muscle.

“What are y’all staring at? Fix your damn plates!” she demanded. The men still didn’t move.

"Babe, do you think you're overreacting?" Jeremy asked. The brothers looked at him in disbelief that he asked that question for they knew what was going to come next.

"O-ver-re-acting?" Moriah said coolly. Each brother pushed their chair back from the table as a glass came flying at Jeremy's head. He ducked just in time. When he got back up he looked at her with anger.

"Woman, are you fucking crazy?" he barked.

"So now I'm crazy?" she asked, rolling her neck.

"Oh, God," Marlon mumbled, closing his eyes and dropping his head. His father was an idiot.

"I think we should probably leave," Jerome whispered to Mehki.

"Leave this table and you will wish you hadn't," their mother hissed, giving him a death stare, then looking back at their father.

"I am legit terrified," Jeremiah whispered to no one in particular. Moriah and Jeremy went back and forth throwing jabs. The brothers just sat there frozen, until Moriah walked off.

"Yeah, take you ol crazy ass upstairs. I'll be up there to lay some pipe in a minute!" he yelled after her.

"I'll be naked and waiting!" she shot back from the top of the stairs.

"Pops!" the men said in disgust.

"Well, how the fuck you think y'all got here?" he challenged, plopping back down in his hair. For Jeremy to only be 65, he could still pass as one of the brothers. He kept himself in shape and he hadn't yet grayed or bald, his locs long, healthy, and intact.

The brothers scooted back up to the table and fixed their plates. They ate in silence for a while, until Moriah reappeared, seemingly in a better mood. She sat down and looked at each of her men as they stared back, confused on whether or not they should keep eating.

"I apologize for my behavior and what I said. I am just upset and anxious about this event going off without a hitch," she explained.

"Ma, it's cool. I mean, we can always talk to our connections and send out a mass email to the attendees who provided one," Jerome offered.

"Yeah, and I can call the award winners and let them know about the change of events personally," Mehki volunteered.

"Sweetheart, and you know I got that new contract with Nu Energy, who now owns Reliant, so we can have the event at Reliant Park," Jeremy suggested.

"I thank you all for..." Moriah began.

"Wait, you got the contract with Nu Energy?" Marlon asked.

"Yep, right from under those Blackstones."

"Pops, why wasn't that discussed with us

first?" Mehki asked through gritted teeth. "We had a meeting with them this morning, and we denied having stolen the deal from them, which now will be seen as a lie!"

"So?" Jeremy shrugged.

"Jeremy, that is a huge deal. Sienna is pissed about that and I told her I knew nothing about it. You are definitely not getting any ass tonight, negro." Moriah threw her napkin on the table and stormed out. Jeremy pinched the bridge of his nose.

"Pops, you know they are our competition, and we have been friendly for some time. You don't think that's something we should've known so we wouldn't be blindsided?" Jeremiah quizzed his father.

"Look, this deal is going to bring in a lot of business for the company. Just tell them it's business, nothing personal."

"But you know that this is personal. Their mother used to be married to Uncle De'Kari," Mehki reminded.

"I don't give a damn. Business is business. If you don't like it, sell your share and find another job," Jeremy finalized, getting up from the table and heading to the back patio. The brothers looked at each other. Shit was fucked up.

5

Bahati was settling into bed, updating her organization's website. They were rallying for Breonna Taylor on Monday morning at the courthouse. Over 3,000 people had signed up to attend. Her phone started going off from an unknown number. She ignored it, and it rang again.

"Please take me off your calling list," she answered.

"Well, I guess you don't want your award then," Mehki's deep, baritone voice came through the phone, disturbing the river inside her again.

"Oh, sorry. I get so many of those robocalls," she apologized.

"No worries," he shrugged.

"How did you get my number?"

"My mother gave it to me."

"You asked your mother for my number? Isn't that an invasion of privacy? I expected that my personal contact information wouldn't be given out with such a prestigious..."

"Bahati, chill. I got the list of numbers of all the award winners."

"Oh, so now you're just running through the list so you can see who would give you some ass? Jerk." She hung up quickly.

Mehki stared at the phone in confusion. He dialed her number again.

"And another thing..."

"Bahati!" he barked, shutting her up instantly. She didn't know why, but that turned her on.

"I got the list of numbers for the award winners because the event has had some last minute changes."

"Oh," she whispered. "Sorry."

"I know you're an activist for women's rights and..."

"Black women's rights," she corrected.

"Yes, black women's rights. I'm not a misogynist or womanizer or anything of the sort."

"Yeah, okay," she sassed. He sighed deeply into the phone. She was going to be a piece of work, but the thought stirred something deep inside him.

"The venue will now be at Reliant Park, at the same time. A car will pick you up at 6 so you can be there by 6:30 to be seated before everyone else is allowed in, also so we can rehearse the program in the new venue."

"Got it," she acknowledged. "Is that it?"

"Yeah, that's all. Have a lovely evening." He hung up before she could respond.

"Dammit, Bahati. What the fuck is wrong with you?" she cussed at herself.

The next morning, she went jogging on

her usual path, praying not to run into Mehki. Up ahead, she could see him in the distance coming towards her. She quickly turned on the next block, hoping he didn't see her. Unbeknownst to her, he had and cut around the next block, waiting at the other end for her to come. He peeked around the corner and saw her coming. He stepped out into her path, causing her to jump and scream. He guffawed as she pulled her earbuds out of her ears.

"What the hell?" she demanded.

"You thought I didn't see you when you cut around the corner? Avoiding me?"

"I don't know what makes you think you're so damn special that I'd be avoiding you."

"Then why'd you change your route?"

"Because...well because..." she stumbled, then paused. "Wait, how do you know my route? Have you been following me?" He straightened up as he saw how she took offense to his words.

"No, I haven't been following you. I..."

"Because that's grounds for a restraining order."

"Bahati, I apologize if I offended you. I didn't mean to..." he stopped as he saw the corners of her mouth curl up before she let out a laugh that made his insides smile. What the fuck was this woman doing to him? He began to smile.

"I see she has a sense of humor," he finally said.

"You should've seen your face," she gasped for air. She was cute when she laughed. He wanted to make this happen for her all the time. As she caught her breath, she looked up at him with her coffee brown eyes.

"I was embarrassed when we ran into each other yesterday. I actually hadn't read the whole letter, so when you mentioned that you were presenting the award, I was thrown off because I just assumed your mother would."

"Is that all?" he pried.

"What do you mean?"

"Is that the only reason you took off like Usain Bolt around that corner when you saw me?"

"Yeah, why would there be any other reason?"

"Just wondering," he lied.

"Well, I'm going to finish my run. I'll see you this evening." She put her earbuds back in and ran past him. He smiled to himself. She was his, and she didn't even know it.

6

Bahati was stepping out of the shower when she heard laughter. Kamaria and Carter must be in the living room. She put on her under garments and moisturized before heading in to greet them. When she stepped into the living room she stopped short, staring at them. They looked gorgeous.

"Damn, we must look good, because she's speechless," Carter laughed, along with Kamaria.

"You looking fucking sexy as hell," Bahati gasped.

"Thanks, babes," Kamaria beamed.

"Carter, I want to apologize for what I said the other day at the restaurant. I really am happy for you and Derwin," Bahati said.

"It's okay. I get where y'all were coming from. Now go get dressed, the car should be here soon," Carter fussed.

Luckily, Bahati had done her hair before taking a shower, braiding her hair like a crown around her head. She was going to wear a head wrap anyway, but she still wanted her hair to look decent. After getting dressed and applying makeup, her phone rang. It was the driver. He was waiting downstairs.

She grabbed her wristlet and walked into the living room. The women were stunned.

"Girl, you're going to give Mehki a heart attack," Kamaria whistled.

"More of a stroke if you ask me," Carter chimed in.

"Y'all stop pumping my head up. I'm already nervous."

"Don't be. You deserve this," Kamaria offered.

The ladies headed downstairs to the awaiting car, only to find it was a Phantom. Carter whistled.

"This has Mehki James-Panton written all over it.

"What do you know about Mehki?" Bahati said, stopping short.

"He always shows up to my events in a fancy car. A different one each time. As well as a different woman each time."

They got in. What Kamaria said stuck in Bahati's mind. She was starting to feel something for this man, and she couldn't control it, but did she want to? Maybe she was just horny.

They pulled up to the front of Reliant in front of a long red carpet, and what looked like thousands of people waiting to snap photos. The driver got out and walked around to open the door for them to get out. As soon as the ladies were out, there was flash after flash after flash.

Their names were being called in each direction. That was one thing about being an activist, big shot lawyer, and top fashion blogger: everyone knew you.

A person with an earpiece directed them on where to stand on the carpet to get all the photo-ops done. After taking what felt like a thousand photos, they were escorted into their seats. They took in the room. For it to be a last minute change, it was decked out. Their eyes went straight to the door as they heard a commotion. In walked Mehki, Jerome, Jeremiah, and Marlon wearing *Nubian King* blazers, khakis, and Vans on their feet. Each woman shifted in their seats as their yonis threatened to soak their panties, or lack thereof.

"Damn!" Carter whispered loudly.

"Damn is right," Kamaria agreed.

Bahati said nothing, her gaze never leaving Mehki. That was until she noticed a woman come up and hug and kiss him on the cheek.

"Isn't that the same woman from The Rainforest Café that served us?" Kamaria asked. Bahati took a closer look and noticed that she was indeed the same woman.

"Yep, sure is," Bahati confirmed, directing her attention back to the stage. She hadn't noticed that the men had been walking towards them until they lined up in front of their table.

"Evening ladies," Mehki said, keeping his eyes on Bahati.

"Evening," Kamaria and Carter said.

"Bahati," Mehki called gently. She looked up at him and smiled, then looked back at the stage. Carter jabbed her with an elbow. Bahati scuffed.

"Well, anyway, these are my brothers, Jerome, Jeremiah, and Marlon. Brothers, this is Bahati and?" he paused, waiting for her to introduce Kamaria and Carter.

"I'm her sister, Kamaria, and this is our best friend Carter," Kamaria piped up.

"Yes, we've met," Jerome said, smiling at Carter. Carter blushed a deeper brown.

"Nice to meet you ladies," Jeremiah said. "Marlon and I are going to take our seats." They walked off to their table.

"I'm going to go find Ma and make sure she's not murdering someone," Jerome joked. He winked at Carter and walked off, leaving Mehki standing there with his hands in his pocket, staring at Bahati.

"Will all award winners and presenters please come to stage left," a woman said over the mic. Mehki stuck his hand out to help Bahati up. She smiled, got up and walked towards the stage.

"Don't mind her, she's just nervous," Kamaria apologized.

"It's cool. You ladies enjoy your evening." He walked towards the stage hoping to find out what Bahati's issue was. When he got backstage, he saw all the award winners and the other presenters. Bahati was talking to another winner off to the side. As he walked over, the event coordinator grabbed his arm.

"All the presenters are over there," she said, directing him to his right.

"Thanks," he nodded.

"Alright everyone," she said. "Listen up, presenters will come out stage left. Award winners, you will come up the stairs to the left to accept your award." She pointed towards the stairs opposite of where Bahati came up. "Once you have your award and say your speech, you'll exit stage right behind the curtains and head backstage where you will wait until all winners have received their awards. The last award will be the Lifetime Achievement Award, which is the biggest award and what major donors are here to see if who has been chosen is worth investing in their organization."

Bahati's eyes widened. She had apparently skipped that part of the letter as well. Mehki noticed her shock and wanted to go over and comfort her. He could tell her nerves were getting the best of her.

"Everyone can take their seats now," the woman said, dismissing them. Mehki caught up to Bahati and gently pulled her arm.

"Hey, don't worry. I know the investors are going to invest a great deal into *Voices of Hue Women*."

"Thanks," she smirked, and began to turn

away. He pulled her arm again.

"What do you want, Mehki?"

"Did I do something wrong?" he asked, confused.

"No, can I go to my seat now?"

"Are you sure I did nothing? You seem upset?"

Bahati rolled her eyes and laughed.

"Go back to your date," she sneered, walking off.

"Bahati, wait," he began after her when he heard the MC of the night come on.

"Ladies and Gentlemen, welcome to the annual Black Women Authors Gala! I am your mistress of ceremony, De'Angela Jones!" The audience clapped and cheered. "This evening we are honoring authors across all genres and awarding an influential person in the community with the Lifetime Achievement Award, probably the youngest in the past 30 years of this gala." Another applause erupted from the audience.

Mehki walked back to his seat with his brothers and parents as De'Angela introduced his mother. She got a standing ovation as she walked up to the stage, escorted by Jeremy.

"Thank you all so kindly for being here, given the last minute venue change. You know, I've been doing this for 3 decades, and I guess it was time to change it up. I started this gala to honor black women who are doing amazing things through written work as well as their activeness in the community. I am honored to know many of these women and to be meeting some of them for the first time tonight. So sit back, relax, and get your pocketbooks ready." The audience laughed and clapped as she exited the stage.

"Why do you keep staring at the woman?" Marlon inquired of Mehki. Mehki focused his eyes on Marlon.

"What?" he asked.

"The woman you introduced us to earlier. Why do you keep staring at her?" Marlon asked again.

"I believe our brother is what you call, smitten," Jerome joked.

"Shut up Jerome," Mehki retorted. That sent Jerome into a fit of laughter.

"Speaking of smitten," Jeremiah said, nodding towards an approaching Amarie.

"I've been looking for you," she swooned.

"What do you want, Amarie?" Mehki asked.

"Awww baby don't be like that." She rubbed his shoulder and he shook her off, causing his brothers to snicker. Mehki kept his eyes on Bahati, but she wasn't paying attention. She was talking to Carter and Kamaria. He breathed a sigh of relief. He knew he needed to explain about Amarie to Bahati.

"Amarie, get gone. It's been over between

us and nothing is going to happen, ever again. "

"Mehki, are you serious? After all we've been through?" He whipped around and bared his teeth.

"Listen and listen good Amarie. You are a gold digging, lying, cheating, conniving ass woman," he seethed through gritted teeth. "I think it'd be in your best interest to save yourself from embarrassing yourself in front of all these people, and stepping the fuck off."

Amarie took a step back and glared at him. She smirked at him as his name was called to present the next award. He straightened up, fixed his jacket, and walked towards the stage with a smile as the audience whistled and cheered.

"Didn't he say to step? Why you still standing there?" Marlon grinned, mocking her. She sucked her teeth and walked off until she heard Mehki begin to speak.

7

"This next award goes to a woman who is beyond admirable. She graduated from Spelman College with a master's in African and African Diaspora Studies. She went on to become a black rights advocate for black women, starting her own nonprofit, *Voices of Hue Women*, who have been rallying behind justice for Sandra Bland, Breonna Taylor, and countless other black women who have lost their lives at the hands of the police and have not received justice. Her book, *I'm Black and I'm Proud!*, is a collection of essays from numerous black women using their voices and speaking up for themselves and the voiceless. No one deserves the Lifetime Achievement Award other than Bahati Carver." The crowd stood up, whistled, cheered, applauded, and just made noise.

Amarie folded her arms and watched as a cheshire smile spread across Mehki's face as Bahati walked up to accept her award. Amarie stormed back to her seat in the back of the room. She watched as Mehki held his hand out to assist Bahati onto the stage. Bahati hesitated and then grabbed his hand to avoid embarrassment if she fell.

"You look beautiful tonight," he whispered in her ear. Bahatai blushed and felt butterflies fluttering in her stomach. This man was so damn sexy and he smelled good as hell. He placed his hand on the small of her back to guide her to the podium and hand her the award. She thanked him and stood in front of the mic as the audience died down.

"Since the moment I received the letter stating that I was to be the recipient of this award, I was tempted to call Moriah and tell her she made a mistake. The work I do is not for praise, awards, accolades, fame, money, or anything else that brings recognition, though I greatly appreciate those things. Growing up in the foster care system, you see a lot of things. You also grow up not having a voice, being bounced from foster home to foster home, not being adopted, no one wanting you, and most importantly no one listening to you.

My sister, Kamaria, and I were lucky enough to be bounced around together, as well as our best friend Carter. Despite not having voices, we made it out of the system and made something of ourselves. We chose careers that allowed our voices to be heard, recognized, and appreciated. Kamaria is the top fashion blogger in the state, Carter is a highly sought after attorney, and I help black women find and use their voices, the most unheard group of people. So this award, though it has my name, is not for me. It is for the little girl who is being molested every night by someone who she's supposed to trust. This is for the girl whose parents didn't want her and neither did anyone else. This is for the college student who went to a party, and was drugged and raped. This is for the woman who works in a male dominated office. This is for the woman who keeps getting passed over for promotions. This is for the woman whose significant other continuously beats her. This is for the woman in the hospital bed about to give birth, and the doctors aren't listening to her pain. This is for the woman who was murdered, and she never got justice. This is for all of you women sitting out in the audience. Thank you."

A thunderous roar filled the room as people cried, cheered, shouted, praised, and clapped. Mehki's heart swelled and tears pooled in his eyes. Though he didn't know this woman, that speech made him fall in love at that very moment. He guided her backstage where they stood and waited for the audience to quiet down and the MC to call the winners back on stage. They gathered and took photos. Once the photos were done, it was time to eat and dance.

Bahati went back to her table where her sister and best friend were still in tears over her speech. They hugged and Bahati joined in the tear fest.

"I am so proud to call you my sister," Kamaria choked out.

"And I am proud to call you my best friend," Carter sobbed.

"Y'all, we are ruining our makeup," Bahati laughed, patting her eyes with a napkin. Kamaria and Carter looked at each other and fell out laughing.

Mehki sat with his brothers and parents while they ate and he stared at Bahati. By her speech, he knew she had a story and he wanted to know what it was. There was something about her that was intriguing that had his mind swirling with questions, confusion, and feelings of love.

"Mehki!" his mother called. He whipped his head towards her. Apparently she had been talking and he wasn't listening, his mind on the way Bahati walked towards the stage in her two piece attire.

"Yeah, Ma?"

"Have you heard a word I've said?"

"No, sorry."

"He's too busy checking out hottie Bahati," Marlon joked, evoking a guffaw from Jeremiah and Jerome. Mehki punched him in the shoulder, making him laugh harder.

"Well go ask her to dance," Jeremy suggested, as the music changed to *Permission* by Ro James. He straightened his jacket and headed towards their table, followed by Jerome and Jeremiah. They lined up in front of the ladies' table. They stopped talking and stared at the men.

"May we have this dance?" Mehki asked for the

three of them, stretching his hand out, followed by Jerome and Jeremiah. Kamaria and Carter accepted Jeremiah's and Jerome's hands, respectively, and they headed to the dance floor.

"What about your date?" Bahati challenged, a sly grin spreading across her face.

"What date?"

"The woman who hugged and kissed you when you and your brothers walked in."

"Oh, Amarie. She's my ex, someone that you don't have to worry about."

"You sure, because the way she's been glaring this entire time, makes me think otherwise," Bahati smirked as she nodded behind Mehki. He turned to see Amarie shooting daggers with her eyes. He smiled and turned back to Bahati, singing her panties off, figuratively of course.

"Now, may I have your permission to dance?" he asked again, stretching his hand back out. Bahati took it without hesitation. She followed as he pulled her to the dance floor. He turned to her and pulled her into his chest. She rested her head against his chest as his hand fell to her lower back, right above her ass. He inhaled her scent and let out a low growl, the scent of shea butter filling his nostrils and the beast inside wanting to be let loose.

They swayed to the music, pelvis to pelvis, hips moving in sync. The way she moved against his manhood had it growing and pressing against her stomach. He began to back up.

"Sorry about that," he coughed, clearing his throat. She smiled and pulled him back in towards her.

"It's okay." They continued dancing with his erection between them. The smooth, silkiness of her skin made every hair on his body stand at attention. This woman was tempting him to act like his hormone enraged teenaged self, but he willed himself to regain control.

"You want to go somewhere private?" she asked.

"I thought you'd never ask." He grabbed her hand and escorted her to a private room down the hall from the gala. It was an office. Once inside, Mehki closed the door and closed the gap between them, sucking in her mouth invading hers with his tongue. The way he rolled his tongue erupted a moan from Bahati. Mehki palmed each ass cheek with his massive hands, lifting her up to sit on the table behind her. He nuzzled his way to her neck, sucking in her flesh, sending a chill through her entire body that arched her back and drew out a gasp.

"Fuck me, Mehki," she begged. Mehki stopped and looked at her eyes, nose to nose.

"Bahati, I want to get to know you. Despite what you may think you know about me. I am not that kind of man. I don't just sleep around."

"I've seen the woman you've had on your arm. I have more class than them, and I'm prettier."

"Both of those things are true," he growled, nipping at her nose.

"Then why won't you have sex with me?"

"Because Bahati, I want to do things the right way with you." She respected his answer despite the opposition between her legs. She leaned up to kiss him just as the door burst open, and Amarie walked in. Mehki snarled.

"So you're in here, about to fuck this bitch just because she won some award? This who you're leaving me for?"

"Leaving? I thought you said she was your ex?" Before Mehki could respond, Amarie cut him off.

"Ex? Bitch we are still together. I just let him sleep with other women."

"I ain't gon be too many more of your bitches," Bahati shot back, hopping off the table and pushing Mehki away.

"Amarie, I told you we were done," Mehki spoke.

"We are not done until I say we are done. Now tell this b..." Bahati threw a left hook connecting with Amarie's nose. Amarie screamed, falling back and holding her nose as Kamaria, Carter, Jerome, and Jeremiah walked in.

"Daaaaaaaaaamn!" Jerome whistled.

"I think you have some unresolved issues. Stay the fuck away from me with your dog ass!" Bahati spat at Mehki, walking out with Carter and Kamaria on her heels.

"Bahati, wait!" Mehki called after her, taking off until Jerome and Jeremiah stopped him.

"Brother, you might want to give her some

space and let her come around," Jeremiah warned.

"And you need to deal with Amarie, for good," Jerome added.

"I'm going to press charges!" Amarie shouted, blood dripping from her nose. Mehki spun on his heels towards her and closed the gap.

"Listen, and listen fucking good. We are over, done, and have been. I loved you, and you ripped my heart out. You cheated, lied, stole my money, used me, and took advantage of my kindness. I no longer love you, and I don't want shit to do with you. As for pressing charges, you won't do a damn thing, and I am only going to warn you once Amarie." He turned and left her standing there, Jerome and Jeremiah right behind him.

They ran out of the arena and saw that the car the ladies came in was gone.

"Fuuuuuuuck!" Mehki roared, squatting down. His brothers knelt beside him placing a hand on either shoulder. Marlon had made his way out.

"Yo, I just saw Amarie, and somebody fucked her shit up," he laughed before noticing his brothers kneeling down. Jerome motioned for him to stop. "What happened?"

"Amarie might've fucked things up with Mehki and Bahati," Jerome answered.

"Oh shit. You did that?" he asked his brother.

"No," Jeremiah responded. "Bahati did."

"Oh she's a keeper then."

"Will you shut up Marlon?" Mehki barked.

"Man what I do?" he asked, holding his hands out.

"You talk too fucking much." Mehki walked past him back into the gala.

8

Bahati sobbed in her sister's lap as Kamaria stroked her loose tresses.

"I can't believe I threw myself at him like that and made a fool of myself!"

"It's his loss," Carter added.

"I was actually just getting myself to believe he was different. But no, he's like any other celebrity."

"Do you really think he's still with her though?' Kamaria asked.

"It doesn't matter. They have some unresolved issues, and I don't have time for it."

"Let's take a trip!" Carter bounced. "We haven't had a girls' trip in a while. How about we leave Tuesday."

"I'm down. Everything is in order for my show next month, and I can blog from anywhere."

"Bahati?" Carter pleaded.

"Don't you have a case with Jerome?"

"Yeah, but he hasn't given me the specifics of his case yet. I'm on retainer."

"Derwin is going to let you go?" Bahati quizzed.

"Derwin doesn't own me, nor does he have a say in my whereabouts. Besides, he's out of town right now for the next couple of months. He's working on the Bryson Ward v. Nebula Thorne case."

"Damn, that's a high profile case to be working," Kamaria commented.

"Yeah, so he'll be gone for a while."

"I guess we can go. I need a vacation anyway," Bahati decided. Kamaria and Carter cheered.

Over the next couple of days, Mehki called, texted, and emailed Bahati to no avail. He understood why she was mad. Hell, he was mad too. Amarie just could not take "no" for an answer. She wasn't always like that. The first three years of their relationship were pure bliss. Then, she caught a whiff of fame after Jeremy retired and the brothers took over the business that she got beside herself.

She was partying on his dime, sleeping with other men, pretending the money was hers, running up tabs, taking private jets with her friends. It all caught up to her when she caught chlamydia and gave it to Mehki. It was the day before their wedding when he got the results and saw how much money she had blown through, finding the bills for everything in one of her purses. That day nearly killed him because he really loved her, and he thought she loved him.

When they broke up, he sought out intensive therapy. He still saw his therapist from time to time, but he had worked through those issues. Now, he felt he may need to increase his visits.

Monday morning, he went on his usual run, hoping to run into Bahati, but who was he kidding. Of course she'd take a different route to avoid him. After his run, he showered and got dressed for the rally down at city hall that was being put on by Bahati's organization. It was to demand justice for Breonna Taylor. He knew that that would be the only way for him to see her.

He made a protein shake and headed out the door. He parked down on Congress and walked over to Discovery Green on McKinney. There were thousands of people there. He had no clue how he was going to find her, at least until he turned around and saw her riding a horse down the middle of the crowd, followed by Kamaria and Carter, escorted by officers riding horseback. He followed behind in the crowd as everyone shouted numerous chants about justice, saying her name, and defunding the police.

Bahati felt an adrenaline rush as they headed toward city hall, thousands of people following her. Even though three thousand had signed up, over 60,000 had shown up, give or take. It took about 45 minutes to get to city hall in the blazing heat and through the crowd of people. Once there, speakers and mics were already set up for her to make her speech. Officers were mounted on horses that stood between them and the people. Bahati took her place, took the mic that was handed to her, and let out a deep breath.

"On March 13, 2020, Breonna Taylor was at home, asleep with her boyfriend. 3 officers were executing a no-knock warrant to an apartment they thought was related to the selling of drugs. Shots were exchanged between her boyfriend and the police, though Breonna was the only one killed. She was innocent. The murder was senseless. The police got it wrong. Now, think to yourself how often the police get it wrong." She waited for a spell as murmurs erupted through the crowd. "Too often, that's how often. More than it should. Those police officers that killed her, Jonathan Mattingly, Brett Hankison, and Myles Cosgrove are still roaming free without a care in the world. Sandra Bland's murder still goes unresolved and is still being labeled as a suicide. Neither of these women is here to testify and speak their truth, or speak at all. So we are their voice, and we demand justice. Black women are going unprotected like we've always been. No one is speaking up for us, protecting us, seeing us, hearing us. We cry out like a wounded wolf in the night, but no one hears us. We get labeled angry, assertive, aggressive, loud, miserable, complainer, victim, and other bullshit terms. I say fuck that and fuck the people who think it. Today, we are going to take action and push for justice to be served. Take out your phones and send this message to the email provided on the screen." She turned and directed everyone's attention to the screen behind her.

Mehki looked on in awe. This woman literally took his breath away, almost to the point that he felt unworthy of her. Once the rally was over and people began to disperse, Mehki made his way to her. She had dismounted from the horse. Kamaria and Carter saw him first as Bahati's back was towards him. Kamaria nodded in his direction, then she and Carter walked away as Bahati turned around.

"You are a phenomenal woman. What you said up there was incredible and I could only hope to continue to hear you speak for those who have no voices."

She eyed him, searching for bullshit in his face, but there was none. He was being genuine.

"Thank you. Did you sign the petition and send the email?" she interrogated.

"Yes and yes. Bahati listen, about what happened at the gala, I wanted to apologize. She and I broke up 5 years ago. I'll admit, over the past few years, we have hooked up from time to time, but I ended that a year ago. She still is trying to hold on, but there's nothing for me there. I want to explore what this thing is with you." Bahati thought about what he was saying, taking it in. She sighed and pulled him by his shirt towards her. He leaned forward and took in her mouth, wrapping his hands around her waist as she wrapped her arms around his stocky neck. He prayed her lips below were as soft and sweet as the lips he was currently kissing.

"Go out with me," he whispered against her lips.

"When?"

"I'm impatient, so how about tonight?"

"I have to pack. My sister, Carter, and I are going to Versailles tomorrow."

"Oh word? Y'all doing it up big," he joked.

"Yeah, it's just a girls' trip."

"Well, I can grab some food and bring it to you. You can pack and I'll watch." Bahati threw her head back and let out a laugh.

"That'd be nice."

"What's your poison?"

"Stella Rosa Rosé."

"I got you. Let me go home and shower again, and I'll be at your place around 8."

"Deal," she agreed.

9

Bahati took a long hot shower, allowing the water to singe off the day and roll down her skin, washing down the drain. She turned the pressure up high to massage the aches she had from riding the horse and then walking back to her car.

She lathered her loofa with her African black soap and scrubbed herself clean. Standing under the shower head as it drenched her 4C tresses, she closed her eyes, taking a few deep breaths. Mehki was coming over. To say she was nervous was an understatement. To have this man in such close quarters with no one else around, she knew she wouldn't be able to control herself.

Shutting the water off, she got out and dried off. After oiling and moisturizing her hair, she made two braids going down the back of her head, and pinned the ends together. She slathered on some shea butter and rolled on an essential oil blend to her wrists, neck, and behind each ear. For her clothes, she chose some mid-thigh shorts and a plain white t-shirt.

Going into the closet, she pulled out her

suitcases and checked that she had everything she needed. She added a few more hygiene items, hair products, and a couple more swimsuits.

Time must've flown because there was a knock at her front door. She hustled through her condo and opened the door. Her smile instantly dropped when she saw it wasn't Mehki standing at the front door.

"What the hell are you doing here?" she asked.

"Is that any way to greet your mother?"

"You aren't my mother. You haven't ever been my mother."

"Oh, you're still mad about me leaving you and your sister in foster care? Tuh," she said and invited herself in.

"You need to leave and don't ever come here again," Bahati warned.

"I see you've done well for yourself," Rashelle said, looking around.

"Did you not hear me? I said get out," Bahati repeated.

"Oh, I heard you," she said, sitting on the couch, "but I'm not leaving. What for? You have room for me to stay here."

"What? How dare you show up at my doorstep after how many years? And think that I would just welcome you with open arms into my home? Get the fuck out, now!" Bahati felt herself about to spiral. She hadn't had one of these episodes in a long time.

"Listen here you ungrateful little bitch," Rashelle seethed as she stood up. "You and your sister owe me for the way my body looks, my hair falling out, me being strung out on drugs, not being able to find a job."

"You're here thinking I'm going to give you money?" Bahati questioned. "You got me fucked up if you think I'm going to give you shit. Get your junky ass out of my house!"

Rashelle charged at Bahati and Bahati met her with a blow to the face that knocked Rashelle on her ass. After climbing on top of her, Bahati only saw red, throwing punch after punch after punch.

Mehki exited the elevator when he heard screams coming from the direction he was going. As he got closer to Bahati's door, he realized the screams were coming from inside. He ran the last few steps and burst in to find Bahati in a raging fit, pounding Rashelle's face in, blood everywhere. Mehki dropped the wine and food on the table next to him and ran to pull Bahati off.

"Stop! Bahati, stop!" he begged.

"No! Let me go!" The shrill cries coming from her squeezed at his heart strings. He knew she was in a state of distress about whoever this woman was.

"I'm going to sue you for every fucking penny you've got, you crazy ass bitch!" Rashelle spat, blood dripping from her nose, eye, and mouth.

" I think it's time you leave," Mehki warned Rashelle.

"This ain't over bitch," she said, spitting a glob of blood on the floor. She slammed the door behind her. Bahati was still trying to break free of Mehki's grasp. He set her to her feet and let her go, backing up. She crumbled and let out shrill screams over and over. He knelt beside her and pulled her to his chest. She was shaking violently. He then felt her relax in his arms and her breathing was returning to normal.

"I'm sorry you had to see that," she apologized.

"Don't be. I'm just glad I showed up when I did or you would be facing a murder charge." She pulled away and sat across from him against the couch. "What happened?"

"That was the woman who gave birth to me. I haven't seen her since I was 7, after she left me and my sister to go get milk. I remember that night vividly. It had been several hours and we were hungry. I thought I could make us some mac n cheese on the stove like Rashelle used to. I turned the stove on. It was a gas stove. The flames were high I guess because I had it on high. I didn't know. Anyway, I poured the noodles into a pyrex dish and set the dish over the fire. I left the kitchen to give Kamaria a bath. Right as she got out of the tub, the smoke detector went off. I guess the dish had shattered from the flames, but by the time we got to the kitchen, it was in flames. There was a, uh, towel, sitting right next to the burner." Bahati's eyes were in a daze as tears fell. Mehki let the tears fall from his eyes as he watched her relive a moment that had clearly started why she does what she does.

"The living room was engulfed. The cheap ass wallpaper was flammable. We almost didn't make it out that night. The firefighters came, and the police. They questioned me, asking me where my mom was. I told them that she went to get milk at 5:37. The look on the officer's face let me know it had been a long time. He said it was currently 8:54. Then, I heard a commotion behind me. I turned around to see Rashelle swinging at a couple officers trying to get by. She yelled, 'Those are my babies! Those are my babies!' I just stared at her. I didn't even recognize her. She was high on something. The officers arrested her, and CPS came and took us. That was the last time I saw her." After she stopped talking, she looked at Mehki. He saw so much pain in her eyes.

"Bahati, I am so sorry that that happened to you. I wish I could take your pain away."

"You can, even if it's temporary."

"Tell me, I'll do anything to never see that look again."

"Make love to me Mehki." He froze, knowing that that was probably not the best idea.

"Don't worry, I have condoms." She pulled out a drawer from the coffee table and threw the gold wrapper at him. She stood up and slowly undressed. He watched and against his will, his manhood gave him away. She stood there naked, her curves begging for him to caress them, kiss them, suck on them. He stood up and slowly undressed, letting her take in his massive build. He removed his shirt, his chest and arms glowing with oil. He dropped his shorts, kicking his shoes off to reveal his thick thighs like she had pictured. His manhood was bulging in his boxers. She gasped as he dropped his boxers. He watched as her pain was subsiding and lust set in. She licked her lips and walked forward to kneel in front of him. He stopped her and pulled her face to his, kissing her gently, then passionately. He palmed her ass and lifted her up.

"Bedroom is straight ahead," she mumbled against his lips. He headed to the bedroom and laid her down. Sheathing himself with the rubber, he crawled between her legs and inhaled her pulsating sex into his mouth. A moan escaped her lips and her back arched. She dug her nails into his scalp and he gripped her thighs with his arms.

"Mehki, fuck!"

He ravished her like he would never see her again, not letting a drop of her juices go to waste and making sure his tongue explored every crevice.

"Ahhh! Shit!"

He flicked his tongue over her bulging clitoris, heat and blood rushing to that spot. Her body was in flames, her core tightening.

"Mehki! Mehki! Mehkiiiiiii!" Her juices squirted in his mouth as she screamed and writhed involuntarily from the intensifying orgasm. He slurped and sucked until she tried to run. He locked her thighs in place.

"Come for me again," he growled. As if her body was only listening to him, it worked against what she could handle and she came again, harder than the last time.

"Ahhhhhhh!" Tears fell from her eyes. She needed this more than anything, and from this man. Mehki released her thighs and climbed between her legs, not even giving her a chance to catch her breath as he eased his way inside her. She dug her nails into his shoulder blades as he filled her. He palmed each ass cheek and hiked her up a little as he went in thrust after deep thrust. His strokes were long and hard. Bahati was fucked speechless. Mehki slowed as he felt himself about to release. She was tight around him and he felt every time she would squeeze. He wasn't ready to bust just yet.

He kissed her deeply, his tongue exploring inside her mouth. She tasted herself on his lips and she purred. She tasted good as hell. She met his slow thrusts with her hips, taking him deeper inside her. He broke their kiss and looked in her eyes as he sped up, pounding her. He wanted to see the pleasure he was giving her.

"Come for me baby," he growled, and just like that, a third orgasm erupted through her, sending her into convulsions.

"Shit Bahati!" he moaned as he met his release. They were both panting as he rolled beside her and cradled her in his arms.

"Bahati, I am here for you and I will never leave you."

"How can you be so sure and you just met me?"

"I asked myself the same question, but I just know I won't leave you. What time is your flight tomorrow?"

"11 a.m." It was currently 10 p.m.

"Well, let's get some sleep."

"Actually, I noticed that you brought food and wine. I was actually starving when you got here, and between beating Rashelle's ass and what you just did to me, I'm famished." Mehki guffawed loudly, and Bahati joined in.

"Remind me to never get on your bad side," he smiled.

"Why?"

"Because if you saw what I saw when I walked in, you wouldn't want to get on your bad side either."

"Another truth moment. I have episodes where I black out. It only happens when something triggers my past, like seeing Rashelle."

"Mon Cherie, you don't have to explain."

"You speak French?" she whipped her

head towards him. He chuckled and nodded his head.

"Français est la première langue étrangère que j'ai apprise."

"Où l'avez-vous appris?"

"I lived in Qatar for a while after college. I wanted to absorb African culture. My mom was big on my brothers and I being rich in our culture. By the way, what does your name mean?"

"It means good luck, or fortune."

"And your sister's?"

"Bright as the moon."

"I do believe that you may be my good luck charm, and I am fortunate to have you," he smiled. She laughed at his corniness.

They got up and got semi dressed to head to the kitchen to eat. Bahati grabbed plates, cutlery, and glasses, while Mehki opened the wine and took the food out of the bag.

"I'm having a hard time understanding how your mother gave you such beautiful and meaningful names, but she is the way she is."

"My grandmother named us. When she died, that's when my mom turned to drugs and became so hateful and vile. My grandmother was everything to her."

"And your pops?"

"Never met him. My mom said he didn't want a family, so he left us."

"Have you ever tried to find him?"

"No. I figured that once we entered the

system, they'd notify him, but my mom was too strung out to even remember his name or anything about him." She took a forkful of the mu shu chicken and rice. It melted on her tongue. She accidently let a moan slip and opened her eyes wide to see Mehki staring with this dark gaze. He smiled at her embarrassment.

"Sorry," she mumbled.

"No need. I actually quite enjoyed watching you enjoy your food." They finished eating and cleared the table.

"I'm going to take a shower, if you want to join," Bahati offered. She turned the shower on and took her oversized t-shirt off. Mehki stood in the doorway and watched as she opened the shower door and climbed in. He dropped his boxers and followed, climbing in behind her. His touch sent an electrifying shock through her body. His dick growing and pressing against her back, he gently leaned her forward and found her opening. Reaching forward, he grabbed her breasts and entered her with such force that she thought she was going to fall. He had a good grip on her.

He thrust in and out, watching her ass slap against his pelvis, the water splashing between them. She placed her hands on the wall in front of her to brace herself for the impact of his repeated entrance into her canal.

"What are you doing to me, mon Cherie?"

"Mehki, fuck me!" she begged. He withdrew, turned her around, hiked her up against the wall, entering her and swallowing her screams with his mouth. She wrapped her legs around his waist and arms around his neck. He pressed his palms against the wall and thrusted faster and harder, feeling the vibrations of her screams in his throat as he kissed her.

He felt her buck and her walls tightened around him, they came together, absorbed in a steamy cloud of ecstasy. After washing each other up and getting dry, they fell in bed still in a euphoric state, Mehki cradling Bahati in his arms. He listened until her breathing changed, letting him know she was asleep, and he followed suit.

10

After wishing Bahati safe travels, Mehki headed home to change clothes and freshen up after their morning sexcapade. Just the thought of it made his dick jump and his lips curve up into a smile. She was going to be gone for three days, and he couldn't wait for her to return. He headed into the office. They had another meeting with the Blackstone brothers, though he knew how this meeting was going to go. As soon as Jordan found out that they indeed had acquired the contract, he was going to be more than pissed.

Mehki walked into the boardroom and greeted his father and brothers. Everyone was dressed relaxed today: polos and khakis. As soon as the men took their seats, the door opened and in came Jordan, Dimitri and Tobias. Mehki took a deep breath and looked at his brothers who didn't seem nervous at all. After quick greetings, the men sat down.

"I called this meeting today to clear some things up," Jeremy began. "Now, yes, it is true that we hold the contract with Nu Energy..."

"I knew y'all bitch ass niggas was lyin'!" Tobias jumped up. Jordan glared at Mehki, but there was nothing he could say to diffuse the situation.

"Now hold on son..."

"Nigga, you ain't my daddy!" Tobias barked.

"Y'all sat here and looked us dead in the eye, swearing that y'all didn't steal this right from under us," Dimitri recalled. Jordan just shook his head and smiled.

"This here," Jeremy whirled his finger around, "belongs to me and my boys. You will respect us in our house."

"Fuck you and your house old man," Jordan sneered standing to his feet.

"We didn't know he got the contract until a few days ago," Jeremiah chimed in.

"And yet you still said nothing. It doesn't matter. Your daddy and his brother ain't nothing but a bunch of lying, cheating, stealing, snakes," Jordan gathered. Marlon jumped up and punched him in the jaw, everyone hearing the connect and the crack, not knowing if it was Marlon's knuckles or Jordan's jaw. Tobias, Dimitri, Jeremiah and Jerome stepped in.

"Hey! Break that shit up!" Jeremy ordered. But no one was listening. Mehki got up to leave when a fist met his jaw. It was from Jordan. They had had many fights, but none of them ever physical. This was now personal. Mehki swung back, cracking a rib and busting Jordan's nose. Blood came spewing out, and Jordan tried to get back up and continue.

Security barged in and hauled the Blackstone men out, closing the door behind them. Mehki looked around, angry at what had transpired. He punched a hole in the wall nearest him and let out a shrilling growl.

"Fuuuuuuuuuuck!" he stormed out, slamming the door behind him, leaving his brothers and Jeremy to gather themselves.

As the women landed, Bahati was in a daze about the previous night and morning spent with Mehki that she had almost forgotten about her mother showing up. She knew she'd have to deal with that when she got back, but for the next few days, all she wanted to do was relax.

"What's got your head in the clouds?" Kamaria asked.

"Shit, Mehki probably got his head in her…"

"Carter!" Bahati snapped her head around. The women fell out laughing.

"So, you gave him some ass then," Kamaria guessed.

"Damn, why do you have to say it like that?" Bahati said, shying away.

"Ladies and gentlemen, you may now gather your belongings and exit the plane," the stewardess directed.

The three of them grabbed their purses and carry-ons, departed from the plane. At baggage claim, they grabbed their one suitcase and headed for the exit to the awaiting car. They rented a driver for their stay. After getting in and the driver putting their luggage in the trunk, they headed to their private villa near Marie-Antoinette's Estate.

"This place is beautiful. How did you book it on such short notice?" Bahati swooned.

"I have a few connections here," Kamaria responded.

They pulled into the driveway and exited the vehicle. Walking up to the door, they were greeted by two lady servants with Sangria. Each of them took one and entered the villa. The place slept six, but they rented the entire place for their stay.

"Ladies, Marina will show you to your rooms, and in 30 minutes, you can head to the terrace for your massages," said Dawina, the head maidservant. The women squealed and followed Marina as she showed each of them to their suites. They each unpacked and headed out to the terrace in their robes. Three tables were set up and each of them took one.

"We could not have done this at a more perfect time," Bahati sighed.

"Why is that?" Kamaria inquired.

"Just because. I needed this. I've been working so hard lately, and I've been feeling the effects of it," she half explained.

"I needed this too. After wrapping up that case with Leanne Jones and Turk Davis, I was ready to bounce," Carter added.

"Speaking of cases, has Jerome mentioned what he needs you for?" asked Bahati.

"Yes, and because of the nature of the case, I can't discuss it with anyone."

"But we're your girls," Kamaria reminded.

"Yes, but this case is sensitive and it will be high profile enough with him just being who he is," Carter explained.

"I'll just ask Mehki then," Bahati shrugged.

"You can try, but no one knows besides me and the other party."

"Damn, that sounds serious," Kamaria concluded.

The masseuses came out and the ladies unrobed and laid face down on their tables. Their massage was 90 minutes, and then dinner would be served in the dining area on the part of the terrace closer to the villa. After the massages, the ladies cleaned up and came back out to a spectacular view. There were candles, soft music playing by a live band, the works.

"Damn Kamaria, you did all this? Shit if you weren't my sister, I'd be trying to marry you," Bahati joked.

"Haha, but no, I didn't order any of this," she said as they sat at the table.

"This is all compliments of a Mehki Panton," Dawina said as she poured their wine.

"Mehki? Damn Bahati, you put it on him like that? Shit, keep doing what you're doing so we can reap the benefits," Carter cheered. Kamaria laughed and Bahati just shook her head.

The maitre'ds brought out soupe à l'oignon as the appetizer. It was the most delicious onion soup that Bahati had ever tasted. Their main course was coq au vin, which was a chicken braised with wine, mushrooms, salty pork, onions and garlic. For dessert was a chocolate soufflé. By the end of the meal, they were full and tipsy off Merlot. As it was getting late, the women headed off to their rooms. As soon as Bahati stepped in hers, her phone rang. She ran to answer it and smiled when she read the caller ID.

"Thank you," she gushed, still feeling the effects of the wine.

"You're welcome," he replied. As soon as his face clearly filled the screen, Bahati gasped.

"What happened?"

"Oh, this?" he asked, nonchalantly pointing to his face. "Just a typical day at work."

"How is that typical when you look like someone beat your face with a bat? Does it hurt?"

"It doesn't hurt as bad as it looks. I'll be fine. How was the flight?"

"The flight was amazing. We received massages once we got here, and dinner was absolutely perfect."

"That's good to hear. I specifically handpicked your wine and meals. Those are my favorite anytime I am in France."

"Well Mr. Panton, you have amazing taste and

an even more amazing palette."

"Mon cherie, you have an amazing taste." Bahati blushed at his innuendo. "So, did you talk to your sister about...?"

"No, and I'm not going to. I don't want to drudge up the past. She doesn't really remember anything. She was 4 when it all happened. I don't want to give her even more awful memories than when we were in foster homes."

"I see your point. Well, rest up. I will talk to you later on."

"Okay, and thanks again. Also, take care of your eye, and don't work so hard that you have matching black circles," she joked. He chuckled. They hung up and Bahati rolled over in bed, feeling as if she was floating. She didn't know if it was from the wine or from Mehki, but she was going to enjoy it to the fullest.

11

A few days later, Mehki was at his office, anticipating Bahati's arrival back to Houston. He had plans to cook for her at his place that evening. It was almost noon, and he was meeting his mother for lunch. She said she had something important to tell him. It sounded urgent, and he hoped no one was dying. He rattled off some information to his secretary and headed out of the office.

He rolled up to valet at Grand Luxe in The Galleria area. He walked in and found his mother sitting across from some man who had his back towards him. He knew for a fact that that wasn't Jeremy. He quickened his face and Moriah stood up quickly to diffuse the situation before it even started.

"Mehki, hey baby," she smiled nervously.

"Ma, what's going on? Who is...?" Before he could even finish, the man turned his head towards him. Mehki's expression hardened as he recognized his father. He didn't look the same as he remembered, but he knew it was him. He had aged so rapidly.

"The fuck is going, Ma?"

"Watch your damn language. Now I know this is the last thing you need, but you will respect me and your father."

"Father? My father is not anywhere in this building." Xavier coughed several times back to back.

"What? You sick or something?" Mehki asked, though he really didn't care.

"Mehki, just sit down, please. Don't make a scene," Moriah pleaded. Mehki scuffed and walked off. He hadn't been in that long, so his car was still sitting out front. He tipped the valet anyway and drove off. He stopped at the store and got what he needed to make dinner for Bahati. He needed to focus on something else. The fucking audacity of that man to show up after all these years.

He parked and ran inside. Bahati's plane should be landing in the next 30 minutes. He whizzed around the store. As he got to the checkout, his phone rang.

"Hello," he answered.

"Hey babe." Just the sound of her angelic voice made everything that happened earlier disappear from his mind.

"Have you landed yet?"

"We just did. We should be out in about 15 minutes. I know I'll see you in a few, but I couldn't wait to hear your voice."

"Oh, really? Is that all you couldn't wait for?" he pushed. He could tell he had her smiling even though he couldn't see her.

"No, that isn't all, but I can't say all that right now," she whispered. He chuckled and paid the cashier.

"Well, I'll see you in a minute, and you can tell me in person. "

"Okay, I'll see you soon." They hung up as he climbed into his car. His phone buzzed again signaling a text message. He opened it. It was from his mother.

You didn't have to run off like that Mehki. We really need to talk to you.

He ignored it and his phone buzzed again as he started the car.

You have read receipts on. Boy, answer me right now, dammit.

He tapped on the bar to start typing, his thumb hovering. What could he say that wouldn't be offensive or disrespectful towards his mother?

Look ma, I don't know what's going on, and if it has anything to do with him, I don't want to know and I don't care to know. I'm about to pick up Bahati from the airport. I'll talk to you later. Love ya.

He exited the text app and threw his phone in the cup holder. He was at the airport in less than 10 minutes. When he pulled up to the passenger pickup lane, he saw Bahati hugging her sister and Carter as they were about to get in separate cars. He pulled up right in front of them.

The ladies smiled and waved at him, elbowing Bahati. She blushed as he got out of the car.

"Ladies," he greeted them.

"Hey Mehki," they sang back.

"Bye, y'all," Bahati shoed at them. They got in their cars as Mehki walked up to Bahati, pulling her by the waist to him and met her lips with his. They tongued each other down for nearly two minutes before coming up for air.

"Hey," he smiled against her lips.

"Hey," she whispered back. He let her go and opened the door for her to get in. After closing the door, he grabbed her bags and put them in the trunk. He got on the driver's side and held her hand as they headed to her condo. She told him all about their trip on the way there. Mehki was quiet the entire time, but thankfully, Bahati didn't notice. When they arrived at the apartment, Bahtai grabbed the food while Mehki grabbed her luggage.

"How about you take a nice long bath, while I cook? I'll even pour you a glass of wine," he suggested once they entered her place.

"Oh? Okay then," she agreed and headed to the bathroom and turned on the water in her Jacuzzi tub, adding bubbles and essential oils. She undressed and unpacked a few things from her bags. As she slipped in, Mehki came in with a glass of Rosé. He sat it on the side of the tub and kissed her forehead. She settled into the hot water and turned on the jets, letting the water pulsate against her body. She must've fallen asleep because she felt soft kisses against her lips. She opened her eyes to see a chocolate demigod kneeling before her.

"The food is ready."

"Is it just now ready or it's been ready?"

"I just turned the burners off and took the roast out of the oven," he smiled. He knew what she was playing at.

"Then get undressed and join me." He chuckled but obliged. Bahati watched as he undressed. The sight of his body never got old . She watched as he tiptoed in.

"Shit this water is hot. Are you trying to send me to hell early?" Bahati shook with laughter as he eased the rest of his body in, grimacing as he sank lower and lower. As soon as he was all the way down, she crawled over to him and straddled his lap. She stroked his member until he was erect. She took his mouth in as he rested a hand on each hip. She moved over him until she felt his head at her opening.

He took a breast in his mouth as she gasped at the sensation of his teeth grazing her nipple. He switched between the two as she lowered herself onto him. He sucked in a breath as his dick spread her walls.

"Shit!" she cursed. She moved her hips up and down his shaft, a rumbling growl expelling from deep inside him.

"Mon cherie," he whispered in her ear. He

nibbled her lobe and a chill ran up her spin, her hips moving faster, rocking back and forth. He moved her head to face him and took in her mouth, digging his fingers into her hips to guide her a little faster and harder.

"I've missed you!" she whined.

"Tu m'as aussi manqué," his accent sending a rush of heat to her lady parts. He felt her walls closing in on him as an orgasm ripped through her, the water in the tub sloshing as she rode the wave.

"Ah! Ah, God! Dammit Mehki!"

"Give in to it baby. Let it take over." She did as he said and gave in, letting the orgasm take complete control of her movements. It was almost like an out of body experience. She felt herself floating above them. He met his own release not long after. She slumped against him and they held each other for a while longer. After drying and getting dressed, they headed into the kitchen where Mehki had already had the table set.

"Wine?" he checked.

"I think I'm good. Water will be fine."

He brought over two glasses of water and sat across from her.

"This looks amazing," she complimented. Before he could respond, his phone was going off in his pants that were now strewn across the back of the couch.

"Thank you," he responded, fixing her

plate. His phone went off again.

"Shouldn't you get that?" she asked.

"No, it's probably my mother."

"If Moriah is calling, you definitely need to get it. I don't want her blaming me for her son ignoring her, and getting on her bad side before I'm even in the family." She froze as the words left her mouth. She hadn't meant to let him know she had been thinking about one day being a part of his family. He smiled at her words and embarrassment as his phone went off again. He apologized and went over to his pants, fishing for his phone. He grabbed it and went into the bedroom.

"Ma, I'm in the middle of something right now."

"I don't give a shit what you're in the middle of. I am your mother and dammit you will answer this fucking phone when I call."

"Ma..."

"Don't 'Ma' me boy! Xavier needs to talk to you. I gave him your number and he will be calling tomorrow whether you like it or not. Hear him out before you write him off." He listened as she went on and on, and he just agreed in the end. When he came back into the dining room, Bahati was halfway done with her plate.

"I'm sorry, but it was soooo good," she relished. He shook his head and chuckled as he took his seat again. "Is everything okay?" she inquired.

"Yeah, it's just my father is back."

"Oh? Where had Jeremy gone?"

"Jeremy is not my biological father. He is my stepfather, but biological to my three brothers. Anyway, my biological father, Xavier, left for good when I was about 9. He had remarried and had another son, but divorced right after his other son was born. We don't speak, his other son and I. He blames me for his mom and Xavier divorcing somehow. I ended up legally changing my last name shortly after my mom and Jeremy got married. Anyway, he's back. My mom asked me to lunch earlier today, and when I showed up, he was there."

"You don't think you can just hear him out? You don't necessarily have to forgive him, but what do you have to lose?"

"Are you willing to hear your mother out?"

"Mehki, that isn't the same and you know it's not," she retorted defensively.

"I know and I'm sorry. I shouldn't've said that."

"If your mother is asking you to do this, then I think it must be something important."

"I know it is. She hated him for a long time and the fact that she's even speaking to him makes me think it's somewhat important. But for now, let's finish dinner. I made an amazing dessert."

"So what we just did in the tub wasn't dessert?" she joked. He guffawed. He was beginning to fall in love and he knew he was going to make her his wife. She just didn't know it yet.

12

The next morning, Mehki received a text from an unknown number asking him to meet at The Breakfast Klub in an hour. He looked over to see Bahati still asleep. He slid out the bed, showered, and got dressed. Once in the car, he sent her a text letting her know he was going to meet Xavier.

When he arrived, the line was out the door. He parked and headed inside. Xavier had texted him and let him know that he already had a table waiting. He recognized him sitting in the back, looking at a menu. He walked over and slid in the booth across from him.

"Man, you sure have grown into a fine, successful young man."

"Yeah, no thanks to you." Xavier's smile dwindled at Mehki's words.

"Listen Mehki, I know I wasn't the father you needed me to be. I wasn't a father to you at all. I know that there is nothing I can do or say to make things right."

"Then why are you here and incessant on talking to me?"

"I don't have much longer to live. I have

months left." He went into a coughing fit like yesterday.

"What's wrong with you?" Mehki felt a feeling that he didn't think he'd ever feel for Xavier: worry.

"I have AIDS, son." Mehki sat up straight and panic set in.

"You what?"

"I have AIDS. I 've had it for a while now."

"What's a while? Wait, don't tell me? Does Ma know? Does she have it? Did you give it to her? Do I have it? No, fuck this." Mehki jumped up from the table quickly, causing other patrons to look on. He ran out of the restaurant and to his car, speeding to his mother's house. He jumped out the car and raced up the few steps to the front door. He used his key to let himself in.

"Ma! Ma!" he yelled, going from the living room, to the kitchen, to her office. "Ma!"

"What in the hell Mehki!" she shouted, coming down the stairs, Jeremy right behind her.

"You wanted me to sit down with this nigga for him to tell me that he has fucking AIDS?" Moriah slapped him something serious, a sting he felt in his whole body.

"You have one more time to cuss at me and so help me God I will light your ass on fire. You hear me boy?" Mehki nodded, a tear rolling down his cheek, not from the slap, but from the fear that he might have contracted the disease.

"Now, yes, he has AIDS. I went to the clinic

a few days ago and so did Jeremy to get tested. I feel you should do the same."

"Do my brothers know?"

"Yes, we told them before telling you. Listen Mehki, I know this is the last thing that you wanted to hear, but I'm sorry baby."

"Ma, why didn't y'all ever get tested before having sex?"

"Did you and Bahati get tested before having sex?"

"What?"

"Yeah, ya moms is good at detecting when someone has been having sex, it's why I could never cheat," he chuckled, walking towards the kitchen as Moriah gave him a slight shove.

"What makes you think that we're having sex?"

"Do you love this woman?"

"Ma..."

"Answer the question Mehki."

"Yeah, Ma, I do. And I know I've only known her for a short time, but I feel like I've known her forever. We confided in each other things about our past that drudge up old feelings and memories."

"Did you tell her about Amarie?"

"Yeah."

"Everything about Amarie?"

"Well, no."

"I think it's time you and Bahati had a real conversation, and you both get tested. But I also want you to really talk to Xavier. I think he can help put together some of those missing pieces you have."

"What missing pieces?"

"Talk to him and find out. Since you're here, you want breakfast?"

"Sure."

Bahati woke up to an empty bed. She checked her phone and saw she had a message from Mehki that he was going to meet with his dad. She sent a smiley face, a kissy face, and heart eyes. She showered and headed down to her office. Her organization was putting a campaign together to raise money for a local women's shelter, which housed mostly black women.

As she pulled up to her office building, she saw the windows were broken and someone had spray painted "BITCH" in red across the front of the building. She got out and pulled her 9mm from the glove compartment. She chose the right day to come in leggings, a t-shirt, and sneakers. She tiptoed in, waving her gun in each direction. After searching the entire building, and satisfied no one was there, she called the police.

"Do you have any idea of someone who would do this?" Officer Daniel asked.

"No, to be honest, I don't." The officer asked a few more questions as pictures were taken. After they had left, her team started arriving.

"Who would do this?" Amina asked.

"Looks like nothing was stolen," Mark assured.

"I think whoever did this, wanted to send me a message," Bahati realized.

"Who would hate you this much? After all the hard work you do for the community." That was Amina.

"My mother," she mumbled, more so to herself. "Can y'all do me a favor? Clean up as much as you can. I'm going to check the security cameras."

"Sure, boss!" Mark smiled.

She never mentioned to the police that she had security cameras, and they never asked. Being that her office was in Third Ward, white officers didn't give a damn about black owned businesses, especially those that cater to mostly black women. She went to her office and pulled up the security footage between last night and this morning. She fast-forwarded it at 32x speed. It was around 2 a.m. on the camera when she slowed things down. She saw someone lurking around the building. A woman. She looked closer and saw that the woman had a sledgehammer in her hands. She watched as the perp swung at the windows and plowed down the front door. Another person came and started spray painting as the woman went in.

Bahati shook her head. She switched to the camera inside that was facing directly towards the door. And it was none other than

Rashelle, and her face was still fucked up. Bahati grabbed her keys and let Amina and Mark know that she was heading out for a while. More of the team was heading in, and she let them know that Mark and Amina would fill them in.

"Pick up, pick up," she repeated as she listened to her sister's phone ring. She got in her car and headed downtown to Kamaria's condo. When she got to the garage, she used her keycard to let herself in. Parking on the fourth floor, she used it again to access the elevator. When she got off on Kamaria's floor, she pulled her keys out, unlocked the door and let herself in. To her surprise, Kamaria was sitting across from Rashelle.

"You fucking bitch!" Bahati raged and charged at Rashelle, swinging on her. Kamaria pulled her off and pushed her back.

"What the fuck Bahati?" Kamaria shouted.

"I told you that bitch was crazy," Rashelle laughed.

"Shut up Rashelle!" Kamaria warned, whipping her head towards her. She looked back at her sister and held her hands out as if to say, "What's up?"

"Not only did this drug addict show up to my home and demand money that she claims I owe her, she broke into my office and vandalized it. Yeah, that's right. I got you on camera." Bahati pulled it up and showed it to Kamaria. Kamaria handed it back to Bahati and turned back to Rashelle.

"I think it's time for you to go," she told her.

"You're going to pick her over me? Your own mother?"

"Bahati was more of a mother to me than you ever were. Just go before I have you escorted out."

"Fine. But you hoes will get yours." She grabbed her purse and walked out.

"Why didn't you tell me she came to see you?" Kamaria challenged. Bahati went and sat on the couch, putting her head in her hands.

"Because I thought I was protecting you, and as we both can see how that worked out."

"Protecting me from what?"

"From being hurt again, seeing her for who she really was. I wanted you to still have those good memories of her." Kamaria came and sat next to her sister.

"Bahati, I'm not a little girl anymore. I don't need protecting. And despite whatever hurt you were trying to keep me from, I know she still left us to do drugs. I will always carry that with me."

"Do you remember that night when we were taken into CPS custody?"

"I remember there was a fire, but that's really it."

Bahati took a deep breath and turned to Kamaria. She told her sister the same thing she told Mehki. Kamaria sobbed, and sobbed, and sobbed. She didn't remember any of that. Bahati held her.

"Are you going to press charges for her breaking into your building?"

"For what? She doesn't have any money. But I am going to get a restraining order against her. Are you going to be okay?"

"Yeah, I'll be fine."

"Okay, well, I'm going to head back to work to get ahead of this campaign. I'll talk to you later.

13

A week later, Mehki was sitting in a coffee shop waiting for his 2 p.m. appointment. He looked up just as the man walked in. He nodded his head and the man came over, sitting across from him.

"Mehki."

"Jordan."

"What do you want, man? Why am I here?"

"To offer you the contract with Nu Energy."

"Why would I want to take this contract?"

"Because it's rightfully yours. And I swear man, I didn't know my father had gotten the contract."

"Does he know you're offering it to me?"

"Does it matter?"

"Yes, because he might try to get it back, and then we'll really have a problem."

"Jordan, what is this really about?"

"What do you mean?"

"I know that this beef isn't just about this stupid ass contract. If you have something that you need to get off your chest, let's have it."

"Okay," he said, leaning forward. "You think that just because your mother is this big-shot author and publisher, and Jeremy owns the largest urban planning company in the state, that you're above everybody else."

"Wait. Isn't your mom a 4 time Grammy award winning artist? And your step dad owns a multibillion dollar company?"

"Your point being?"

"This can't be about whose parents make more or are more famous. Cut the bullshit and really let me know what's up."

"You weren't there Mehki."

"Where?"

"When my mom and De'Kari divorced, you weren't there for me."

"What are you talking about? I was there."

"No, you weren't. You were too busy playing with your brothers."

"They're my brothers, the fuck? You're really wild'n right now."

"Yeah, but I was there before them. I was there when Xavier left."

"And I was there when your pops left and when he got incarcerated. Jordan, I have always been there. You're my brother man, doesn't matter that we aren't blood." The two men stood up and hugged. Mehki's phone buzzed. It was Bahati. She had been blowing him up all week. He wasn't avoiding her, but he knew he needed some space, especially since waiting on the test results from his blood test.

"Must be a woman," Jordan mentioned.

"What? Oh, naw. It's cool."

"Doesn't look like it's cool by your face man. I'm all ears."

"Okay, check it. I've been dating this woman, Bahati, and..."

"Bahati Carver?"

"Yeah, you know her?"

"Who doesn't know her? I mean I don't know her personally, but I know her work."

"Yeah, she's pretty amazing."

"Then why the fuck are you ignoring her calls?"

"Because I don't know if I have AIDS yet."

"Nigga what? I know we fell off, but I need you to back up some and fill me in."

"Xavier came back and told me that he's dying from AIDS. Said he's had it a while. My mom got tested and suggested I get tested."

"What does that have to do with you avoiding Bahati?"

"We've had sex, a number of times without protection."

"Don't you think you should put her on notice?"

"I mean, I figured if the results came back negative, I wouldn't have to tell her."

"But you do realize that by ignoring her, you're going to have to give her a damn good reason, especially if you're ignoring her for something that she didn't do."

"I know. And she's going to be pissed."

"I think you need to go talk to her today."

"You're right. Later man." They dapped each other up

"Oh, and before you go, keep the contract with Nu Energy," Jordan told him.

"Are you sure man?"

"I'm sure. There will be other projects." They went their separate ways, Mehki headed straight to Bahati's house.

"Is his phone still going to voicemail?" Carter asked.

They were lying across Bahati's bed.

"Yeah. I haven't heard from him in a week." They had only been dating almost two months and had talked nearly every day. Bahati was becoming worried that she may have done something.

"You sure y'all didn't have a fight or disagreement?"

"No, but he still didn't tell me what happened while we were in Versailles. He FaceTimed me that first night and his face was all busted up. He said it was work related."

"But that was a while ago." A knock at the door turned both of their heads. "Were you expecting company?"

"No," Bahati frowned as she headed to the front door, Carter standing in the doorway of Bahati's bedroom. Bahati peeped through the peephole to see Mehki on the other side.

"You've got some fucking nerve showing up here after a week of ignoring my calls and text messages!" she accused as she swung open the door.

"Oh, shit," Carter whispered to herself.

"Listen, Bahati, I'm sorry. I've just really been going through some things and I didn't know how to explain what was going on."

"I don't give a damn. When you're dating someone, you're supposed to communicate whatever is going on, good or bad. You just stopped calling and sent my calls to voicemail. I saw you read all my texts. So come up with something better than that lame ass excuse." She folded her arms, blocking the doorway.

"Can I just come in and we talk, privately?" he asked, looking at Carter. Carter turned her lips up and folded her arms, mimicking Bahati.

"Very well then. I met with Xavier."

"I remember that. That was the last message I received from you."

"Yeah, well, the meeting didn't go too well," he hesitated, rubbing his hand down the back of his neck.

"What does that have to do with me? With us?

"That's why he's back. He's dying from AIDS."

"What?"

"Yeah, he said he's had it for a while, not sure how long, but he suggested my mom get tested, as well as Jeremy, my brothers, and, well, me." The horror on Bahati's face pulled at his heartstrings. He walked towards her with outstretched arms, but she backed away.

"So you're saying, you could've given me AIDS?"

"Yes and no."

"Don't fuck with me Mehki!"

"I already got tested. I got the results this morning, and I'm negative. So are my brothers, mom, and Jeremy."

"So, instead of forewarning me, you decided to keep this from me and get tested so you could then let me know whether or not you have it? Is that right?" Her eyes pooled with tears.

"Bahati, listen. What I did was fucked up. I should've told you the minute I found out, but I didn't know how to tell you. I was scared myself, and angry. This man, who I haven't seen in over 15 years, comes out of the blue to tell me he's dying from AIDS. How else should I have reacted?"

"Oh, you want me to feel sorry for you, huh? Oh poor Mehki, his daddy has AIDS and is dying. Fuck you! I should've been your first call since we have been having unprotected sex. Now I have to go and get tested."

"Well, you might want to wait about 3 months since it takes that long to show up, if you have it," Carter chimed in. Bahati whirled her head around, and Carter held her hands up in surrender before backing into the bedroom.

"Bahati, I really am sorry, mon cherie."

"It doesn't even matter anymore, Mehki. I

think it's best if you leave. Don't contact me anymore. We are done." She slammed the door in his face, leaning her back against it, and sliding down it as the tears fell. Carter came out and sat beside her friend, holding her.

14

Eight months had passed since Mehki and Bahati had broken up. He called and texted every day. He sent flowers and gifts to her job and home. In that time, Bahati had been tested twice for everything in the book. Everything came back negative, except one pregnancy test. She was a week away from being 9 months pregnant with Mehki's daughter. She hadn't told him and was still debating whether or not she should. Carter and Kamaria had begged her to, but she was of course being stubborn. In that time, she had put on 4 different events for *Voices of Hue Women*, and she traveled a great deal.

It was the beginning of October, and she knew she had to tell Moriah. Not because of the award she won, but because she deserved to know she had a granddaughter on the way. She grabbed her phone and dialed her number.

"Moriah Panton speaking."

"Hi Mrs. Panton, this is Bahati, Bahati Carver."

"Girl, I know who you are. You're the only person I know with that beauty of a name. How are you?"

"Thank you, and I'm fine. I was calling to see if you wanted to grab lunch."

"Of course. I know of this nice little bistro over on Montrose."

"Luis's, I heard their tomato basil soup was amazing. Is noon okay?"

"Sure, I'll see you then." They hung up and Bahati got dressed. She headed to the bistro and valeted her car. Moriah was already there sitting at one of the outside tables. She waved Bahati over. As she got closer, Moriah stood to give her a hug.

"Well look at you, pregnant and glowing. I can't believe it's been that long since I've seen you." They took their seats.

"Yeah, I've been keeping a low profile so as to not get stressed."

"May I take you ladies' order?" the waiter asked.

"Yes, I'll have the tomato basil soup, an extra order of breadsticks, a caesar salad and an iced tea," Bahati ordered.

"You know, I think I'll have the same." The waiter took their menus and went to put their orders in.

"So, how far along are you?"

"I'm going on 9 months next week. She doesn't seem to be wanting to evacuate anytime soon." They both laughed.

"A girl? Aww. How I had wished that you and my son would end up together. That could be my first grandbaby in there."

"That's actually why I called you here. She is your first grandbaby." Bahati's eyes welled with water.

"What?" Moriah blinked.

"She's Mehki's daughter," she sobbed.

"Oh sweetheart," Moriah said, getting up to hug her and hand her a napkin. "Why are you crying? This is the best news I've received in a long time."

"I don't know. I'm always crying now over the littlest thing. I cried this morning because I couldn't see my shoe to put my foot in." Moriah snickered and then they both laughed. "I also thought you 'd be upset since I hadn't told Mehki."

"I assume you have your reasons. I also assume it has to do with Xavier." Moriah took her seat again as the food came.

"I just don't get why he waited, and then he ghosted me for a whole week. Then he shows up at my door out of the blue and tells me this, claiming he didn't know what to say or how to tell me. How else am I supposed to react?"

"I told Mehki to tell you the day he found out. I knew the two of you were fooling around, and now I see I was right," she gushed, looking at Bahati's belly. Bahati took a few bites of her salad, bread and soup.

"I'm going to tell him. I just don't know when."

"I would hope before the baby arrives," Moriah suggested.

"Yeah. Can you not tell him though? I think he needs to hear it from me."

"Oh honey, you have my word." They chatted and finished their lunch, then said their goodbyes.

That evening, Mehki and Jerome headed to their parents' house for dinner.

"What do you think is so important that Ma wants us there an hour earlier than usual?" Jerome asked.

"I don't know, but I swear if she brings up Xavier's name, I'm leaving." Xavier had been calling and texting Mehki over the past six months to no avail. Mehk ihad nothing to say to the man. As they pulled up, they saw that Jeremiah and Marlon were already there. They walked inside to see everyone sitting at the table already.

"It's about time y'all got here," Marlon quipped.

"It's 6:45. We're 15 minutes early," Jerome shot back.

"It doesn't matter. Wash your hands and have a seat," Moriah directed. They went to wash and came back. Once seated, Jeremy blessed the food.

"Amen," they all said.

"Now, before we dig in, Mehki, I ran into Bahati today," Moriah said matter-of-factly.

“Okay,” he said, confused.

“Why the hell didn’t you tell that girl about getting tested the day I told you to?”

“Moriah,” Jeremy warned. She cut her eyes at him.

“Ma, seriously? I had just found out and needed to let it sink in.”

“Boy, that’s her life too that could’ve been altered.”

“Could’ve been?

“Yeah. She told me she has been tested twice since then and they came back negative. You need to make things right with her.”

“Ma, she won’t even talk to him. He’s been sulking like a lil…” Marlon laughed.

“You better watch your mouth,” Moriah warned. Marlon stopped laughing.

“Marlon’s right Ma, about the not talking to me part,” Mehki added, peering at Marlon out of the corner of his eyes.

“Well you better do something.” The rest of the men began to fill their plates as Mehki and Moriah went back and forth. The house phone rang and Jeremy jumped up to answer it. He ran back in the dining room and everyone looked up at him.

“It’s Xavier. He’s in the hospital. They don’t think he’s going to make it through the night.” Mehki hopped up and ran out the door, his brothers behind him. They jumped in their cars and sped to the hospital, Moriah and Jeremy not far behind.

15

They all sat in the waiting room. Mehki paced back and forth. He didn't know what made him want to get here so quickly. He was nervous and shaking. Why did he feel this way about his father?

"Family of Xavier Welsh?" the doctor called, coming into the waiting area. They all stood up and behind Mehki.

"Xavier is comfortable, but he is asking to see a..." she looked down at her clipboard, "Mehki."

"That's me," Mehki spoke up.

"Follow me."

He followed her through the double doors. He could hear his mother sob. They walked down the hall and turned right and stopped at the second door on the left.

"Don't be alarmed. The rashes are normal for those who refuse medication."

"Refuse medication?" he questioned.

"Yes, did you not know that his HIV escalated to AIDS from refusing medication?"

"Xavier and I are not close." The doctor nodded and opened the door. Mehki heard the beeps of the machines. He looked around the dimly lit room until his eyes rested on Xavier. Over the past six months, he had aged and became thinner. He didn't recognize this man that he used to play catch with and attend football games. He sat in the chair beside the bed. And as if Xavier felt his presence, he slowly opened his eyes and smiled.

"Aren't you a sight for sore eyes?" he crooked. Mehki grabbed the water off the tray and held the straw to his mouth. Xavier took three large gulps and cleared his throat which sent him into a coughing fit. Mehki waited anxiously for the coughing to subside. When they did, he spoke first.

"Why did you leave?" he choked out.

"I know you won't believe me, and I know it sounds selfish, but I loved your mother. And when she said that she didn't want me, I couldn't take it."

"You were married, with a whole other kid."

"Yeah, and that's why I got divorced. I lied and told my ex-wife I cheated, but really, I couldn't get over not being with your mother."

"So you decided to leave me too?" Mehki let the tears fall as he looked at his father, who was also tearing up.

"Mehki, I know that I can't change things, but I don't want to leave this earth with you hating me, or thinking that I didn't love you. I do love you, both of my sons." Mehki dropped his head and wiped the tears. "Listen, I made some big mistakes, including however I got AIDS. I had a lot of sex with a lot of women. I shot up drugs at one point. I've been clean and sober for over 10 years. But I figure this is karma for what I put you, your brother, your mother, and his mother through." Mehki's shoulders shook as he sobbed. Xavier reached out a hand and Mehki took it, both of them squeezing.

"I don't hate you."

"I don't blame you if you did." He started coughing again. Mehki grabbed the water, but Xavier refused. Mehki sat on the bed next to him. Once the coughs subsided again, Xavier looked his son in his eyes.

"I love you Mehki."

"I love you too, Pop." Mehki watched as his father took his last breath. The door swung open, but Mehki didn't turn around.

"Is he dead?" a male's voice asked. Mehki slowly turned around to see his brother, Xavier Jr. He nodded. Xavier Jr. broke down.

"This is your fault! It's because of you and your whore of a mother that he turned to drugs and left me and my mother!" Mehki jumped up, knocking a tray over and ran up on him. He swung and Xavier Jr. moved, catching Mehki in his side with a jab. Mehki doubled over but got up quick, hitting Xavier in the chin with an uppercut. Xavier Jr. fell back and Mehki jumped on him. They tussled for a while, throwing punches until Mehki's brothers came in to break it up.

"What the hell is going on?" Moriah demanded. Mehki shook his brothers off and stormed out of the room, leaving the hospital. He got in his car and drove home.

When he got there, Amarie was waiting. He parked and got out, walking past her and unlocking the door to his house. She followed. He went straight to his bar and grabbed a bottle of Hennessy. He sat on the couch, opened it, and took a swig. Amarie took this as her chance. He clearly was upset and hadn't asked her to leave. She knelt between his legs as he took two more swigs from the bottle. She reached into his sweatpants to pull his member out. She stroked it and watched it harden, licking her lips.

She took him all the way in her mouth. He took another drink and watched her head bob up and down his shaft. He felt the head of his dick hit the back of her throat and cursed. He let his head fall to the back of the couch as she worked him like she had always been good at doing. He rested a hand on the back of her head to push himself further down her throat. The sound of her gagging made him push her head down further.

He took another drink as he moved her head up and down until he released his hot nut down the back of her throat, stiffening beneath her. He released her head and watched her wipe a tear away from gagging. She stood up and lifted her skirt to show she had no panties on. He leaned over and pulled a drawer open from a side table and handed her a gold wrapper.

"Seriously?" she questioned.

"Put it on me," he ordered.

She tore open the condom and rolled it down his shaft. She places her hands on his shoulders to position herself so his head was at her opening. She eased her way down him and gasped as she widened the further down she went. He glared at and placed the bottle on the side table. He gripped her thighs and lifted her up and down him. He closed his eyes as she moaned and screamed his name, thinking of the woman he really wanted to be getting him off: Bahati.

"You're going too hard Mehki!" Amarie complained, but he didn't care. He wanted to bust this nut, he needed to bust this nut. Her ass slapped hard against his thighs as he slammed her up and down until his core tightened and he filled the condom.

"I'm coming!" she screamed. He let her thighs go and let her finish. She convulsed and threw her head back. He softened as she finished. She moved over to sit beside him. "You want to talk about it?"

"Not really," he said, taking the condom off and going to flush it. When he came back she was taking a few swigs from his bottle. "You hungry?" he asked in passing to the kitchen.

"No," she responded, walking into the kitchen.

He took some ingredients out to make a sandwich. She came up behind him and wrapped her arms around his waist. He stiffened at her touch. "I'm so happy you came to your senses."

"Just because we fucked, doesn't mean that we are getting back together." He continued making his sandwich.

"No, but it's a start."

"Amarie, I just lost my father. I don't have time for this right now."

"Jeremy died?" she recoiled.

"No, my biological father. He had AIDS."

"Do you have it too?"

"No." He ate his sandwich in three bites. He washed it down by opening another bottle of Hennessy.

"I'm sorry, Mehki. What can I do?"

"Get undressed and let me fuck you how I want." He glared at her. She hesitated, but then figured this was her chance to show him that she had changed and could be the woman he wanted. Mehki spent the rest of the night ramming his member in all her holes.

16

"I'm so nervous," Kamaria shook.

"You'll be fine. Everything looks perfect," Bahati offered, hugging her sister.

"Girl, you put on this event every year," Carter reminded.

"You're right," Kamaria agreed, taking a deep breath.

"Time to rub the belly for good luck," Kamaria squealed, rubbing and kissing her sister's belly. "Now don't you arrive and upstage auntie's show," she cooed. Bahati and Carter laughed as they left to find their seats. They were seated on the first row at the end of the runway. As they chatted, Carter froze.

"What's wrong with you?" Bahati asked. "You look like you just seen a ghost." She laughed and then followed Carter's gaze towards the left of the stage. Mehki and his brothers were coming in, but it was who was on Mehki's arm that made Bahati's heart drop.

"I can't believe he had the nerve to show up with that bitch on his arm at your sister's show," Carter whispered. Bahati kept her eyes on him until their eyes met. She saw his expression change when he noticed her belly. He slowly sat in his seat and she smirked. Her gaze broke when Kamaria came out on the runway and everyone cheered.

Mehki kept his eyes on her. He couldn't believe she was pregnant, and he was almost certain that the baby was his.

"Yo, I think you may have a problem," Jerome whispered to him. Mehki nodded his head.

"Did you know she was pregnant? I know you've been hanging out with Carter."

"No, and we have not been hanging out. She's giving me legal advice."

"About what?"

"Don't worry about it.

"Ladies and gentleman," Kamaria began. "Welcome to the 5th Annual Hue Beginnings Fashion Show, brought to you by yours truly, Kamaria Carver." The audience erupted with applause. "The proceeds for the show and the auction of the pieces you see this evening, will go towards The Voice of Youth Foundation. So sit back, relax, and enjoy the show. Also, go ahead and take your wallets out so you can have your coins ready." The audience laughed as she headed backstage.

An hour later, the show was over and it was time for the after show party. It was being held in one of the numerous ballrooms in The Galleria. Bahati and Carter found their reserved tables and took a seat, waiting for Kamaria.

"Don't look now, but baby daddy is headed

this way," Carter warned, getting up to get them some drinks. Mehki sat down next to Bahati and turned towards her.

"Is it mine?" Bahati looked at him and smirked.

"Why do you care?"

"Why wouldn't I care?" Bahati rolled her eyes and scoffed.

"Yes, she's yours."

"She?" he repeated. "She's a girl?" He cheesed from ear to ear. Carter came back with their drinks and sat down. "How far along are you?"

"I made 9 months today."

"Then why are you here? Why aren't you in bed, resting your feet?"

"Because I wanted to be here for my sister. I'm not inept, Mehki. I'm pregnant."

"Yeah, I know, but you shouldn't be out."

"And who are you, my daddy?"

His gaze darkened at her words. He didn't know if she knew Xavier had died or not.

"Bahati, I'm not joking," he said through gritted teeth.

"Regardless, your girlfriend is on her way over here." He turned to see Amarie heading their way with a scold on her face. He knew it was about to be drama.

"Hey baby, I was looking for you," she drawled, placing a hand on his shoulder. "Oh, you got knocked up. I knew she was a whore." Carter jumped up at the same time as Mehki. He stood between them.

"Not now Amarie. And don't call the mother of my daughter a whore." Amarie took a step back, as if he had struck her.

"Mother...of...your..." She couldn't finish her sentence. "How do you know it's yours? She could be lying to trap you."

"Like you did 5 years ago?" he reminded her. Tears filled her eyes.

Bahati felt a sharp pain in her side. She knew it was a contraction. Water pooled at her feet. She hadn't worn underwear.

"Eww, are you peeing?"Amarie asked, disgusted. Carter and Mehki both looked at Bahati as Kamaria headed over.

"My water just broke," Bahati cried.

"I'll call the midwife," Carter offered as she grabbed her phone off the table.

"I'll drive to the hospital," Mehki said.

"No!" all three women barked.

"She's having a homebirth, so we need to get her to her condo," Kamaria explained.

"No, take her to my place. Give the midwife my address." He rattled it off to Carter. Bahati was in no shape to argue. Mehki helped her to her feet.

"Are you serious right now?" Amarie scuffed.

"Amarie, I think your presence is no longer wanted," Moriah said, as she, Jeremy, and Mehki's brothers walked up.

"Mrs. Panton, but I..."

"Bye ho," Moriah glared. Kamaria and Carter snickered. Mehki carried Bahati out of the mall and to his awaiting limo. Everyone else took their own cars. Bahati began to practice her breathing techniques that Athena had taught her.

"What can I do?" Mehki asked.

"Nothing. I think you've done enough," she breathed, looking at her belly. He let out a deep chuckle.

"I know this isn't the time for this, but I love you Bahati, and it's not just because you're having my baby." She looked up at him.

"You're not even going to question whether or not she's yours?"

"I did the math," he said, twisting up the side of his mouth. Bahatai laughed until another contraction jolted her back to reality. He grabbed her hand and she squeezed it through the next contraction. He winced as her grip tightened. They pulled up to his place 15 minutes later. Mehki felt like his right hand would be permanently contorted. The contractions were now 2 minutes apart. Baby girl was coming fast. Mehki's brothers were already waiting outside his house to help. The midwife, Kamaria, and Carter were setting up inside.

Jerome opened the door and Jeremiah and Marlon carried Bahati out.

"If y'all drop her, I swear to God I'll kill you both," Mehki promised. They carefully carried her inside, taking heed to their brother's words. The pool was set up in his living room, and the women were pouring warm water into it. Jeremiah and Marlon set her on the couch. Bahati began to undress.

"Bye!" Mehki told his brothers. They laughed and headed to his back deck. He helped her to finish undressing and got undressed as well, down to his boxers.

"What are you doing?" she asked.

"I'm getting in with you. I'm not letting you do this alone."

"I've been doing this alone the past 9 months."

"Yeah, but that was your decision. Right now, you don't have one. And do you really want to argue about this right now?" Before she could protest, another contraction came. She shrieked and grabbed his wrist.

"Get her into the pool," Athena ordered him. He did as he was told and carried her into the pool. He sat behind her as Athena showed him how to use his fists to apply pressure to her hips during each contraction. As Bahati moaned in pain, he pressed his fists against her hips. Kamaria and Carter poured warm water over Bahati. Mehki watched as the woman he loved labored. She had never looked more beautiful.

"Alright, this labor progressed rather quickly. It is time to push," Athena announced. "Push on my count. 1..2..3.." Bahati bared down and pushed, clasping Mehki's hands. "Mehki, maneuver your way around this side to catch your daughter." Mehki stared blankly.

"Huh?"

"Move on this side between her legs." He did as she said while Carter and Kamaria took his place behind Bahati outside the pool, each woman holding either of Bahati's hands. Mehki settled in between Bahati's legs. He saw fear in her eyes.

"Bahati," he said gently. "Mon cherie, you got this." She looked at him through blurred vision. Tears filled her eyes. She nodded, took a deep breath and pushed again.

"What the hell is going on here?" Everyone turned to look in the direction of the voice except Bahati and Mehki. Mehki reached between her legs as their daughter made her way out.

"Bitch, can you not take a fucking hint? He doesn't want you!" Kamaria stood up and stepped in Amarie's direction.

"What do you know?" Amarie smirked. "Baby, tell these bitches that we're together." She looked over at Mehki as he lifted his daughter out of the water and held her to his chest, making sure not to move too far since she was still attached to the placenta.

"Mehki!" Amarie hollered.

"You need to do something about that bitch. I know I just gave birth, but I will get out of this pool and beat her ass, again." Mehki smiled at Bahati and handed over his daughter. He rose out of the pool like a chocolate knight. He walked over towards Amarie.

"You are no longer welcome here or anywhere

else that concerns me, my daughter or my future wife."

"Wife?" Amarie barked. "You're going to marry that bitch just because she had your baby?" Kamaria swung around Mehki, connecting to Amarie's jaw. Mehki held Kamaria back.

"Let me do this. Go over there and tend to your sister and niece." He grabbed Amarie by the arm and dragged her outside. "Listen and listen good. I don't love you. I don't want you. I don't like you. Yes, in a moment of weakness, my judgment was cloudy and I used you. I told you what it was then, and that hasn't changed. You are a conniving succubus. I think at one point you did love me, but that changed. You just want what comes along with being with me. Now that woman in there," he continued, pointing towards the door, "I am going to marry her, and I am going to be the best father to that little girl. Both of them have my entire heart. I don't need, nor do I want anything from you. Now, I am only going to say this once. Leave my fucking house."

Tears ran down the sides of her face as what he said sunk in. She turned and ran towards her car. Mehki watched until he couldn't see her taillights anymore. He went back inside and saw his mother holding his daughter. Bahati was nowhere in sight.

"Where's Bahati?"

"She's upstairs in your bed," Jeremiah answered.

"Y'all let her walk up the stairs by herself?" he demanded.

"Nigga chill. Naw, she ain't walk up by herself," Jerome retorted. Moriah walked over to him and handed him his daughter.

"Go to her, and make her a part of this family, now." He leaned down as she planted a kiss on his forehead. He carried his daughter and the bag with the placenta up the stairs. When he walked into his room, his heart fluttered. Bahati was asleep, and she still looked fucking good even after giving birth. He walked over and lay down next to her. He nestled the baby next to her exposed breast and watched as his daughter latched. He smiled. Bahati stirred and batted her eyes open to first look at their daughter and then at him. She smiled.

"Hey, baby daddy."

"Hey, baby mama. What's her name?"

"Khadija Xavia James-Panton."

"Xavia?"

"Yeah, your mom told me about your dad. I'm sorry, Mehki."

"Thanks. So, we're getting married Monday at the courthouse. I would be remiss to go against my mother's orders and not ask you to marry me."

"When did you ask? Because if I'm hearing things correctly, you just told me that we are getting married."

"Look, Bahati, I love you. I don't want to be with

anyone else but you. I knew I wanted to marry you the day before y'all went to France. I was going to propose when y'all got back, but things got crazy. I'll be damned if my daughter grows up in a house without both her parents who love her and each other."

"What makes you think I love you?"

"I know you love me, without a doubt." He rolled over to his nightstand and pulled out a black box. He opened it and turned it towards Bahati. She gasped. It was a rose gold band with a huge princess cut diamond in the middle.

"Bahati Carver, will you do me the honor of being my wife and mother to our future kids?" She nodded as tears rolled down her cheeks. He put the ring on her finger and leaned over their daughter to kiss her.

EPILOGUE

Two weeks later…

"We are gathered here today, not to mourn a loss, but to celebrate a life." The pastor continued with his message. The funeral of Mehki's father was held at the Pristine Cemetery. Mehki sat in the front row with his wife and daughter. Joining them was his mother, Jeremy, Xavier Jr., and his mother. After the eulogy, a few people got up to speak about Xavier. Then it was Mehki's turn. He looked at Bahati and she smiled, squeezing his hand. He got up and walked to the other side of the casket.

"Growing up, Xavier and I were inseparable when it was time for me to go to his house. We did everything together. When he left me, a part of me hated him, only a small part. But mostly, I blamed myself. For the longest I thought about what it was that I did to make him leave me." He looked at Jordan, who knew all too well what it was like to have their father leave and disown them. "Even through counseling, I was told that it wasn't my fault, but for some reason I couldn't accept that. On his deathbed, he told me the truth, his truth, and for once, I don't blame myself. I love you pop." Mehki threw a rose onto the casket and sat back down with his wife.

After everyone came to pay their last respects, they watched as Xavier was lowered into the ground. Xavier Jr. came over to Mehki and Bahati.

"I want to apologize for what I said about you and your mother. I was angry, being childish, and wanted you to hurt like I was hurting."

"It's cool man," Mehki accepted. He opened his arms to hug his brother. "This is my wife, Bahati, and our daughter Khadijah."

"Nice to meet you," Xavier Jr. said.

"Same," Bahati replied.

"Maybe we can hang sometime," Xavier Jr. hoped.

"For sure." The men hugged again, and Xavier Jr. left.

"You okay?" Bahati asked as she nestled a fussy Khadijah to her breast. Mehki watched in awe. "Why are you looking like that?"

"Mon cherie, you are an amazing woman and mother. When this six week shit is up, you're getting pregnant again."

"What?" Bahati shrieked, startling the baby. Mehki laughed, and they headed to join the rest of their family.

BROKEN PROMISES

1

Carter woke up around noon to the feeling of someone staring at her. When she opened her eyes and they focused, she shrieked and jumped back in the bed, hitting the headboard. It was Derwin.

"It's noon. Why are you still sleeping?" he demanded, sitting in a chair at the foot of the bed, eyeing her skeptically as if she were about to tell a lie. He wore white linen pants, a brown linen shirt, and some Sperry's.

"What are you doing back? I thought you'd be gone for another two weeks?" she asked, rubbing her eyes.

"I ask the questions!" he snapped, causing the hairs on her body to stand straight up. She hated when he got like this. Sometimes he would get physical. One particular time he came back from traveling early because she hadn't answered her phone. He choked her until she passed out and then beat her while she was unconscious.

"Please Derwin, you just got back. Can we not do this?" she pleaded.

"You were out hoeing weren't you?" he

sneered, easing out of his chair.

"No!" she shrieked defensively. "Bahati had her baby last night, and we stayed at her fiance's house to help out." He inched closer.

"Who is 'we'?" he asked, now on the side of the bed.

"Me, her sister, the midwife, her fiancé, and his parents," she explained, shaking, omitting the part about Mehki's brothers being there.

"Anyone else there?" She shook her head quickly from side-to-side, shrinking back as he was now right next to her, towering over her like a skyscraper. Before she knew it, her face stung from the smack of the back of his hand.

"You fucking lying bitch!" he foamed at the mouth. He grabbed her by her hair and yanked her out of the bed with one swift move.

"Derwin, stop!" she begged, clawing at his hands, kicking. He slammed her head against the floor. She heard ringing in her ears, and then a sharp pain in her abdomen as he kicked her repeatedly. She curled into the fetal position. He stomped on her side, spitting vulgarities at her.

"You stupid whore! I know who Bahati's fiancé is. I saw the pictures of him and her and his family at his house, including his brothers. You were in the background of some of them. You think you can lie to me, huh?"

She felt sharp stings all over her body. He had taken his belt off and was giving her lash after lash after lash. After a while, like always, she became numb and just took it. He would eventually stop. He fell back onto the floor, out of breath as she couldn't seem to find hers. Her vision blurred right before it went all black.

Several hours later, Carter felt warm drops on her face. It smelled of ammonia. She opened her eyes to see Derwin standing over her, pissing on her face. He threw his head back and laughed. She tried to move, but the searing pain that coursed through her body kept her frozen in place. He shook his manhood to let out the remaining droplets and then zipped his pants back up.

"Get up, clean up this mess, and make me some dinner." He walked out the room, slamming the door behind him. She shook violently as she sobbed. She had endured this for too long. Carter grew up in the foster system. No one ever wanted her. When she was 18, she went off to college at Spelman. She met Derwin while at Spelman. He was her first real relationship.

After graduating, Derwin moved to Houston to attend Thurgood Marshall School of Law, and Carter followed. Everything was great in the beginning until two years ago. Something in Derwin changed around the time she started gaining momentum and securing high profile clients, and he became mean, aggressive, violent, vehement, and dark. Every now and then, he would break up with her, and then come back saying sweet nothings that she fell for time and time again.

No one knew that he beat her, not even Kamaria and Bahati. She was supposed to be meeting them for dinner, but she knew there was no way he was going to let her out the house. She crawled to her knees, sharp pulsating pains knocked the breath out of her with very move. When she finally made it to her feet, she stared in the mirror across the room. She hadn't slept with any clothes on. There were dark purple bruises all over her body, along with welts from the belt. She grabbed her phone and sent a message to their group text as tears fell from her chin.

Carter: Bae came back early, so we're going to stay in for the night and get reacquainted with each other's bodies.

She had become good at making up excuses as to why she couldn't meet with them, and they never suspected anything

Kamaria: Ewwww. You could've left that part out.

Bahati: That's cool. Baby girl won't get off the titty anyway and her daddy is getting jealous, so I need to tend to my babies.

Carter winced as she tried to smile, truly happy for her best friend, but also somewhat envious. Not in a way that she hated her, but more so in a way that she wanted that same thing for herself, and she knew she wasn't going to get that with Derwin. She sent them both kiss emojis and locked her phone.

She began sobbing again as she limped achingly to the bathroom. She turned on the shower, turning the knob all the way to hot. Steam filled the bathroom. She opened the shower door and painstakingly got inside.

2

"You might want to sit down for this," the doctor said. Jerome slowly sat down, not knowing what type of news to expect. He had been waiting on the results of the test for a few months now.

"I have some good news, and some not so great news," he continued.

"Give me the good news first doc," Jerome hesitated.

"Good news is, the DNA test came back positive and Genesis is in fact your daughter." Jerome jumped up throwing a fist in the air, tears streaming from his eyes. He was married to Melina Blackstone, sister of the Blackstone brothers for 5 years. After they divorced, Melina found out she was pregnant. She never told Jerome until a few months ago. The little girl was two now. He met her on one occasion and instantly had a feeling she was his. When he demanded a DNA test, Melina refused to let him see her anymore. She was pissed that he questioned whether or not she was his, but he had every right to.

Melina had gotten into drugs a few months before their divorce after she lost her job at the number one marketing agency in the city. She took it pretty hard and Jerome tried to be there for her, even taking her to see a series of therapists. One night she went out and didn't come home for a few days. Jerome had a PI search for her and found her in a crack house. He sent her to rehab for 60 days, and when she came back, everything was good for a few days until she did it again, this time almost overdosing.

After she was released from the hospital, he sent her back to rehab. She checked herself out and was found servicing several men in an ally in Trinity Gardens. Jerome couldn't deal with it anymore, so he filed for divorce.

It broke his heart when it was time for her to sign the papers that she signed them and walked off, never speaking to him again until a few months ago. When she told him about Genesis, he did the math and realized that she potentially could've been someone else's kid. Melina didn't want money or anything from him. She just wanted to let him know he had a kid.

Now that he knew she was his, he was going to fight for custody of her. He had a CPS agent look into where they were living, and they were living in a homeless shelter. He wanted Genesis taken out claiming that Melina was on drugs, but she had been clean for a year. The social worker said there was no grounds for taking the child. She was clearly nourished, clean, and happy. Jerome didn't care. He knew he could give his daughter a better life.

"Okay, doc," Jerome said, coming down off his high. "What's the bad news?"

"We ran some tests on the girl as the social worker instructed, and she has acute leukemia." All air left Jerome's body. The walls felt like they were closing in as he stumbled to sit back in his seat. The doctor rushed to his side to keep him from tipping over.

"Mr. Panton, can I get you some water or something?" Jerome shook his head. It felt like his heart was slowing, threatening to stop.

"Mr. Panton, it's not a death sentence. Apparently, her mother has been keeping up with her treatments and doctor's appointments. However..."

"There's more?"

"Yes. She's currently in remission but needs a stem cell transplant and..."

"I'll do it. I'll do whatever I need to. Get my blood tested to see if I'm a match."

"Are you sure?"

"The fuck? Hell yeah I'm sure. Shes my fucking daughter!" Jerome boomed.

"Alright. Here's the paper to get the bloodwork done in the lab downstairs." The doctor smiled.

"You knew I would agree to this didn't you?" Jerome smirked.

"Mr. Panton, I have been your doctor for 15 years. I think I know you by now." Jerome and the doctor stood up and shook hands. He hustled down to the lab to get his blood drawn. He couldn't wait to tell Carter.

After leaving the doctor, Jerome headed over to his parents' house. Mehki was getting married today. They had planned to go to the courthouse, but since finding out Marlon was an ordained minister, they figured it best to have the wedding at their parents' house.

"My man is tying the knot today," Jeremiah quipped.

"Are you sure about this man? Marriage isn't all that," Jerome chimed in.

"Tuh, says you. Just because yours didn't work out by no fault of your own, doesn't mean mine won't," Mehki shit back.

The men continued getting dressed when Jeremy walked in.

"I am a proud man, Mehki. You made me a grandfather, and I'm gaining a daughter," Jeremy beamed. Jerome looked down as the words hurt a little. He wasn't ready yet to tell everyone about his daughter until it was the right time.

"Thanks pops," Mehki said, pulling Jeremy into a hug. "Now, go find my wife and get ready to walk her down the aisle." The men laughed as Jeremy headed out.

"You ready?" Jeremiah asked.

"More than ever," Mehki responded.

The men headed to the kitchen to get ready to walk out the back door. The backyard was set up with white folding chairs lined with white tulips, Bahati's favorite flowers. There were tables setup for the reception with blush tablecloths, and baby blue roses as the centerpieces. All their close friends and family that could make it last minute were there. Marlon lined up first, followed by Jeremiah and Moriah, Mehki, Jerome and Carter, and finally Kamaria, the maid of honor.

"You look stunning," Jerome whispered to Carter. She gave him a slight smile and looked forward. Derwin had come with her to the nuptials, and she didn't want to give him any reason to make a scene. Jerome frowned at her lack of acknowledgement.

"Is there something wrong?" he asked, leaning in, placing his hand on the small of her back. She winced before moving. She had done a pretty good job with her makeup. Luckily she was a deep dark brown, so the bruises were easy to cover.

"I'm fine. Let's get ready to walk," she said through gritted teeth, her eyes forward as the double doors opened. Jerome stared for a minute longer and then turned his attention forward and smiled as they walked down the makeshift aisle.

As he got closer to where Derwin was sitting, he had a scowl on his face as he watched the two walking arm in arm. Carter winked at him to try to ease his clear disdain for the situation, but his expression didn't falter.

After everyone was in their place, the music changed and everyone stood up, looking back towards the house. The doors opened and everyone gasped at the sight of Bahati in a long blush gown, embroidered with sequins along the ends. Jeremy was on her right as she carried a sleeping and nursing Khadija on her left. Everyone smiled as Carter shed a tear, and so did Mehki.

As they walked down the aisle, everyone sat down row by row. When they got to the altar, they stopped in front of Marlon and Mehki.

"Who gives this woman to be wed?" Marlon asked.

"I do," said Jeremy, Kamaria, and Carter. Mehki came down and replaced his father's position. He looked down at her and their daughter.

"Baby, I fucking love you," he whispered. She beamed up at him.

"Uhhm," Marlon said, pretending to clear his throat. "We are gathered here today to witness the nuptials of my brother and my soon to be sister. As the youngest, I am proud to be blessed with such an honor. Usually, I am looked over in this family and..."

"Marlon, dial it back," Jeremiah whispered as the crowd laughed.

"Right. Mehki and Bahati have each decided to say their own vows." Carter watched and listened in awe as the two exchanged beautiful, heartfelt vows to each other. Kamaria cried. When it was time to exchange the rings, Bahati lifted Khadija up and adjusted her breast as Moriah came up to get her granddaughter.

"I now pronounce you husband and wife. You may kiss the bride," Marlon announced.

"Come her girl," Mehki said, grabbing Bahati by the waist as she giggled. He kissed her passionately, borderline sexually.

"Okay that's enough," Moriah joked, setting the crowd into a fit of laughter. They stopped kissing and stared at each other.

"Ladies and gentleman, I present to you Mr. and Mrs. Mehki Josiah James-Panton!" Everyone stood and cheered.

After the ceremony, the wedding party went to change into their reception outfits. The ladies wore sundresses, and the men wore linen short sets. Carter went to the restroom to touch up her shoulders, face and back. She was lucky her bridesmaid dress was long and the sundress. The door opened and her head whipped around. It was Jerome.

"Y-y-you can't be in here," she stammered, hurrying to get her stuff and get out before Derwin caught them.

"Carter did I do something?"

"No, but I have to go."

"Wait, I have some good news. I don't need you on retainer anymore. It's official now. I need you to represent me."

"Great, make an appointment with my secretary," she scurried to the door and when she opened it, Derwin was standing there.

"Hey baby, nothing happened," she said quickly.

Derwin said nothing and didn't even look at her. His eyes were on Jerome. Though Jerome had him by a foot, and body wise his muscles were double the size of Derwin's, Derwin wasn't intimidated.

"Jerome Panton," Jerome introduced, offering Derwin his hand. Derwin never took his eyes off Jerome's.

"Let's go," he told Carter.

"But the reception just started," she protested.

"I said let's go." Derwin walked off and Jerome watched Carter's expression go from sadness to a mix of sadness and terror.

"Carter..." he started as she walked off.

When he made it back outside, Carter was over by Kamaria and Bahati, the man nowhere in sight. He made his way over to Mehki and his brothers.

"Congrats man," he told his brother.

"Thanks. She made me an honest man."

"Isn't the saying that a woman is made into an honest woman?" Jeremiah asked. They all fell out laughing.

"Well, I'm going to go ask the sister of the bride to dance," Jeremiah announced, rubbing his chin as he strolled over to the women. Mehki and Jerome shook their heads.

"I'm going to go grab some wings before pops eats them all," said Marlon as he took long strides towards the food.

"Hey man, do you know anything about Carter's boyfriend?" Jerome asked. Mehki took a sip of his drink.

"Not really. I know that Bahati and Kamaria don't like him. Why?"

"It's just, when she and I were in the bathroom earlier..." Mehki's drink sprayed from his mouth.

"Y'all were in the bathroom?" he asked as his eyes bucked.

"Not like that. I wanted to tell her that I no longer needed her on retainer and that I actually need her to represent me now, and..."

"Man what kind of legal issues do you have? We can help?" Jerome hesitated. Out of all his brothers, he and Mehki were the closest. An inner battle took place as he wondered if he should tell him. He sighed.

"I have a daughter."

"What? By Melina?" Jerome nodded.

"Are you sure she's yours? I mean I know Melina..."

"She's mine. I got the DNA results this morning. Look I know this is your big day, and I don't want to put a damper on it."

"Naw, man, you good." Mehki listened attentively as Jerome told him the story.

"Wow. Congrats man. You have a picture of her?" Jerome pulled his phone out and showed his brother the photo of Genesis. "She looks just like you, with a hint of Ma." Jerome chuckled and nodded his head in agreement.

"So what do you need Carter for?"

"I want full custody."

"Why?"

"I haven't spoken to her mom in two years, and even though she's been clean for a year, there's no telling what my daughter has been through. And now I know that her leukemia is in remission, I want her to be in the best care, and I can provide that."

"You don't think that will make Melina relapse?"

"You think I give a fuck? She kept this from me for two years. I missed my daughter's birth, first words, first steps, first tooth, everything man. She took that from me." Mehki nodded his head. He understood.

"So when are you going to tell Ma and Pops? You know they'll be excited, especially Ma."

"Man, I don't know yet. I'm still trying to see when I can see her, and have her for the day. I want to tell them when they can physically see her. But back to Carter. When we were in the bathroom and dude came, he looked at me like he wanted to kill me. Like I had done something. And the look on her face, she was clearly terrified of him."

"I don't like to get in other people's business, but it sounds like you need to keep y'all relationship strictly business."

"Why wouldn't she tell me she had a boyfriend though?"

"Fiance."

"They're engaged?"

"That's what Bahati told me. Though she doesn't think they'll ever get married since they've been engaged several times before." Jerome let his brother's words sink in. He had actually felt something for Carter.

"Aww shit, you feeling her, huh?" Before Jerome could answer, Bahati came over.

"Excuse me brother-in-law, I'd like to dance with my husband slash baby daddy," she interrupted, running a finger down the center of Mehki's chest. Mehki started cheesing and walking towards her.

"You two love birds go ahead," Jerome smiled.

"This conversation isn't over," Mehki told his brother as Bahati pulled him to dance. Jerome watched as his big brother danced with his new sister. He wanted that. He deserved that. He had hoped he'd get that with Carter.

3

Carter sat at her desk the next afternoon going over case files. She had a meeting with Jerome in 30 minutes. After getting home late last night, she saw that Derwin had not only packed his things, but destroyed her house and left her a note that he was going away for a while and to not contact him. Where she should've felt a sense of relief, a sense of loneliness set in. She knew she shouldn't've felt that way, but she felt like she did when she first got into foster care: abandoned. Derwin didn't love her, and she knew that that was for sure.

Her assistant beeped in letting her know that Jerome was there. She told her to send him in. She looked in the floor to ceiling length mirror on the right wall of her desk to make sure she looked presentable and that none of her bruises were showing. She was still sore and banged up from the other night, and she possibly had a concussion. She thought about going to the hospital, but they'd ask too many questions.

The door to her office opened and what walked through the door took her breath away. He had on a fedora with a pinstripe button up shirt, khaki shorts, Ray Bans shades, and some Brogue designer shoes. She could smell his Armani cologne from where she stood, that sent a signal between her legs that she hadn't gotten in a while. His entire existence spoke to every part of her.

"Good afternoon, Mr. Panton," she said, walking towards him, holding her hand out to take it. He removed his sunglasses and fedora to stare at her blankly.

"No need to be formal. This isn't the first time we met," he smiled. She stood there with her hand still out.

"I know, but this is business, and when it's business, I like to keep things formal," she insisted. He eyed her the way he did at the wedding, making her shift a little as she stood there. He could tell he had an effect on her and that boosted his ego. He took her hand and shook it slowly, staring into her eyes. His hand sent an electric surge through her body. She didn't know what kind of man he was, and as bad as she wanted to, she felt like she was too damaged.

"Please, have a seat," she directed to the chair on the other side of her desk. "So, what's going on? I know you said that you need me to represent you."

"Yeah, I need to file for full custody." She stared at him in confusion. She didn't know he had a kid, and it seemed like neither did his family.

"I'm sorry, that's reserved for people who have children," she explained. He leaned forward and placed his arms on her desk.

"I know what that's for. My ex-wife recently told me that I had a daughter."

"Well, we would have to get a DNA test done first to establish paternity and then..." He pulled out an envelope that she hadn't noticed he was carrying, and handed it to her. She took it slowly, keeping her eyes on him. She opened it and pulled out some papers. Jerome watched as she eyed them, looking so serious and professional. His dick jumped. Something about a woman being about her shit and taking it seriously was a definite turn on.

"Well, seems legit," she said.

"It had better be. As much money as I paid for a rush on the results."

"Alright, let's get started then." She set the papers down and turned to her computer to pull up a document to take notes. She asked him a series of personal questions such as his birthdate, which was coming up, his social, address, all phone numbers, his job name, and his salary.

"Damn, I feel like with you having all of that information, I should at least get a date," he joked, half serious. She only smiled a little and kept typing.

"Okay, Carter, stop," he sighed. She turned to look at him, still with a serious face. "What's going on? Seriously. You were cold at the wedding, and you're being cold now. I know you have a fiancé, but that doesn't mean we can't be friends." She opened her mouth to speak, but then thought better of it.

"Mr. Panton, I..."

"Woman, if you don't call me Jerome. Mr. Panton is my father."

"Fine, Jerome, I think right now, since I am on your dime, we should be getting this done."

"You know my salary. I don't give a shit about that."

"But don't you care about your daughter?"

"What the hell kind of question is that?" he barked, jumping up from his seat. Carter shrieked and held her hands up as if he were going to strike her. He eyed her reaction and froze. His heart stopped.

"Carter, what are you doing?" he asked softly. She opened her eyes and saw the expression on his face. She quickly put her arms down and straightened her clothes.

"I think that what we have is enough for today. I'll get back to you when it's time for the next steps." She got up to shake his hand and stumbled, knocking everything off her desk and nearly falling. Jerome was quick and caught her as she passed out.

4

"What the hell happened?" Bahati demanded as she, Kamaria, and Mehki ran up to where Jerome was sitting in the waiting room. After Carter had passed out and hadn't woken up after 15 minutes, he had her secretary call an ambulance.

"I don't know. We were talking about my case. Then she asked me did I even care about my..." he stopped, realizing he was about to tell them about Genesis. Both women were staring at him, waiting for a response. "She asked me a personal and sensitive question, and I yelled at her. But then she did the weirdest thing. She screamed and held her arms up like I was going to hit her."

"Did you?" Bahati asked, bucking at him.

"Mon cherie, chill," Mehki said, pulling her back. "He didn't hit her, now did you?"

"No, I didn't hit her. What the fuck? When she stood up to tell me that we were done for the day, she passed out. I couldn't wake her, so I told her secretary to call an ambulance. That's when I called y'all." He turned to look at Bahati. "The dude she's dating, has he ever hit her?"

"Not that I know of. I've never seen any signs of domestic violence. No bruises, nothing."

"Well, her skin is rather dark, so maybe they don't show," he gathered, moreso to himself.

"Let's not jump to conclusions," Kamaria offered. "What did the doctor say?"

"Nothing yet."

"Family of Carter Malone." They all turned around in the direction of the voice. It was a black female doctor. They all walked over to her.

"We're her sisters," Bahati lied, kind of. As long as they had known each other, they might as well have been sisters.

"Ms. Malone has a concussion from what seems like a blow to the head. She has some cracked ribs, internal bleeding, and quite a few bruises." Bahati ran to the nearest trashcan and vomited. Kamaria felt like all oxygen had left her body, and began hyperventilating. The doctor dropped her clipboard, and she and Jerome caught Kamaria before she fainted. They carried her to a nearby couch.

"Is there any good news doc?" Jerome demanded.

"Yes, she will be fine. My only concern is the severity of these injuries. They coincide with being violently beaten, kicked, and punched. I also noticed welts all over her body consistent with the width of a man's belt." She eyed both men.

"It wasn't us," Mehki said, holding up his hands in defense.

"You're saying a man beat her?" Bahati asked, finally walking over.

"It looks that way. It appears that he was very angry, given the nature of the injuries."

"I'm calling the police," Bahati said, quickly rummaging in her purse for her phone.

"No need," said the doctor, pointing behind them. Two officers were at the nurses' station. "It is protocol to call the police when these types of patients come in." The doctor walked over to the officers and spoke with them for a second before directing them towards Bahati, Mehki, Jerome, and Kamaria.

"I'm Officer Jones and this is my partner, Officer Reyes. Can you tell us who may have done this?"

"I believe it was her fiancé," Jerome answered, telling them about the night of the wedding.

"Where is he now?" Officer Reyes asked.

"We don't know," Kamaria said, slowly sitting up. Bahati ran to her side to help her.

"If you see him, please give us a call. Do not interact with him." Officer Jones handed each of them a card before both officers left. Since they had no proof it was Derwin, the officers couldn't really do anything.

"Two of you may come in to see her," the doc said as she came back over to them. Kamaria and Carter followed her.

"Yo, this is wild," Mehki whistled, running his hands over his head. He took a seat next to Jerome.

"I knew it. I just knew it. That night I asked you about that, I knew it Ki," Jerome kept repeating. He let the tears fall and his brother pulled him into a side hug.

"I know Rome, I know."

"If I ever see him again, I will kill him." Mehki knew his brother was serious, which led him to his next question.

"How bad do you have it for her?"

"As bad as you have it for Bahati."

"Shit. Have y'all even been on a date yet?"

"No, but it doesn't matter. I never thought I'd catch feelings for anyone after Melina, but this right here, that woman in there, caught me by surprise."

"I know the feeling. But it'll be alright. Don't do anything stupid, and take your time with her. You know their history. Let her come to you."

In the hospital room, Kamaria and Bahati glared at Carter. They were too angry to be sympathetic.

"I know what y'all are thinking," Carter crooked. Her throat was dry from being unconscious for several hours.

"Bitch, do you think we give a fuck?" Kamaria asked.

"And I for damn sure know you don't know what we're thinking," Bahati added.

"Y'all are thinking why didn't I leave."

"No! We're thinking why the fuck didn't you tell us!" Bahati shot back, tears flowing like a river down her cheeks. Carter's eyes pooled as she looked at her friends and the concern written all over their faces. They truly loved her, and she felt bad for not telling them.

"I didn't want y'all to get upset."

"Bitch look at us! We are beyond upset!" Kamaria cried.

"I'm sorry," Carter sobbed. The two women walked over to her and stood on either side, leaning down to hug her.

"Don't be sorry. But please tell us you aren't going back to him," Bahati warned.

"He left last night after he trashed my house."

"He what?!" they both asked.

"Yeah. I got home late after the wedding. He was pissed that I didn't leave with him."

"Wait, so he didn't beat you last night?" Kamaria asked, realizing that it didn't add up.

"No. The morning after Bahati had Khadija, he was there, waiting for me to wake up. He came home to surprise me. He asked where I was and what I was doing the night before, and I told him you had the baby at Mehki's house. He asked who all was there, and I told him everyone except Jerome, Jeremiah, and Marlon. He apparently had already seen the pictures on social media and found out I was lying. He pulled me by my hair out of the bed and threw me on the floor. He kicked me, punched me, whipped me with a belt, and then peed on me. I blacked out."

Kamaria and Bahati were bawling as Carter told them the story.

"I'm going to fucking kill him!" Jerome roared, causing all three women to turn their heads towards the door. He stormed out. He went back through the waiting area in record speed. Mehki jumped up to follow him.

"Rome, wait!" he shouted, running after him. Jerome flew down the few flights of exit stairs and across the parking lot. Mehki pulled him by the shoulder to get him to stop.

"Bro, what the fuck happened?" he asked.

"That muthafucka punched her, kicked her, and peed on her!" he growled, his eyes turning dark as he foamed at the mouth.

"What?" Mehki paused, letting the words sink in. "Wait, but what are you going to do?"

"I'm going to do what I can to find him, and I'm going to kill him." He turned to get in his car.

"What about Genesis?" Mehki asked. Jerome stopped, one foot in the car and one on the ground. He stood there for a minute. He knew why his brother asked. If he did this, there was no way he'd get custody, and there's no way he'd ever see her again. He took his foot out of the car and slammed the door. He turned to Mehki. Mehki pulled him in for a hug, and they both cried.

5

Carter woke up the next morning, still in the hospital. They wanted to keep her overnight for observations. She noticed a figure sitting in a chair. She tensed up and crawled backwards on the bed.

"Hey, hey, it's just me, Jerome," he said, coming towards her. She settled down and began to cry. He sat on the bed next to her and held her in his arms. He felt her relax against him. His anger was coming back, but that'd have to sit at bay for now. Carter pulled back and wiped her eyes.

"I'm sorry, this is so embarrassing," she laughed nervously.

"What is?"

"This whole situation."

"You have nothing to be sorry for and nothing to be embarrassed about. His punk ass is the one who's going to be sorry."

"Jerome, promise me you won't do anything stupid. You could lose this case before it even gets started."

"You're right," he nodded.

"So, I already talked to Tasha, my assistant, and she filed the paperwork yesterday evening. Your ex-wife should be getting served some time over the next week."

"Wow, that's fast. I've seen some of my boys get served months later."

"That's why I'm the best of the best. Derwin hated that. I beat him out on a lot of cases and..." She stopped as she realized she was talking about him.

"Wait, your fiancé is a lawyer?"

"Ex-fiancé. He left me two days ago, and yes, he's also an attorney."

"What kind of attorney?"

"Same as me, family and criminal law."

"So wait, he is a family law attorney, which I'm assuming covers domestic violence, and he put his hands on you?" Carter nodded as she realized that she also represented clients of domestic violence, and now, she found herself on the other end of it. More embarrassment set in.

"I know what you're thinking, and you can stop thinking it," he smiled. "You aren't stupid. Love can sometimes put blinders on us."

"I didn't love him," she said curtly.

"Then why'd you stay?"

"So I wouldn't be alone. I know how that sounds, but you don't understand. Growing up how I did, you are always alone and feel abandoned. Yeah, I always had Bahati and Kamaria, but I've never felt like someone wanted me. My parents didn't want me, no one wanted to adopt me, my teachers were always kicking me out of class. You could never understand what I've been through, with your fancy clothes, big house, long money. You grew up with a silver spoon in your mouth and parents who would do anything for you and your brothers. So yeah, that's why I stayed. You can leave now."

She folded her arms and looked toward the window. He opened his mouth to speak, but there was nothing he could say that wouldn't cause her to become more upset.

He stood up and walked towards the door. He turned to look back at her to see if she was looking, but she was still looking out the window. He walked out the door and closed it. Carter turned and stared at the closed door before she sunk down in the bed and cried.

A week had gone by and Jerome hadn't heard from Carter. He attempted to call her a few times but stopped. He knew she wouldn't answer. He replayed their last conversation in his head all day every day. He was sitting at his desk drawing up plans for a new high rise apartment building on Kirby. The contract was one of the highest that they ever had, and yet, he could not concentrate.

He just stared at the computer until he heard a loud commotion outside his office door. There was screaming and cursing. As he walked closer to the door, he could hear loud and clear.

"Get your fucking hands off me! Where

is my bitch ass ex-husband?!" Jerome closed his eyes and dropped his head. It was Melina, and she must've been served the papers for court.

"Shit," he whispered, opening his office door. "Melina!" he barked. "Get your fucking ass in here!" She stopped screaming and looked at him, as well as the rest of his office staff. "The rest of you, get back to work. I'll handle this."

"You got damn right..." Melina started.

"Shut the fuck up and get in my office," he growled in a low, snarling town. She rolled her eyes and walked past him into his office. He slammed the door behind them, and she jumped.

"You've got some fucking nerve showing up to my fucking job, acting a fucking fool!" His glare made her shutter momentarily, but she regained her composure.

"I don't give a fuck! How the fuck do you think you can just take my child away from me? You don't even fucking know her, and she doesn't know you! On top of that, she has an illness, and she needs me."

"I am well aware that she has acute leukemia and is in remission. I also know she needs a stem cell transplant. I'm waiting on the results as we speak to see if I'm a viable donor. So don't tell me what the fuck I do or don't know about my child." Melina took a step back in shock at this revelation. The tears pooled in her eyes as she looked at him in disbelief.

"After all we've been through, after all I've

been through, you would take the one thing that means the most to me?" she whispered through sobs.

"Melina, I think that I'd be better able to take care of her."

"What, because you have money? Genesis is happy, healthy, and well taken care of."

"A homeless shelter is no place for a child and you and I both know that, so let's not play this game."

"But, she's my baby."

"One whom you have hidden from her father for two fucking years. I've missed some of her most important milestones, Melina. She will not grow up thinking she doesn't have a father or that I didn't want her. Over my fucking dead body she won't."

"So your only solution is to take her?"

"Until you can get on your feet Melina and find a place for the both of you to stay where you don't have to look over your shoulder." He stopped and narrowed his eyes at her. "Where is she?"

"At daycare. You think I'd leave her there alone?"

"How can you afford daycare?"

"I have a temp job through the government and they take care of daycare expenses. I just started last week."

"Hm, I see." Jerome was thinking he'd check the credibility of that.

"Jerome, I really am trying. Please don't take her from me."

"Melina, this isn't permanent. Just for now, I think she should live with me."

"I swear to God Jerome, if you go through with this, I will make your life a living hell."

"Can't be worse than the hell you put me through at the tail end of our marriage."

"You bastard! You knew what I was going through."

"And I tried my damnedest to help you over and over again. And what did you do?"

"Don't put all the blame on me."

"No? What did I do to play a part in you getting strung out on drugs?" She looked around, searching for answers that were nowhere to be found. "Just as I thought. Get out of my office. I'll see you in court."

She glared at him as her breathing became ragged. She took a deep breath and let out a shrill scream before she spun out of control trashing his office. He stood there filming everything on his phone. He knew this would be evidence he could use in court to exhibit her emotional instability. Security came barging in. Jerome held up a finger for them to wait a minute. She threw the glass vases, trying to shatter the shatterproof glass windows.

When she sank to the floor and cried violently, he nodded for the men to leave. He had his secretary bring some water in. She handed

Jerome the water and then closed the door behind her. He walked over to Melina and sat on the floor.

"Here Melina," he said, offering her the water. She took it and gulped it down. She sat up and leaned against his desk. They stared at each other for a long time.

"Jerome, please, I am begging you. Too many people have already tried to take her from me."

"Melina, I am not trying to hurt you. I am doing what is in the best interest of Genesis health wise and environment wise. She needs to be in a stable and safe environment."

"You won't take her, and I'll make damn sure of it." She threw the cup at him and stormed out of his office. He jumped up and got his brothers on the phone to meet him at his place in a couple hours. He grabbed his wallet, cell, and keys and jogged out of his office. He requested that his secretary get his office cleaned up and headed to Carter's law firm.

6

Carter was in a meeting discussing an upcoming case with other attorneys in her firm. She heard loud voices outside the door before it burst open and her heartbeat walked in, huffing and puffing.

"I need to talk," he breathed. "It's an emergency." She eyed Jerome and knew something was wrong.

"Okay, everyone, we will take this up tomorrow." Everyone gathered their things and filed out. When the last person left, she turned to glare at Jerome as he was doing something on his phone. "How dare you just barge up in here like you…" She stopped as he shoved his phone in her face. She took the phone and watched as a woman was apparently having a tantrum. "Who is this?"

"My ex-wife, and she's destroying my office. I don't know what kind of pull you have, but I need temporary custody of my daughter now. Melina is clearly unstable." Carter continued watching the video in disbelief.

"I'll see what I can do, but I won't make any promises." She handed him his phone back.

"There's more, but I don't know if you can help."

"What?"

"I need to know if her government job is legit and if my daughter is enrolled in daycare and which one."

"I can do that. I'll have that info to you before the day is over." He nodded and stared at her.

"Fuck it," he said as he closed the gap between them and pulling her face to his. He expected her to back up, but she didn't. She was kissing him back. His tongue found his way into her mouth and wrestled with hers. She let out a soft moan against his lips. His hands slipped down to her waist and he pulled her closer as she wrapped her arms around his neck. Suddenly, she pulled back.

"I shouldn't have done that," she apologized, looking down embarrassed. He placed a finger under her chin and lifted her head.

"Don't ever apologize, love. I kissed you, so if anyone should be sorry, it's me, and to be honest, I'm not sorry. I have to go, but I'll be expecting to hear from you about that information." He pecked her on the lips and then left.

Carter stood there in a daze. She rubbed her fingers across her lips and smiled. Heading back to her office, she called Josephine in. She was another attorney and also a close friend. Josephine came in, closing the door and sitting down across from Carter, elbows on the desk and chin in hands.

"Spill the tea. What was fine ass Jerome James-Panton doing here all disheveled and needing to see you?"

"I can't tell you that just yet. But I need you to do me a solid and keep it on the low."

"When have you ever known me to flap my mouth unless it was on my man's dick?" Carter laughed because she was right. Josephine held water tighter than a virgin.

"Jerome is filing for custody of his daughter who he just found out about a few months ago. She's two and his ex-wife just told him. Well, she showed up at his job and wrecked the whole place. So I'm going to file a motion stating unstable behavior so he can have temporary custody until after the court hearing."

"Damn. Okay, what you need me to do?" Carter scribbled something down and handed the paper to her.

"I need you to find out everything you can about her. He says that she told him she had a government job. I need to know where and how long she's been working there. I also need to know any past jobs, how long she's been sober, and where she lived before the shelter."

"Okay, and what are you going to do?"

"I have to go down to the hospital and subpoena the child's medical history. Then I need to go to the rehab facilities Melina was at and subpoena their records, as well as to the hospital the child was born to see if she was born with any other abnormalities or if she suffered from any effects of the drugs."

"Damn, you doing a whole lot for this man. You must really like him?"

"I'm doing my job, and I need you to do yours. Thanks."

"Okay, I got you," Josephine purred as she got up to leave. Carter shook her head and got to work on the subpoenas.

Jerome was pouring the last glass of Hennessy as Marlon walked in his house. Jeremiah and Mehki were already there.

"Great, Marlon is finally. Let's get this over with so I can go home and fuck my wife," Mehki said.

"Didn't she just give birth?" Jeremiah asked as Marlon shook his head and Jerome laughed as he sat down.

"Yeah, and?" They all howled with laughter.

"On a serious note, why are we here Rome?" Jeremiah asked.

"Okay, so I already told Mehki, but I think it's best I told you two as well. I just found out I have a daughter with Melina, and I am currently trying to get custody of her."

"The fuck?" Marlon muttered.

"Does Ma and Pops know?" Jeremiah asked.

"No, and right now, I don't want them to

until they can meet her."

"Have you met her?" Marlon questioned.

"I have and I fell in love the first moment I held her. She smiled at me and rubbed my cheek. But there's more. She is in remission from acute leukemia, and I am waiting on the results of some tests to see if I am a good stem cell donor."

"Whew," Marlon whistled, rubbing a hand over his head.

"Damn, Rome. Man, why you ain't tell us before now?"

"Hell, I don't know. I debated even telling Ki. But I need y'all support more than ever, and I'll need y'all as character witnesses."

"Man, you know we got you," Mehki reminded.

"Thanks y'all. Means a lot."

"You have an attorney yet?" Jeremiah inquired.

"Oh yeah, he has an attorney," Mehki chuckled as he swallowed the last of his drink.

"Let me guess. Carter?" That was Marlon.

"Yes, Carter is my attorney," he smiled.

"Ah ha, something went down between y'all," Mehki pointed out. "Let's hear it."

"After barging into her office and basically having word vomit, I kissed her, and I mean I really kissed her, like tongued her down." His brothers whistled and howled as each one patted him on the back. "I fucking hate y'all childish asses." He shook his head, smiling. He felt so blessed in that moment to have his brothers.

Later that evening, Carter sat in her home office going over the records she got for both Melina and Genesis. She grabbed her phone and called Jerome.

"Hey, got something for me?" he asked.

"Yes. She was telling the truth about her job, and Genesis is in daycare. I'm texting you the info now. I also got her records and Genesis' records, medical history, rehab, everything. I think you might want to see these. I can schedule a meeting for..."

"Text me your address," he interrupted.

"Uh, Jerome, I don't think that that's such a good idea. I don't usually have clients come to my home."

"Well, then you come here. I'll send you my address." He hung up and she received a text a minute later. She let out a huge sigh and started to text him back, then deleted the message. Against her better judgment, she packed up the files and got dressed, and headed to his house.

It was dark, but when she got to the gate, she was sure it was his house. It was very similar to Mehki's. His house, too, was built from shipping containers. It was two stories and lit up in every window. She pushed the button on the little box.

"Well hello love, come right on in," he drawled smoothly.

"Calm down, Carter. You are here strictly

for business reasons, not pleasure," she coached herself. The gate opened and she drove up to the front of the house.

As she got closer, she realized that his house sat on quite a few acres of land. She parked and grabbed her briefcase out of the passenger's seat. She got out and closed the door, standing there for a moment. She took a deep breath and walked towards the door. Before she could knock, Jerome opened the door. He stood there in pajama pants and nothing else. Carter looked down so he couldn't see the lust that was snitching on her, in her face.

"Hey, thanks for coming over. I'm sorry I got impatient. This is really important to me," he said, his deep voice sending shock waves between her legs.

"I would greatly appreciate it if we kept this professional. So please put a shirt on."

"Right, sorry. Come in." He moved back as she walked in the house. She looked around the living room and saw that he had good taste in décor. It was simplistic, but definitely manly.

Jerome closed the door and headed upstairs to grab a shirt as Carter headed to the dining room table. She pulled out the files and began to spread them out all over the table.

7

Jerome came back and watched as she sorted them. She hadn't noticed or heard him come back. He scanned her body from head to toe, taking inventory on the different ways he could make her scream his name. His dick jumped as she bent over, his palms itching to grab her ass. He leaned against the door frame as she made her way to the other side of the table, and then finally noticed him, jumping back in surprise.

"You scared me," she gasped, her hand on her chest. He noticed the deep v-neck in her shirt, displaying her large, round mounds. He licked his lips and smiled.

"My bad. You want something to drink?"

"Um, water is fine." She continued spreading the files out as he walked into the kitchen to grab two bottles of water. He came back as she sat down, handing a bottle to her. She opened it and took large gulps, trying to cool herself off.

"Thirsty?" he noticed, raising an eyebrow.

"Yeah, thanks. So I figured we'd start with when she went to rehab the first time," she directed, grabbing the file directly in front of her. "I noticed that she didn't stay long, only 15 days. Is there a reason why?" Jerome frowned and walked over, taking the file from her.

"No, she was there for 2-3 months I think. I remember because I went to visit her every day."

"Well, these are the official records." He perused them and shook his head.

"This isn't accurate." He dropped the file and went to his home office, grabbing a folder out of his filing cabinet. "Here is the file I received and signed," he said as he came back in and handed it to her. She looked it over and smirked.

"This was doctored. Here look," she said, placing the files side by side. "Look at the signatures. This one has yours, the one you gave me, and this one was signed by a Margarie Sanders."

"Her mother checked her out of rehab?" he asked himself. "Then how the hell was she there everyday? Explain that."

"I wish I could, but looking at a lot of her records, she lied to you. You said the second time she went to rehab was for 3 months. I looked at the visitor logs and your signature was there every day the first 30 days, but not the next 60." She handed him another file.

"That's impossible. I was fucking there every day!" He slammed his fists on the table, causing Carter to jump back. "I'm sorry," he quickly said. "I didn't mean to trigger you, it's just, I really loved her and I tried so hard to help her and now it looks like I didn't give a shit."

"I think that someone who worked there while she was there, doctored the documents you were given, and she may have helped them to do it."

"I just can't wrap my mind around the fact that she would do that. Then again, she is keeping my kid from me." Carter watched as he went through more files, cursing and talking to himself. She made notes throughout that could possibly help him. She also made notes to get a copy of the staff roster for the times Melina was there, compared to now.

"It says here that her last stay in rehab was a year ago. If she was in rehab, where the fuck was my daughter?" he asked.

"She was..." Carter grabbed and flipped through a few files before giving him one. "... staying with Melina's parents." He let out what sounded like a sigh.

"I can't believe this. I was so close with her parents until they blamed me for her drug addiction and then relapsing." Carter's heart ached for him. He was apparently distraught at finding this out, which made her want to work even harder to help him get custody of his daughter. They spent the next 3 hours going over each file, and Carter making notes to draw up in a deposition.

"I think that we have everything for now, besides, it's late and I have court in the morning.

I will type all this up and work on getting you temporary custody."

"Thanks Carter. I don't know what I would do without you." He helped her gather up all the documents and she filed them in her brief-case. She picked it up and went to grab her purse at the same time Jerome did, their hands meeting on the handle. She looked up at him, and he gave her a smoldering look that made her gasp. She let go of the purse and briefcase as he pulled her in, sucking in her mouth and palming her ass.

She jumped up and wrapped her legs around him as he walked them to the couch. He sat down, and she straddled him. He placed soft kisses along her jaw line and then to her neck, ending in between her breasts. He unbuttoned her shirt and took it off. He was thrilled to see her bra snapped in the front. He unhooked it and her breasts fell out of the cups in his face. He sucked in one nipple and palmed the other breasts as she grinded her hips on his lap, her sex over his hard erection.

"Ahh," she moaned as he gently nibbled on her breasts. He leaned them forward, breast still in his mouth and stood up. He walked towards the stairs, not needing to see anything in front of him. He built his house and knew the layout with his eyes closed. He ascended the stairs and went straight to his bedroom, sitting her on his California king sized bed. He dropped his pa-jama pants, showing he had no boxers on. Unbeknownst to her, he had hoped that this evening would end here in his bedroom.

Carter took her bra off. Jerome removed her shorts and soaked panties. Her pheromones flared his nostrils and darkened his expression. He took her hands and brought her to her feet, turning them around to where his back was to the bed. He laid back and scooted up on the bed.

She planted her feet flat on the bed and her hands on her knees. She rocked her hips back and forth, throwing her head back at the feeling of his dick pushing inside her. Jerome watched as she pleased herself on his dick. He wet the index finger of his left hand and reached under her, pushing inside her ass. She stiffened and then relaxed as he moved it in and out. He took her clit in between his right thumb and index finger, gently making circular motions.

"Jerome!" She whined. She held onto either side of his waist, digging her nails in as she bounced up and down.

"Fuck!" he growled, the vibrations sending her into overdrive.

"I'm about to come!" she said, shaking as her orgasm threatened to dismantle her. She moved her hands to the sheets on either side of him and gripped them as she came.

"Ahhh shiiiiiiiiit!" She screamed. He watched her face contort and felt himself brick up even harder at the fact that his dick made her come. Her walls gripped him every time she swallowed him with her gushing pussy. She rode him hard for a few more seconds and then collapsed on top of him, struggling to catch her breath. He removed his hands from her ass and clit, and wrapped his arms around her waist. Underneath her, he rocked his pelvis up and down, pushing in and out of her. Her walls would release as he pushed in, and contract as he pulled out, the same sensation as if he were getting head.

"Damn baby, this pussy is dangerous," he whispered in her ear. She lifted her head and shoved her tongue in his mouth, teasing his beast that was trying to escape. He moved in and out of her expeditiously, the hunger in him rising. She moaned against his lips and tried to break their connection, but he kept one arm pinning her waist down as he fucked her harder, and one behind her head to keep her lips to his. He swallowed her moans and screams as she came again. Her walls shed a new layer of lubrication, coating his dick in all her lust for him. Both hands moved to her shoulders and pulled down so he could enter her deeper as he met his own release, cursing against her lips.

"Fuck! Shit baby!" He sprayed his nut inside her, still pumping in and out, not wanting to waste a drop. Despite having shared test results prior to having sex, he didn't wear a condom, and didn't care if she got pregnant. In his mind, she was already his wife and the mother of his children.

"Shit Carter, you got some bomb ass pussy. Got damn." She giggled as she slid off him. He gently rolled her to her back.

"What are you doing?" She asked.

"I'm about to see if you taste as good as you feel."

"Can we take a break first?"

"Just let me get a third orgasm out of you, and then we can." At the sound of his request, her clit started pulsating, clearly opposing taking a break. He made his way between her legs. Slowly, his tongue parted her lips and made its way up and down her clit, almost like her clit stimulator did. She gasped as she gripped the sheets and closed her eyes.

"Ahh, Jerome!" she pleaded. She looked down as his head moved between her legs, his tongue taking control and dominating every part of her pussy. He moved in between her crevices to sucking her clit into his mouth. She thought how nasty he was with it and passionate. Her breathing hitched as he continuously sucked on her pearl. Her hands quickly moved to his head to keep him in place, letting him know he had hit her sweet spot.

"Shit Jerome! I'm bout to come!" she screamed as she moved her hips under him. She held the back of his head with one hand, and his shoulder with the other as her core tightened along with the rest of her body. He felt her jerk and gripped her thighs so she couldn't move. He sucked her orgasm out and sent cries of his name through her body and out her mouth. He bricked up again as she started trying to push him off. He let her go and came up, her juices dripping off his face. He moved between her legs and pushed inside her again. They spent the rest of the night entangled in each other, coming back to back.

8

Jerome lay there the next morning beside Carter and stared at her as she slept peacefully. Last night had taken his mind off everything that was going on. Carter was who he needed in his life, besides his daughter, to make it complete. He watched as her breasts rose and fell as she breathed softly. She began to stir, and her eyes fluttered open. She looked around before looking over at him to see him smiling at her. Heat rose to the surface of her cheeks as she remembered what happened the night before.

"Good morning, love," his baritone voice heating her pussy yet again.

"Good morning. What time is it?"

"A quarter to 8."

"I have court in a couple hours."

"Well, that means we have a couple hours to continue what we started last night," he suggested.

"Oh really? Last night wasn't enough for you?"

"Was it enough for you?" he frowned. She giggled at the seriousness in his face. She then laughed as his brows furrowed even more. His frown turned into a grin as he realized she was joking. He began to tickle her and kiss on her neck, sending her into a fit of laughter until he moved between her legs and thumbed her pearl. They spent the next hour in a replay of the night before.

Jerome walked into his office to see he had several messages from Melina. He threw them away and walked into his office to see her sitting there with a man.

"The hell are you doing here Melina?"

"Sir, I suggest you calm down," the man warned.

"Man fuck you! This is my office, and the both of you are trespassing. Now leave, or I'm calling security." Melina and the man looked at each other.

"Very well," the man began. "I just want you to know that I am John Bates, attorney at law, and I'll be representing Melina Panton."

"And?" Jerome shot back.

"We thought we would come and talk to you about rethinking taking Melina to court to fight for custody."

"Without my lawyer present? You of all people should know that this isn't proper protocol."

"Speaking of your attorney, I think you should know some things about her." He put an envelope on Jerome's desk, and Melina smirked as she got up to leave, Bates following behind her. Jerome's jaw tensed as the door closed. He sat down and snatched the envelope, ripping it open. Inside were photos of Melina having sex with several different men, as well as documents stating that she had been banned from several cases for sleeping with the client, ultimately losing the case.

"What the fuck?" his anger tripling as he flipped through the pages. He pulled up Google on his computer and did some research to try to find this information to see if it was public, and if he just missed it. Nothing came up. Either this was fake, or it wasn't public information and was being covered. He threw the papers on the floor as Jeremiah came in.

"Yo, what's up, second big bro?" He walked in and looked at the photos all over the floor. "Is that...Carter?" He asked, picking up a photo.

"Yeah," Jerome mumbled.

"Why do you have these?"

"Melina's lawyer came in talking about reconsidering the custody battle. Come to find out, Carter slept with a few clients and they ended up losing their case. Man, I can't lose this and let my daughter suffer."

"You slept with her, didn't you?"

"Yeah, man, last night and this morning. I wonder if this is what she does with men who she knows are going to lose."

"Man, don't jump to conclusions. Did you search for this?"

"Nothing came up. Makes me think that she's covering it up somehow, maybe paying them off."

"I mean I know she's a bomb ass lawyer, but does she really have that much pull? And wouldn't she be disbarred if this were true?"

"Which makes me think that she is covering this up."

"Well for right now, we have a meeting to get to. This is going to have to wait, Rome." Jerome nodded and followed his brother to the boardroom. They had a meeting with a potential client.

After Carter's case was done and won, she headed to Bahati's house to see her niece and catch up on things. Bahati answered the door in a bodycon dress and stilettos.

"Um, are you going somewhere, because we did have plans to just chill?" Carter questioned.

"Girl, I haven't really been anywhere, and I just wanted to dress up."

"Aww, you did this for me?" Carter joked as she walked in and hugged her best friend.

"No bitch, I did this for me." They headed into the living room where Kamaria was rocking and talking to Khadija.

"Aww, Auntie Carter is here now." She reached for Khadija as Kamaria backed up.

"Aht aht ho, wait your turn."

"Hey, if y'all drop my baby, I'm fucking

both of you up," Bahati warned, shooting darts with her eyes at them both. They laughed as she went into the kitchen to grab some drinks. Carter held out her arms and Kamaria surrendered the sleeping baby. Carter rocked and cooed as Bahati came back in and set the drinks down.

"So what's been going on ladies? I feel like it's been forever," she started.

"I've been getting ready to attend this fashion show coming up in a couple months. It's in Valencia," Kamaria bragged.

"Valencia, as in Spain Valencia?" Bahati asked.

"Yep!"

"That's amazing Kamaria!" Carter congratulated.

"Yes, that's going to be good for your career," Bahati added.

"Exactly, and, it's being held at the Nubian Fashion House for their grand opening."

"Well, I for one am excited for you. So what's been going on with you Carter?" Carter looked down sheepishly at Khadija as she slept so as to not give away that she slept with Jerome.

"You dirty ho, you slept with Jerome didn't you?" Kamaria accused.

"Damn, how did you know?" Carter asked.

"I didn't, but you just told us. Spill." Carter sighed and went into detail about the night before and this morning.

"You should've warned me prior to telling

us all that nasty shit, exposing my baby's ears to such explicit ho shit," Bahati said, turning up her nose and walking over to get her daughter.

"Well, then how the hell she get here?" Carter laughed. Bahati stuck her tongue out and laid Khadija in the pack and play.

"So what does this mean for y'all?" Bahati asked.

"I don't know. I mean I have feelings for him. He's caring, generous, thoughtful and genuinely cares about my well-being. He's so different from Derwin."

"Um, yeah, he's a Panton. They all hit different," Kamaria joked, then realized what she said. "I didn't mean like that, but like they are a different breed of men."

"I know what you meant," Carter reassured.

"And how would you know Kamaria?" Bahati questioned. "You need to tell us something?"

"No, I just meant that just the way they carry themselves, you can tell they're different. That's all," Kamaria stammered. She had been sleeping with Jeremiah for a while, but she wasn't ready to tell them. She took a long sip of her wine as Carter and Bahati stared at her. They smiled and their smiles turned into giggles then laughter. "I hate y'all."

"Anyway, Mehki told me about his daughter and how he's trying to get custody. Does he have a good case?"

"He has a solid ca..." The front door swinging open interrupted her sentence. They all turned their heads and saw a raging Jerome storming in with Mehki not too far behind.

"Man don't be busting up in my house like you own the place!" Mehki called after him.

"So this is a joke to you, huh?" Jerome demanded.

"What are you talking about?" Carter asked, standing to her feet.

"You thought I was stupid enough for you to play me?"

"Jerome, what is going on?" she asked.

"Rome, man calm down," Mehki said, placing a hand on his brother's shoulder. Jerome shrugged him off, his eyes boring into Carter. He threw the papers and photos on the coffee table. She slowly bent down and picked them up. Jerome watched her expression.

"Tuh," he said, "that's all I need to know."

"Jerome, I can explain these."

"Forget it. I'm not about to be another body for your count. My daughter means way too much to me for some slutty ass lawyer to fuck things up for me."

"Jerome, now you're out of line," Bahati jumped in.

"Maybe, but your friend here shouldn't be practicing law." He turned and headed towards the front door. He turned around and glared at Carter. "Oh yeah, and in case you were wondering, you're fired." He slammed the door behind him, waking the baby.

"I'm going to kick his ass," Mehki sneered. He took Khadija and headed upstairs.

"What was that about?" Bahati asked. Carter's eyes filled with tears as she flopped on the couch and sobbed. Bahati and Kamaria sat on either side of her.

"These pictures aren't even real. They're photoshopped. I never told you guys, but a few years ago, Derwin tried to ruin my reputation as a lawyer. This case was kept quiet. We even went to trial and everything. He made up this story that I was sleeping with my clients. I don't know how he doctored these photos, but that isn't even my body in any of these pictures. We got to court, and I had a digital tech come in and he basically reimaged the photo to its original state. Derwin's license was revoked in the state of Texas, but he can practice anywhere else. This case was sealed. I don't even know how Jerome would've gotten ahold of these."

"Well, we're going to find out," Kamaria promised.

9

Jerome found himself outside his parents' house. He hadn't planned on telling them about Genesis, but he needed them right now. They were the only ones he could trust. As he got out of the car, his mother walked out the front door and stood on the porch, her arms outstretched. He sped up his pace and hugged her and did something he rarely ever did: he cried. Moriah rubbed his back and squeezed him tight as her son let it all out in her arms.

"Whatever it is, baby, it's going to be alright," she promised. They stood there for another few minutes until he got himself together.

"Is Pop here?" he asked, wiping the tears away.

"No, he is playing golf with his buddies. Is it something you can't tell your mother, the woman who carried you for 10 months and pushed you out her vagina?"

"Ma, seriously?" he asked, scrunching up his face. His mother chuckled. "It's not that, I just wanted to tell y'all together, but I need to get this out and I only trust you and Pop."

"Well let's go inside and I'll pour us some

brandy." He followed her inside, shutting the door behind them. He stretched out on the living room couch and waited for his mother to come back. He needed things to move along a little quicker now that he didn't have an attorney.

"Alright, I'm listening," his mother said, setting his glass on the coffee table and having a seat across from him. He sat up and took a long sip, then placed the glass back down.

"I have a daughter." Moriah's glass stopped midway to her mouth, then she set it back on the table.

"Don't fuck with me boy."

"Ma, I'm serious. Melina gave birth to her two years ago and just told me a few months ago. And before you say anything, yes, I got a DNA test done and Genesis is mine."

"Genesis?" his mother repeated, her eyes lighting up. "I have another grandbaby?! When can I see her?"

"That's the thing, she won't let me and I filed for full custody. She has my child living in a homeless shelter. It's a nice one, but no child of mine is living in a homeless shelter. Besides, she is in remission from acute leukemia. I got blood work done to see if I'm a match. Still waiting on re..." His phone rang, interrupting them. He pulled it out his pocket and it was the doctor. His eyes widened.

"What is it baby?"

"It's the doctor. I think these are the results."

"Well answer it!" his mother pushed.

"Hello?"

"Good afternoon, Jerome. I have good news. You are a match for your daughter."

"I am?" Jerome stood up, his eyes becoming misty. His mother watched, her own eyes pooling.

"Yes. So should I schedule everything?"

"Yes, doc, any day and time, I will be there."

"Ok then, see you soon." They said their salutations and hung up. Moriah ran over to her son and wrapped him in her arms, squeezing him tight.

"This is great baby. Okay, first thing's first, you need to call that Carter girl and get her..."

"No, Ma. That's the other reason I'm here. She was my attorney, but then I found out she sleeps with her clients that she knows aren't going to win, then gets pulled off the case and ultimately the client loses. I just fired her."

"Boy, are you stupid?" his mother asked, slapping him upside the head.

"Ow, Ma what was that for?"

"You really think if that was true she would be the top attorney in this city?"

"I think she may have either paid them off, or she has the case sealed because I couldn't find anything on it." His mother slapped him upside the head again. "Ma, can you stop?"

"Jerome Donell James-Panton, you listen, and you listen damn good. Go back to that girl and rehire her. I know damn well that whatever somebody told you, ain't true."

"How would you know?" She squinted her eyes and stepped closer to him.

"Get your ass over to that woman and apologize for whatever dumbass tantrum you threw and rehire her. I want to see my grand-baby." Before he could protest, his phone rang again. It was one of his boys that worked at the hospital.

"Hey Jay, what's up?"

"Rome, you need to get down here right now."

"What's wrong?"

"Melina was just rolled into my OR. She overdosed and we just pumped her stomach. She'll make it, but I think there's something else you should know. She had a little girl with her at the time, and man, she is the spitting image of..." Before Jay could finish, Jerome hung up and flew out the door. Moriah knew Jay and that he worked at the hospital, and by Jerome's reaction, he knew he was headed to the hospital. She called her husband and her other sons and told them to meet at the hospital.

Jerome swerved into a parking space and ran at full speed into the hospital.

"I need to speak to Jay Richardson!" he barked. Running in circles, he repeated himself until security came.

"Man back the fuck up off me!" he demanded as the officers tried to cuff him.

"He's good!" Jay called, running to them. "He's good." Jerome shook the officers off.

"Where is she?" Jerome asked.

"She's sedated right now..."

"You sedated a toddler?"

"No, I was talking about Melina."

"Man, fuck her. Where's my daughter?"

"With CPS, follow me." Jerome followed Jay down the hall to a waiting area where his daughter was playing with some toys inside the kid area. He dropped to his knees.

"Genesis," he sobbed. The little girl turned around and flashed a huge smile. She walked over to him.

"Daddy!" she squealed. He picked her up and broke down, holding her tight to his chest. Just then, his family came in, including Bahati, Kamaria, and Carter. He hadn't noticed. He rocked back and forth with his daughter. Everyone watched on, not a dry eye.

"Sir," said one of the social workers. "I'm Gracie Banks." Jerome stood up, not letting his daughter go.

"You're not taking my child," he glared back.

"We're not taking her. We were actually waiting on you. We got a request sent into our office from the law offices of Malone, LLC. Typically a judge would have to sign off, but given the current circumstances, you are the next of kin."

"Can he take her home?" Moriah budded in.

"Yes," Gracie smiled, "he can take her home." His whole family cheered. "We will be in contact with you to do a walkthrough of your home and assess her living environment."

"You got it," he said, taking her card and giving her his. The social workers left and he walked over to a chair, placing his daughter on his lap.

"Daddy," she said again.

"Yeah, I'm your daddy." He noticed Moriah walking over. She knelt down in front of him.

"Hi, Genesis," Moriah whispered. "I'm your grandma."

"Gamma," Genesis said in her toddler language. She reached for Moriah, and Moriah picked her up, hugging her close as the tears kept coming. Jeremy walked over and kissed Genesis' forehead.

"And I'm you grandpa."

"Ganpa," Genesis smiled. They all laughed and surrounded them and Jerome. Carter stood on the outside looking on. She smiled and then left. Jerome had gotten so caught up in the moment, he hadn't noticed until he was looking for her.

"Hey, where'd Carter go?"

"Why do you care?" Bahati questioned.

"Mon cherie, not now," Mehki warned. Bahati turned her lips up and rolled her eyes, turning her attention back to Genesis playing with Khadija in Moriah's lap.

10

Carter sat in her office a month later, finalizing some paperwork for Jeremy to hand over to the next attorney who would represent him.

"You have a visitor," Josephine said, peeking her head through the door.

"Who is it?"

"They wanted to stay anonymous."

"Send them in." Josephine walked back out and her breath caught when the visitor walked in. It was Jerome.

"Hey, Carter," he said softly, closing the door and sitting in the chair across from her.

"Hey, Jerome. What are you doing here?"

"I came to apologize. I truly am sorry Carter. Bahati told me everything and then bit my head off along with Kamaria."

"Oh," was all she said.

"I know it's been a while, and I should've come and said something before now, but being a single dad is work, more work than I thought. Plus, I've been getting ready for this stem cell transplant for Genesis. It's no excuse, but..."

"Jerome, you don't have to explain. Bahati has been keeping me in the loop." Jerome raised an eyebrow as Carter's hands shot to her mouth.

"So, you've been keeping tabs on me?" he smirked, teasing her.

"Yes," she admitted. "I have been asking about you because I still care and have feelings for you. I also wanted to make sure your daughter was okay."

"She's fine. I had them run a drug test on her, and she's good, thankfully. Her mother is in rehab for the time being under 24 hour surveillance."

"Did you find out anything about when she was in rehab before and the documents?"

"Yeah. There was a worker there, who was fired back then, that she was sleeping with and he was helping to falsify her information and doctor video footage."

"Oh, she's good."

"Yeah, good enough that I fell in love with her. But enough about her, are you free tonight? I really want to make it up to you."

"I wish I was, but I have these documents to get over to your new attorney. Have you chosen one yet?"

"Yeah, you." Carter looked at him confused.

"Me? Don't you think that's a conflict of interest?"

"I don't care. You're the best in the city, and I need the best on my team."

"You do know that you're going to get custody right?"

"I do. But I still want you to represent me."

"Well, okay then," she agreed.

"So about tonight?"

"What about Genesis?"

"My parents are keeping her for the weekend, like they have been every weekend. You'd swear she was their child."

"Well, she is their first grandchild, and I know Moriah is happy to have another grandbaby."

"Tuh, Ma is not the issue. It's my pops. That little girl has him wrapped around her little finger."

"I'm sure she has her father wrapped too," Carter smirked.

"That's not the point," he deflected. They both laughed.

"I'll be over at 8," she said.

Jerome was pulling the lamb out of the oven when the timer on the air fryer went off, letting him know the potatoes were done. He pulled them out and put them on a paper towel covered plate to cool. He took out some Stella Rosa wine and poured some into two wine glasses on the table. He placed the food on the table when his doorbell rang. It was 7:50. He jogged to the door, smiling. His smile quickly faded when he opened the door to see Melina standing there.

"What the fuck?"

"You miss me?" she slurred.

"Melina, I think for your safety, you should leave."

"Aww baby, don't be like that." She stumbled in and he caught her before she hit the floor. "See, you still care," she laughed sloppily. He stood her up and propped her against the door frame.

"Go Melina," he warned, his jaw twitching.

"Why? You expecting ya lawyer girlfriend?" Melina's eyes closed as she smiled. He glared at her.

"I'm only going to say this once more before I physically make you lea…wait, how did you get through the gate?"

"Your dumbass never changed the code," she cackled, rolling back and forth against the frame.

"I'll make a note to change that. Now go." He tried to close the door and she stopped him, quickly sobering up.

"I'm not going anywhere until you drop this case right now." She pulled a 9mm out from the back of her pants and pointed it at his chest. He snarled at her. "Yeah, that's what I thought, now back the fuck up." He took a couple steps back, and she came into the house, closing the door behind her. "The fact that you still have a weak spot for a woman who is in distress is pathetic, but I used to love that about you." She waved the gun for him to back up and sit on the couch.

He obliged, for the time being until he could devise a plan to get the gun away from her.

"I see you haven't changed the place much since we split," she noticed, looking around, still holding him at gunpoint. She looked back at him. "Why didn't you try to continue to make things work with us?"

"Are you serious? I tried several times, Melina, and not only that, but you kept relapsing and now I know that you never finished your entire time in rehab none of the times you were there. You played me and took advantage of my love for you." He looked down at his watch. It was 8:15.

"You can stop looking at your watch. Your little ho isn't coming. She's a little preoccupied right now," she smirked. Jerome froze, his expression darkening.

"What the fuck do you mean?" he growled.

"Well, it's up to you whether she lives or dies. Now, where is my daughter?"

"What did you do to Carter?"

"Fuck her! Where is my daughter?" She released the safety on the gun. Her eyes were glossed over. She was high on something, and he knew he'd be able to overpower her.

"You'll have to kill me."

"Oh, I plan to, right after I get my daughter back. My plan is to kill your whole family."

"Oh yeah," Jerome let out a dark chuckle.

"Only one of us will make it out of this house alive, and I guarantee it won't be you."

"Funny, seeing as how I'm the one with the g..." Jerome charged at her and she left off a couple shots. They wrestled and a few more bullets sprayed. They both froze and he felt blood oozing over his hands.

11

Carter had just put her shoes on and grabbed her purse before taking one last look in the full length mirror in her living room. She smiled at her reflection. She grabbed her keys and headed to the door, only to open it and see Derwin standing there. She gasped before he struck her, knocking her out cold.

A little while later, Carter came to with a raging headache. Her arms were tied behind her back and to her ankles. She was lying down and was being thrown around. She realized she was in the trunk of a car. She tried to scream, but there was tape over her mouth. She felt around for something to cut the tape with. She couldn't find anything. She lay her head down and her face felt something cold. It was a nail. She did her best to roll over and grab the nail with her hands. Once she grabbed it, she worked her way through the tape against the bumpy ride. Once her hands were free, she ripped the tape off her mouth, letting out a low yelp. She then cut the tape off her feet.

The car came to a stop and the engine was cut. She placed her face against the floorboard of the trunk and put her hands behind her back to appear still tied up. The car door opened and slammed shut. She heard footsteps coming towards the trunk. As soon as it opened, she kicked Derwin in the groin. He hit the ground instantly, letting out a deep growl in agonizing pain.

Carter jumped out and ran, thankful she chose to wear flats and jeans. It was dark and heavily wooded, but she kept running. Two shots rang out and Carter stopped. She turned around slowly to see Derwin stumbling towards her, his hand covering his groin.

"You bitch!" he spat. Carter backed away from him. She didn't realize that behind her was a tree root sticking out of the ground. She tripped and fell backwards, tumbling down a hill. She screamed as she picked up momentum. Thoughts ran through her head of never seeing Bahati, Kamaria, and Jerome again. She closed her eyes as she slammed against the ground at the bottom of the hill.

Her head bounced hard against the ground. Every part of her body ached. She heard leaves rustling as Derwin was sliding down the hill towards her. He stumbled towards her, catching himself before falling. He shook the fall off and walked over to her, grabbing her by her bun and rolling her over.

"Agh!" she screamed in pain at him pulling her hair. She was face-to-face with him now, rage filling his eyes. She saw nothing but pure hatred.

"You know, I wasted the last few years with you. I don't even know what I saw in you in the first place," she spat. The sting of his palm against her already aching flesh pulled out a yelp from her.

"You are such an ungrateful little bitch! I tried to love you, but you always tested me with your lies. You're nothing but a whore." He slapped her again, this time across the other side of her face. Tears threatened to roll down the side of her face, but she blinked them away. She wouldn't dare let him see that he had her scared.

She tried to wriggle free, but he had her arms pinned down with his knees, cutting off the circulation.

"Where do you think you're going?" he sneered, ripping her shirt open. He unhooked her bra with one hand as he held the gun in his other. He sucked on a nipple, then bit down hard.

"Agh!" she cried out in pain. He moved his way down her, his knees now pinning her hands down. Carter knew right then, he was going to try to rape her. He used one hand to maneuver between his legs and undo her jeans, pulling them down by lifting his hips. She tried to get a leg through to knee him, but he punched her again, ringing blaring in her ears. She had double vision as she tried to not pass out.

He undid his pants, releasing his erection. He moved off her hands and was able to quickly pin them above her head. He moved between her legs and before he could enter her, she brought both legs up crossing them around his neck. He let go of her hands trying to pry her legs open, dropping the gun in the midst of it all.

She jammed a thumb into his right eye, blood shooting out. He cried in pain like a wounded animal. She released him from between her legs and kicked him with her flat foot in the face, knocking him back.

She scrambled to stand and pull her jeans up. Her head was spinning and she stumbled back to her knees. She could hear Derwin still screaming in pain a little distance away. Once she regained somewhat normal vision, she stood up slowly and buttoned her pants. She turned in every direction and chose one to go in. She limped at first, but then her adrenaline started pumping. She sprinted as fast as she could as if she were going to hand off the baton to a teammate.

She didn't know where she was going, but she had to get out of there. Up ahead she saw a clearing. It was a road. She got to the road and kept running. All those years of running track and jogging every morning was coming in handy. She saw car headlights coming toward her. She ran into the middle of the road waving her hands. The car screeched before slamming into her.

12

Jerome woke up to bright white lights. His vision took a while to become clear, but when it did, he realized he was in the hospital. He tried to sit up, but a sharp pain made him change his mind.

"Take it easy brother," Marlon said, coming to his side, followed by Jeremiah and Mehki.

"What happened?" he croaked. Mehki grabbed a cup off the food tray and held the straw to his mouth for him to drink. The brothers looked at each other. "What happened?" he repeated.

"Melina tried to kill you," Jeremiah finally spoke.

"What?"

"I was at home when I heard gunshots going off," Jeremiah continued. Jeremiah and Jerome lived next door to each other, sharing the same plot of land. "I ran over and the door was open. Melina was lying in a pool of blood. She was already dead. I ran to you, and I felt a pulse. I called the ambulance and the family."

"Shit," Jerome mumbled. His head was aching as the rest of his body. "Man, I was preparing dinner for Carter and...Carter!" It hit him that she never showed. Melina's words replayed in his head. "Melina said that she was preoccupied or something." He looked at each of his brothers' faces as they held their heads down.

"I'm sorry Jerome," Mehki whispered.

"Why? Where is she?"

"She was struck by a car," Jeremiah explained. "She's in ICU right now and last we heard, it didn't look good." Jerome's eyes watered as he lay back on the pillow. His brothers gathered around him as he cried.

Later that day, Jerome woke up to his mother sitting bedside.

"Ma," he said, rubbing his eyes.

"Hey baby. How're you feeling?"

"Like I got hit by a truck."

"That's expected after a surgery and stem cell removal."

"Huh? Stem cell removal?"

"Yes. Your doctor decided that while you were in surgery, and that your wounds weren't critical, that it'd be best to go ahead and remove some stem cells to give to baby girl."

"Ma, where's my daughter?" he asked, his eyes misting.

"Baby, she's fine. She's with your father in recovery. Seems her body is taking to them well." Jerome let out a sigh of relief. It was already a possibility that Carter might not make it. He couldn't lose his daughter either. "She's a fighter, a strong little something. I know she gets that from you." She looked at the door as two officers stood there. "Baby, these two officers have been waiting for you to wake up." His mom got up to leave when the officers came in.

"Ma, can you stay?"

"Sure baby," she responded with a smile, walking back over to sit down.

"Sorry to have to do this now, but the more information we get now, the better," said Officer Reyes. "Can you tell us why Melina Panton was at your house?"

"She was looking for Genesis, our daughter. She just showed up. I was preparing for my girlfriend to come over so we could have dinner."

"Did she seem out of it? Like she was on something?"

"Yeah, her eyes were glossy like they used to be when she first started using, back when we were married."

"So, then what happened?"

"Officers, I can actually show you better than I can tell you. Ma, please hand me my phone." Moriah dug through his pants pocket and got his phone, handing it to him. "I have security cameras set up all around my home with video and audio." He pulled up the camera in his living room that also captured the front door. He handed the phone to Officer Reyes and waited as both officers watched and listened.

"Is there a way you can send this over to

the precinct for evidence?" he asked.

"Yeah, I can send it now." Officer Reyes handed back his phone and rattled off the email address to send it to.

"We have a few more questions if you don't mind."

"No, go right ahead."

"When's the last time you've seen Derwin?" Jerome's brows furrowed.

"At the wedding. Why are you asking me about him?"

"According to the doorman at Carter's condo and a neighbor, he was seen carrying her out."

"And security didn't do anything?" Jerome barked.

"Apparently, he had paid them off to turn a blind eye. When the accident hit the news, they came forward." Jerome's jaw clenched as Moriah rubbed his shoulder.

"Is he the one who hit her?"

"No, it was an innocent driver who didn't see her until the last second. The driver has been here the past couple of days waiting for her to wake up. He feels guilty."

"Is that all?" he asked, signifying he was done talking to them.

"Yes, Mr. Panton. Thank you for your time, and we hope you have a speedy recovery." The two officers left and Jerome closed his eyes, lying his head back on the pillow.

13

A week went by before Jerome was able to take Genesis home. His house was cleaned up and in order when he, his brothers, his parents, Kamaria, and Bahati drove him there. His mother had cooked and frozen a month's worth of food for Jerome and Genesis. Genesis had recovered pretty well and was due for a checkup in 3 weeks. Carter had still not woken up.

Moriah tended to Genesis and Khadija as Jerome, his father, and his brothers heated up some of the food Moriah hadn't frozen. They sat around the table and ate in silence. All anyone could hear were forks against plates, and Moriah and Genesis playing in the playroom.

"Derwin was arrested, in case you were wondering," Marlon offered.

"I wish he hadn't been so I could kill him," Jerome said, not looking up from his plate.

"Now Jerome, had you done that, you'd have lost Genesis," his father reminded. Jerome said nothing. Mehki's phone rang, interrupting the silence.

"Hey, mon cherie," he answered. "What? When? Okay, I'll tell him." He hung up and looked at Jerome who was staring back at him. "Carter's awake." Jerome jumped up and ran to the playroom.

"Ma, she's awake." He ran to kiss her and Genesis before heading out the door.

When he got to the hospital, he asked for directions to her room. Upon entering her room, Kamaria and Bahati turned to him and parted so he could see a smiling Carter. She was bruised pretty badly and bandaged up. Tears rolled down his cheeks as he walked over to her, sitting in a chair beside the bed. Kamaria and Bahati excused themselves.

"Hey," she said.

"Hey," his baritone voice vibrated through his tears.

"The girls told me everything. How are you? How's Genesis?"

"We're good. She's with my mom. How are you?"

"In a lot of pain."

"Carter, tell me what happened."

"Well, I was getting ready to leave and I opened the door and Derwin was there." He listened attentively as she told him the rest of the story, right before getting hit by a car. "The man came in earlier to apologize, but I told him it wasn't his fault. He still blamed himself and paid my medical bill. He was some sort of millionaire."

"Wish I could've met him and thanked

him," Jerome smiled. They both fell silent for a spell, staring at each other.

"I know that initially when we got together, a child wasn't in the plans so soon, but..."

"Jerome, I knew Genesis would be with you full time when you told me that the DNA test proved she was yours."

"Right, well, I understand if that changes things."

"It doesn't. Besides, she's going to need a mother, and since I can no longer have kids due to the accident, she's the next best thing." Tears streamed down her cheeks as she came to terms that physically having a child was no longer possible. Jerome kissed her and promised to always love her.

EPILOGUE

Two months later...

Carter was out of the hospital and had moved in with Jerome and their now daughter, Genesis. Carter agreed to adopt Genesis, and since her mother was not there to have to sign over her rights, the process went fairly quickly.

"Hey mama's girl," Carter cooed, kissing Genesis on the forehead. The little girl squealed as Genesis tickled her. Carter was finally back working, but mostly from home. During the day, Genesis stayed at her grandparents' house while Carter worked, and then they'd drop Genesis off or Jerome would pick her up on the way home. They had fallen into a routine fairly quickly.

"My two favorite girls," Jerome cheesed as he came into the playroom.

"Daddy!" Genesis sang as she ran over to him. He scooped her up and twirled her around, evoking laughter and screams out of her.

"Hey babe," Carter said, getting up to kiss him. He kissed her back deeply.

"Ewww, kissy, kissy!" Genesis giggled.

"How was work?" Carter asked.

"Awesome actually," he responded, putting Genesis down so she could go play with her toys. "We took on a new client for a build overseas. So, we will be traveling to Ghana at the end of the month."

"Babe, that's huge! Congrats! I'd love to visit there one day."

"Did you miss the part where I said 'we'?"

"Wait, what?" Carter's eyes lit up as she jumped in his arms.

"Yeah, we leave next month."

"Good thing I put in my year sabbatical."

"What? Why?"

"Well, I want to spend more time with Genesis before the new baby comes." She smiled as he stared at her, eyes widening.

"You're...pregnant?"

"Yep!"

"But I thought that you couldn't."

"Well, I went to the doctor this morning since my period never came a week ago, and I am pregnant, about four weeks." Jerome fisted the air as tears of joy glistened against his chocolate skin. He pulled her into his arms and tongued her down.

LOVE & WAR

1

Kamaria stepped off the plane in Valencia. It had been a long flight, though the amenities were exquisite. Flying in a private jet that she didn't have to pay for was always a perk. When she received the invitation for the grand opening of The Nubian Fashion House in Spain, she thought she'd died and gone to heaven. She spent countless years as a noted fashion blogger, but an invitation like this meant she was well on her way to being in the top tier of the industry.

"Bienvenidos, señorita," the limo driver greeted.

"Gracias," she replied. She spent her time at FIT after graduating from Spelman studying abroad in Spain. She threw herself into the culture and absorbed it all, including the language.

She followed the driver to the awaiting stretch limo on the tarmac, not too far from the jet. The man took her bags and loaded them in the trunk before opening her door to get inside.

The team at The Nubian Fashion House put her up in the penthouse suite at the Caro Hotel in the Seu-Xerea neighborhood. They went all out for their attendees. She knew of several other fashion bloggers that were going to be there, though none of them seemed to like her.

As they pulled up to the hotel, Kamaria gasped at its beauty. The driver opened her door and she got out to walk inside. As the driver gave one of the bellhops her bags, she spun around the foyer inside, taking it all in. She still hadn't gotten over the fact that there are certain experiences only people in her field get to experience for free.

"Kamaria?" She stopped short as she spun to see none other than Jeremiah James-Panton. Damn he looked good. He was dressed in white slacks, a navy and wine striped button down with the top two buttons unbuttoned, loafers, a red wine colored fedora, and Armani sunglasses. He dripped money and sex appeal.

"Hey, Jeremiah," she finally managed to get out. He walked over and gave her a hug. It had been months since they slept together. Kamaria was tired of the constant women coming around, and she wanted to focus on her career.

As he embraced her, his cologne traveled through her nostrils like steam, heating her insides. She closed her eyes for what felt like forever until she heard heels clacking and stopped relatively close. She opened her eyes and saw some woman glaring at her.

Kamaria quickly jumped back. Jeremiah looked confused until he turned around.

"Hey baby, this is Kamaria, my sister-in-law," he explained, wrapping his arm around the woman's waist. "Kamaria, this is Beatriz Morris."

"Yeah, the fashion model," Kamaria nodded. "I saw you in the fashion show during Paris Fashion Week." Beatriz's lips curved up as her expression changed.

"Really? How did I look? Did I look fat?" It registered in Kamaria's head that Jeremiah was not with this woman for her brains. She smirked before answering.

"You looked great. It was nice seeing you Jeremiah, and nice meeting you Beatriz." She walked towards the concierge to check in. She didn't even turn to look back. After getting her keys, when she turned around, Jeremiah and Beatriz were gone. She let out a sigh and went up to her suite. When she got off the elevator on the top floor, she followed the arrows around to her room.

She stuck her key card in, opened the door and was floored. Spain really knew how to do it up in a hotel. The baseboard of the walls lined with gold with pictures on them that she couldn't quite make out. The ceiling had a mural of Les Demoiselles d'Avignon. In the foyer was a round table with a bouquet of fresh flowers. There was a card. She took the card out and it was from The Nubian Fashion House.

We are so glad that you accepted our invitation to our grand opening. We hope that you find the accommodations to your liking.

Best,

The Nubian Fashion House

She stuck the card back on the stick and smiled. If only they knew that the accommodations far exceeded her expectations. She headed to the shower to freshen up for dinner. There was a group dinner for all of the bloggers in the hotel restaurant. The glass encased shower had a large square shower head hanging from the ceiling, and granite tile walls with speckles of gold, which she assumed were real.

She got cleaned up and dressed in a form fitting, knee length black dress. She grabbed her purse and phone, ensuring her room key was in her purse. She opened her room door and stepped out, nearly running into someone.

"I'm so sorry," the man apologized.

"It's okay," she responded, finally looking up to see Jordan Blackstone staring down at her. She remembered him from a few of Mehki and Bahati's gatherings. He was Mehki's best friend.

"Jordan, right?" she asked, smiling back.

"Yeah, and you're Kamaria, Bahati's sister?"

"Yep, that's me."

"What brings you all the way to Spain?" They walked towards the elevators, and Jordan pushed the button.

"I was invited by The Nubian Fashion House. You?"

"Same. They wanted someone from my

company to be here for photo ops since we helped in constructing their building, along with Panton Scaping." That's why Jeremiah was here, she thought to herself. The elevator doors opened and they got in. Kamaria pushed the button for the lobby. As the doors started to close, someone's hand stopped them. It was Jeremiah.

"Hey, Jordan," he said, dapping him up. He scooted in between them as Kamaria moved further away.

"Hey, man. What, your brothers sent you out here?" Jordan asked.

"Hell yeah. Mehki's wife just had another baby three months ago, and Jerome and his wife are trying to get pregnant again. Marlon? Well, you know how Marlon is." Both of the men laughed as Kamaria stared straight ahead, willing the doors to finally open.

"Hey Kamaria, you look nice," Jeremiah finally said. She gave him a quick smile as the doors opened, and then rushed out. She headed towards the restaurant which was completely reserved for the attendees of the grand opening. She found her name plate and took a seat.

"I see, we were put at the same table," Jeremiah said, sitting next to her. She didn't even acknowledge him.

"Hey baby," Beatriz said, sitting in the seat next to Jeremiah. Kamaria smirked as Jordan came and sat beside her.

"Looks like they put all the Houston

people together," he noticed.

"Seems that way," Kamaria said, smiling at him. "So what do you do at Blackstone Brothers?"

"Oh, he does the same thing Mehki does," Jeremiah interjected.

"I believe I was talking to Jordan," she scolded.

"Well, he's right, kind of," Jordan spoke up. "I oversee the projects and contracts that come in, and then delegate. My brothers, Tobias and Dimitri, have their respective positions as well."

A waitress came around and took their drink and food orders. After she left, Kamaria gave all her attention to Jordan, pretending Jeremiah wasn't even there.

2

Jeremiah grew envious as he watched Kamaria all in Jordan's face, and Jordan was all in hers. Beatriz was rambling on about something he had no clue about. He knew he had fucked up with Kamaria time and time again, but he couldn't help it. Settling down and being monogamous was not in his nature. But he was starting to believe that that may not be true.

These foreign feelings of jealousy were creeping in the more he sat and watched the two flirt and feel one another's arm.

"How long are you staying? I know that we all have to be in the Virgin Islands in a couple days," he heard Kamaria ask Jordan.

"Yeah, man, since you're the big boss, don't you have to get back and oversee everything and delegate?" Jeremiah smirked, mocking Jordan. Jordan ignored the jab and Jeremiah.

"Actually, I took the time off to attend my best friend's wedding. Maybe while we are there, we can get to know each other better," he told Kamaria.

"I'd like that." Jeremiah felt himself getting heated. The waitress came with the food and drinks. They all barely said more than two words as they enjoyed their meal. After everyone was finished, Kamaria spoke first.

"Well, that was amazing. I'm stuffed."

"We aren't too far from the beach if you want to walk the food off," Jordan offered.

"Sure!"

"Oh baby, let's go walk on the beach. That sounds so romantic," Beatriz gushed. Kamaria rolled her eyes, and Jeremiah smiled.

"Sure, why not?" Jordan stood up and held his hand out for Kamaria's. She took it and they headed out first. Jeremiah stood up and wasn't too far behind, and didn't pay attention to Beatriz still sitting there waiting to be helped to her feet.

Walking barefoot in the sand, Kamaria linked arms with Jordan.

"It's so beautiful here," she swooned.

"Not as beautiful as you," he responded. Jeremiah scoffed at the both of them.

"Let's go somewhere private," Beatriz whined. "I'm horny." Jeremiah cut his eyes at her, warning her before she said anything else. He shook her off his arm, and she jumped back.

"Fine, I'm going back to the hotel!"

"Well, get gone then." Beatriz ran off.

Kamaria and Jordan snickered at them and kept walking.

"I'm actually pretty tired," Kamaria admitted.

"I'll walk you back to your room," Jordan offered.

"Yeah, I think we all should head back," Jeremiah chimed in.

"Actually, I got this Jeremiah. You should probably head back and make sure Beatriz made it okay. You know how our black women are going missing," Jordan said. Jeremiah sucked his teeth and trotted off. Jordan and Kamaria fell out.

"You know he has it bad for you right?" he asked.

"I don't care. He can't keep his dick in his pants, and he isn't the monogamous type. I don't need that kind of energy in my life." Jordan nodded his head in agreement.

Once back at the hotel, Jordan walked Kamaria to her suite. Stopping at her door, he gave her a hug, neither of them noticing Jeremiah peeking from his room.

"Would you like to come in for a nightcap?" Kamaria asked.

"I'm not sure that's such a good idea," he said, smiling and rubbing his chin, his head cocked to the side.

"We're adults, and if anything should happen, let it be," she whispered, pulling him into her room by his shirt. Jeremiah slammed his door shut. He flopped back on the bed, pissed. He knew he had fucked up, but wsn't going to give up. Beatriz hadn't come back yet, so he called

Mehki.

"This better be good. I was about to lay the pipe on Bahati," Mehki answered.

"Man, you have all the time in the world to do that."

"And I want to do it right now."

"Hey, Jeremiah," his sister-in-law called.

"Hey, sis. Mehki, listen, I really fucked things up with Kamaria."

"I thought you knew that already."

"Yeah, but I didn't realize how bad until she took Jordan into her room."

"Jordan? Jordan Blackstone?"

"Yeah, who else?"

"Oh, well Jeremiah you might as well let that go. No offense, but Jordan actually is Kamaria's type," Bahati chimed in.

"What?"

"I'm just saying, I know my sister better than anybody. She's had her eyes on him a long time."

"So you're saying I don't have a shot with her again?"

"All I'm saying is, don't get your hopes up. My sister isn't the type to put up with your fuckboy shit."

"Hey, that's my brother," Mehki said in the background.

"And you know he's a fuckboy, fucking all them hoes and expecting a woman like Kamaria to put up with his shit."

"Give me the damn phone," Mehki said. Jeremiah could hear him taking the phone.

"Ignore her," he apologized.

"No, she's right. I am a fuckboy." The other end was silent. "You aren't supposed to agree."

"Man, look, that's always been you, and I've just gotten used to it."

"But why haven't you ever checked me? Or Marlon or Jerome?"

"You're a grown ass man, Jeremiah. I'm not about to tell a grown ass man how to act. You know you more than anyone, and that's just what you like."

"But I want what you and Jerome have. And Ma and Pops."

"Well, fucking all these women is not going to get you there. Ain't no woman going to put up with that shit." Jeremiah let his brother's words sink in. If he wanted Kamaria, he was going to have to show her better than he could tell her.

3

Kamaria gripped the sheets as Jordan drove deep inside her canal. The way he caressed her body and gently sucked on her neck while deep stroking from behind had her screaming his name. Jeremiah never fucked her like that. He was more beating the pussy up and Jordan, well, he was passionate, almost like he took pride in pleasing a woman.

He pulled out and gently guided her to her back as he went head first between her legs, his tongue dominating her pearl. She dug her nails into his back as he worked her like he had known her for years. He was more skilled than anyone she had ever been with.

Jordan sucked on her middle, becoming more aroused from her taste and pheromones. Her screaming his name had him on edge. She shook as her cream moistened his face. He moved up her body and plunged inside again, both lost in the throws of passion, heat, and ecstasy.

He guided his tongue in her mouth so she could taste every bit of her essence. She moaned against his lips, sending sensations to his entire nervous system. Their hearts beat against each other as he rocked his hips back and forth.

They reached their peak together, grasping and groping in the dark with nothing but a sliver of light from the moon peeking through the window.

The next morning, Jordan was gone, but she hadn't expected him to stay. Sitting up on the edge of the bed, Kamaria smiled. She needed it last night. There were some feelings for him, but she needed what he could give her in that moment even more.

After showering and getting dressed, she headed down to get breakfast at the buffet. She put some food on her plate and made some tea. She looked around for somewhere to eat, and her eyes landed on Jeremiah, sitting alone working intensely on something on his computer. She smiled and made her way over.

Sitting across from him, his eyes never left the computer. She took a sip of her tea and then cleared her throat.

"Hey, Kamaria," he mumbled, still not looking up. She felt a little bit salty that he wasn't jumping at the fact that she was sitting with him.

"Good morning. You must be really into whatever is on your screen."

"It's this business proposal from a client of ours. They want to expand the project that we had already started on. Given that the location they want is occupied by row houses, we aren't willing to contribute to the gentrification of that area." Kamaria frowned. She'd never known him to be the type that actually cared about things like that. Then again, she hadn't really gotten the chance to know him or even gave him a chance. It was always sex.

"So, what are you going to tell them?" He finally looked up at her and his dick grew an inch. Her hair was pulled back into a thick, bushy bun. Her lips were painted a deep red that matched the top of her dress. The depth of her dimples when she smiled, made his dick grow another inch. Her mocha skin had a sunkissed glow to it, and she smelled of lavender and shea butter. He had forgotten what she had asked.

"Sorry, what was your question?"

"I asked, what were you going to tell them?"

"Oh, right. Well, we have a virtual meeting scheduled later on once it's morning there. I was just responding to the group email. Hey, you want to go for a walk in the town? I heard there's this great museum."

"Sure." He answered some more emails as she ate her breakfast. She did need to get out and take some pictures for her blog. Once they had gone back to their rooms and gotten what they needed for the day, a car pulled up in front of the hotel.

"You got us a car?" she asked, raising an

eyebrow.

"I mean, we can't really walk to where we're going."

"But the center of town is only a few blocks away, and I'm wearing appropriate shoes. I don't mind."

"Could you please just get in?" he begged. She eyed him carefully, then sighed and hesitantly got in. She didn't know if she was going to regret this later on or not. He closed her door and then went around, getting in on the other side.

"Vamos, por favor," Jeremiah told the driver. The driver pulled off and headed into the heart of Valencia.

After riding for about an hour, they finally pulled up to a gate that surrounded a massive estate. Kamaria sat up in her seat.

"Please don't tell me this is one of your family's houses." Jeremiah laughed.

"It's not."

"Then where are we?"

"You're about to see." The car pulled up to the gate far enough so that the voice box could be reached from Jeremiah's side of the car.

"Tu nombre?" someone said.

"Jeremiah James-Panton."

"Que bien." The golden gate began to open and they drove through and up the winding road to the house.

The lawn was well manicured, and she saw gardeners trimming the hedges along the house and the gate. The flower beds were gorgeous and lined the entire front of the house. The driver pulled under the pergola that was atop several decorative pillars. Stopping at the steps, Jeremiah got out and ran around to open her door.

"I will wait over in the drivers' port," the driver told them. Jeremiah nodded.

"Drivers' port?" she asked.

"Yes, it is a port around the back of the house where the drivers can relax and wait until their passengers have finished their business. It is very prominent here." Kamaria lifted an eyebrow at him, and he guffawed.

"Come on," he said, grabbing her hand. They walked up the several steps as a door to the house opened. A woman came out in a business suit.

"Bienvenidos, yo soy Linda."

"Hola, me llamo Jeremiah y esta es Kamaria."

"Very well," Linda said, turning to go back in the house.

"Are we supposed to follow?" Kamaria asked.

"I think so," Jeremiah whispered.

"Come!" Linda barked. Jeremiah and Kamaria jumped as they quickened their pace into the house. Linda closed the door behind them as they took in the foyer and the spiral staircases to the second landing.

"Who lives here?" Kamaria leaned in and whispered.

"You're about to find out," he smiled. They both looked up as none other than Persia St. Laurent stood at the railing looking down. Kamaria gasped.

"Jeremiah!" Persia drawled in her Spanish accent. She glided down the steps and embraced Jeremiah, placing a kiss on each cheek. Kamaria stood there stunned.

"Persia, so good to see you again,' Jeremiah smiled. Persia stood about 5'9, even with Kamaria. She had long, black coils that she wore loose. Her skin was that of golden milk chocolate. Her lips were plush and painted a velvety purple, her breasts large and on display. Her hips slightly poked out and her glutes seemed firm. She took a once over of Kamaria and beamed.

"I assume he did not tell you that he was bringing you here?" she asked. Kamaria shook her head.

"Does she speak?" Persia asked Jeremiah. Kamaria snapped out her trance.

"I'm so sorry, I'm just a huge fan of yours. I've been following you for years, and I love your clothing."

"Yes, Jeremiah tells me you're a fashion blogger, and a noted one at that."

"I am, but that's not important. I know we just met, but, would it be okay to interview you and take pictures of you and your place?"

"I like this one," Persia smiled, linking arms with Kamaria. They spent the next several hours, talking, snapping photos, eating, and enjoying the day. Jeremiah watched from a distance as Kamaria went into work mode. Watching her work and being so excited about what she did, made him realize that she was it. She was the one. He had been with his fair share of women, but none compared to her, not even in the same ballpark.

Jeremiah snuck off to a quiet room for his conference call without the women noticing.

"You know, Jeremiah speaks so highly of you, and his face lights up when he says your name. I have never seen him like that with anyone."

"How long exactly have you known him?"

"I met him in fourth grade when my family spent some time in the states. We moved in sixth grade back here, but we kept in touch. We dated briefly in college, but we both knew that friendship is where it stopped. But my dear, it is you he wants, and it has been you for a while. Now, before you rebuttal," she continued as Kamaria opened her mouth to speak, "I know he sleeps with a lot of women, but they are easy. You give him a challenge. Men tend to go more for women who won't put up with their shit. But, trust me, give him a chance." Kamaria smiled and they hugged.

An hour later, they were saying their farewells to head back to the hotel to get ready for the grand opening of the fashion house. On the way back, Kamaria ranted and raved about Persia. She then made sure to send all the photos to her assistant to back up on a hard drive for when she got back to the states.

Back at the hotel, they parted ways to their respective rooms to shower and get dressed. An hour later, Jeremiah stood at the entrance of the hotel in some white slim fit pants, a fitted black tee, black and white Sperry's, and a black and white striped blazer.

He looked up just in time to see Kamaria step off the elevator and take his breath away. He couldn't believe that she could look any more beautiful than she already was. Her hair still pulled into a bun, she lined her bun with hair jewelry that matched the royal blue and red wine knee length dress she wore. She had on some red wine Valentino stilettos. The top of her dress was strapless, and her strapless push up bra had her breasts sitting right. His dick jumped in his pants, and he had to readjust.

His expression changed when he saw Jordan coming out of the elevator right behind her. They linked arms and were walking in a different direction. Now he was pissed he let Beatriz leave because he was going to show up to the opening alone. He cursed and got in his awaiting car.

4

When Kamaria stepped off the elevator she caught a glimpse of Jeremiah. She had really thought about what Persia said, but she knew that Jeremiah wasn't ready to be monogamous with her.

While getting dressed, Jordan called and let her know that he had had an emergency with a deal not falling through, and wanted to make it up to her by taking her to the opening. She agreed.

Despite spending the day together, and Jeremiah introducing her to Persia St. Laurent, Kamaria respected his efforts, but that wasn't enough. She knew what he was doing by taking her there, and yeah, he got brownie points, but in her 31 years of living, she learned that men will go all out for a woman just to get what he wants and then treat her like shit again.

On the way to The Nubian Fashion House, Kamaria and Jordan talked about their day, both having had quite a bit of excitement. Kamaria found that Jordan was easy to talk to. He listened attentively and waited for her to finish before speaking. Being best friends with Mehki definitely meant he was a good guy.

Once arriving, he opened her door and they walked arm-in-arm. They found their reserved seats on the front row, her being in the middle of him and Jeremiah. This was going to be an interesting night. They sat and drank some champagne and ate hors d'oeuvres. As the speaker came to the stage, Kamaria noticed Jeremiah walking in with Persia on his arm.

She shook her head in dismay and turned her attention back to Jordan. She tuned out the speaker and didn't pay attention until the lights were turned off as the show started. Kamaria made sure to snap as many photos as possible. After all, she was there on business. She caught a few glimpses of Jeremiah and Persia whispering and giggling. She was pissed, even though she shouldn't have been. She was here with Jordan.

After the show was over, she was more than happy to get away from them. She networked while Jordan spoke to the owner of the company. It was two in the morning when they got back to the hotel.

"That was an amazing grand opening. You all did an amazing job on the construction of the building," Kamaria complimented.

"I can't take all the credit. Your brother-in-law and his brothers helped out," he said.

"Yeah, well, it still looked great. I guess this is goodbye for now. You're leaving tomorrow right?"

"Yep. My plane to the Virgin Islands takes off tomorrow morning."

"Mine is tomorrow afternoon." They stood there and stared at each other. Jordan stepped in as she stepped back.

"Listen, last night was great, but I think we should slow things down. I just had a weak moment," she said.

"Ok, cool. I, uh, I understand. Good night."

"Good night, Jordan." He walked down the hall to his room. She stood there for a moment before she heard screaming. She turned towards the direction that Jeremiah's suite was in and walked towards it. She put her ear to the door and could hear a woman screaming as the headboard banged against the wall.

"Got damn, Persia!" Jeremiah growled.

"That bitch," Kamaria whispered to herself. She stormed to her room and began packing. She got her phone and changed her flight to within the next two hours. She checked out of the hotel and was on her way to the airport by three.

She boarded a little after five and stretched out on the bed in her pod. It was going to be a long flight, so she got comfortable and went to sleep.

She woke up to the stewardess asking if she wanted some lunch. She ordered and went to the bathroom to freshen up a little. There was a knock on the bathroom door, and to her surprise, it was Jordan.

"Hey, what are you doing here?" she asked.

"I decided to change my flight. I have some business to take care of before the bridal party festivities tonight." Heat radiated from her body with the sultry and seductive look he gave her. She pulled him into the bathroom and finally joined the mile high club.

After their little sexcapade, they went back to her pod and finished what they had started. A few hours later they were landing in the Virgin Islands. It was almost 6 p.m. there. A car was there to pick up Jordan, but Kamaria rode with him as well since they were going to the same place. They checked into the Air BnB and went to their rooms on opposite sides of the mansion. Her sister and Mehki booked the place to house all their guests.

When Kamaria got to her room, she quickly connected to the Wifi with her laptop and finished up some work. She had a deadline to meet for the article about The Nubian Fashion House grand opening. She opened up her photos and that is when she saw the photos with Persia. Persia's words instantly replayed in her head, and she became slightly upset.

"Lying ass bitch." She said through gritted teeth.

"Who's a lying ass bitch? I know you not talking about one of us?" Bahati said, rolling her neck. Kamaria jumped as Bahati and Carter came in. She hadn't heard the door open.

"Hey, y'all!" she smiled, getting up to hug them. Carter held her hand out to stop her.

"Aht aht, who's a lying ass bitch?" she asked.

"No one," Kamaria sighed. Bahati plopped on the bed and folded her arms while Carter stood in the same spot with her hands on her hips, waiting.

"Fine," Kamaria caved. She told them all about Valencia from beginning to end. When she was done, neither Carter nor Bahati said a word. They looked at each other and then back at Kamaria.

"What?" she asked.

"Well, um, Persia is here. We just saw her walk in with Jeremiah," Bahati said softly.

"Are you shitting me?"

"Kamaria calm down."

"Fuck that, Carter! That bitch sat in my face and went on and on about how he had feelings for me, and how he wanted me! She told me about their past and how it didn't work out, and now, the bitch is here with him?" By this time, Kamaria was crying. She sank on the bed next to Bahati and nestled her head in her sister's lap while her sister stroked her hair.

"Well, if it makes you feel any better, we thought his plus one was Beatriz," Bahati offered.

"No, she left early while we were in Valencia," Kamaria sniffed.

"Well, look on the bright side, you still have Jordan," Carter shrugged.

"I don't even have feelings for him. He was just someone to do because I couldn't be with Jeremiah, and now I have to watch him all over this woman whom I've admired for the longest time."

Neither woman knew what to say to her that could remotely even make her feel better.

"Well, this is my wedding weekend. I know you're feeling like shit, but this weekend is about me," Bahati finally said. Carter and Kamaria laughed as Bahati pretended to pout. Carter and Bahati left so that they could all get ready for this evening's festivities.

The guests all met on the beach for a bonfire dinner. They had personal chefs make their meals and serve them around the fire. There was lots of laughter, drinking, and eating.

"Where're my nieces?" Kamaria demanded.

"With the nanny upstairs," Mehki said, turning his lips up as if he were upset that they weren't part of the party.

"Yeah, I'll be going up in a sec to pop my titty out for Lena," Bahati groaned.

"Hey, don't be depriving my baby of that liquid gold woman," Mehki joked, slapping her on the ass. Everyone fell out. The laughing quickly subsided as everyone's attention turned towards the house. Kamaria turned to look at what everyone was so captivated by. Her heart stopped as Jeremiah and Persia came arm in arm towards them. Persia caught Kamaria's gaze and smirked.

Kamaria's heart began to race as they came closer. She felt like she was going to vomit.

"Waddup tho?!" Jeremiah called to his brothers. They all hugged and dapped each other up while exchanging introductions.

"Everyone, this is Persia St. Laurent, which I am sure all of you know," he gloated.

"Hi everyone," she waved shyly. Kamaria's eyes bore into Jeremiah. Jordan came and sat by her. He watched as she followed Jeremiah and Persia around with her eyes.

"You love him don't you?"

"What?" she asked, snapping out of her trance. "No, I don't love him. We used to sleep together, that's it."

"Then why do you look like you want to throw her into the fire?"

"Because she's a hypocrite," she mumbled.

"Well, he's a fool for not committing to you." She turned to look at Jordan and smiled. She leaned in to kiss him. He lifted her chin with the crook of his index finger. Once their lips separated, they gazed into each other's lust filled eyes.

"I would like everyone's attention please," Jeremiah announced. "This week is to celebrate my big brother and Bahati having the wedding they've wanted. Now, two kids later, they are making it a reality. I had a conversation not too long ago, and I was told I was a fuckboy." Everyone laughed.

"And I took that to heart. So, as of today, right now I am giving up my fuckboy ways." He turned to Persia. "We've known each other a long time, even briefly dating. I cheated, I lied, I schemed, and you left. I deserved to have my car set on fire and my clothes incinerated." Laughter roared among all the guests.

"But I would be remiss to let you go again. Persia St. Laurent, will you marry me?" Everyone looked on in shock. No one said a word when Persia accepted the proposal. Carter and Bahati looked over at Kamaria whose eyes puddled. She got up and ran off, back to the house and straight to her room.

5

After Kamaria left, Mehki, Jerome, and Marlon pulled Jeremiah towards the water to talk privately.

"Nigga, what the actual fuck?" Mehki barked. "Have you lost your fucking mind? So that conversation we had about Kamaria didn't mean shit?"

"Look, I tried to do something to show her I was worth another chance."

"And what was that? Buy her flowers?" Jerome chimed in.

"No, I introduced her to Persia while we were in Valencia. I knew that she idolized her, so I figured that that would win her over. Then she showed up to the opening with Jordan."

"Let me see if I have this straight," Marlon said. "You introduced the woman that you have been pining over for over a year to a woman that you are now going to marry and proposed to in front of said woman you've been pining for? Is that right?" He looked around at his brothers for confirmation. They nodded. He stepped closer to Jeremiah and slapped him upside the back of his head.

"Man what the fuck is wrong with you?" Jeremiah challenged, stepping to Marlon.

"What the fuck is wrong with me? Man what the fuck is wrong with you? Do you know how stupid that shit is that you just did? Do you realize how you just literally lost every chance you had of being with Kamaria?"

"Look, we aren't really getting married. We are just trying to make her jealous," Jeremiah confessed. It was Jerome then Mehki who slapped the back of his head this time.

"If one of y'all slap me again, I'm fucking somebody up," he warned.

"Naw, you need to be worried about Ma fucking you up when she finds out," Mehki said.

"You always were a snitch ass bitch," Jeremiah scoffed.

"Maybe so, but this snitch as bitch has a wife and two kids. And what do you have my friend? Oh, that's right, not jack shit." The brothers laughed as Jeremiah stormed off towards the house, Persia at his heels.

Once back in the house, he went to the men's wing of the house. Truth be told, he was slightly worried about what his mother was going to do and say once she found out. His father too. How had he fucked this up? After kicking his own ass for a couple hours, he decided to go to Kamaria's room and talk to her. No answer. He knocked several more times to no avail.

He went downstairs and towards the kitchen. Through the window to the back of the house, he saw Kamaria and Jordan having sex in one of the cabanas. His chest rose and fell rapidly. But he could only be mad at himself. He stormed back to his room and slammed the door. As soon as he lay on the bed, Marlon came in, closing the door behind him.

"Can't sleep?" he asked.

"Naw," Jeremiah mumbled. Marlon came and lied on the other side of the bed like they did when they were little and needed to talk. They were the closest in age.

"Come on, tell me," Marlon said.

"Do you like being single, Marlon?"

"Who likes being single?"

"Well, you've never mentioned any girl or having any interest in anyone. Are you gay?" Marlon guffawed at his brother's assumption. Fact is, many people thought he was gay, but he was far from it.

"No, I'm not gay. I'm just not into objectifying women and sleeping with as many as I can like you three."

"I mean, if you were gay, I'd be cool with it."

"I'm not gay. But I will tell you something that no one knows. I'm…still a virgin."

"Oh trust, everybody knows that," Jeremiah said matter-of-factly.

"What? How?"

"Marlon, look at you. You scream 'virgin.'" Marlon sat up and looked at his pajamas. He had on a silk two piece button down set. He began to laugh at himself. His brother was right. Jeremiah joined in on the laughter.

"Look, there's nothing wrong with being a virgin. Fucking a bunch of women ain't all it's cracked up to be."

"Then why do you do it?"

"Fear."

"Fear? Of what?"

"Commitment." Marlon nodded in understanding. "I've never been committed to anything or anyone."

"That's not true, brother. You're committed to you career, you're committed to the family, you're committed to fucking a bunch of women," he joked, getting a smile out of Jeremiah.

"Yeah, but those things mean a lot to me, well except smashing a bunch of women. I want to be committed to one woman, and that woman is on the back patio fucking Jordan."

"What?" Marlon asked, his eyes wide. He got up and went to the window to see Kamaria and Jordan still going at it. "Damn, he is tearing that ass up!" Jeremiah threw a pillow at him. Marlon laughed and came and laid back down.

"Look, if you really want her, you need to prove that she is who you want, and that you are a better man than Jordan."

"What about Persia?"

"I don't know why you brought her dumbass here. What the fuck were you thinking?"

"I wasn't. I was being petty because my feelings were hurt."

"Does Persia even know that this is all to get Kamaria back? Because as I recall, you hurt her pretty bad. She was really in love with you, bro."

"No, she doesn't know."

"So you're using her? Jeremiah, do you know what she's going to do when she finds out? She might try to kill you."

"I know," he said, sitting up and turning to his brother. "That's why I need your help." Marlon jumped up and headed to the door.

"When it comes to that psychotic bitch, you're on your own." He walked out the door, closing it behind him.

The next morning, Jeremiah felt something tight and wet gliding up and down his morning erection.

"Fuck," he whispered. He had been dreaming about Kamaria and thought it was still a dream. The sensation became even more intense, and he was about to let one off until he opened his eyes to see Persia riding him with no condom. He pushed her off before using his hand to release his nut.

"What the fuck, Persia?"

"I could ask you the same thing nigga." She sat up and eyed him curiously. "Who were you dreaming about?" He sat up and looked at her. He could tell her the truth, but a funeral would definitely ruin his brother's wedding. He could lie and string her along, but that would lessen his chances even more with Kamaria. It was a lose-lose situation.

"I was dreaming about you," he finally said, lying.

"Then why did you push me off?"

"Because you know fucking well we use condoms. You've always tried to trap me, Persia. And I told you, I am not having kids outside of marriage."

"But we are getting married, so why wait?" she asked, climbing back onto his lap. She waited as he got his thoughts together. He would eventually have to tell her. But right now, he needed the rest of the week to go smoothly. He reached up with his lips and took her mouth into his. He caressed her back and made his way up to her hair and tugged gently, pulling her head back.

His tongue attacked her neck in the very spot that he knew would make her body quiver. He took one breast and sucked in her nipple and as much of her breast as he could, then moved on to the other. She grinded against his rising wood. He reached over in the nightstand and pulled out a condom. He strapped up, never taking attention away from her body.

He lifted her up over the head of his shaft

and brought her down, filling her tight walls. She wrapped her arms around his neck as he guided both of them. At one point, he did love her, and he did want to marry her. But he was young then, and being monogamous never crossed his mind, no matter how much he felt for her.

But the only person who he could see himself being monogamous with was not the woman on his dick. He rolled them over to where he was on top and he drilled inside her like he knew she liked it.

"Ah, Jeremiah! Baby, yes!"

He sped up the tempo until she was shivering and shaking beneath him.

"I'm coming!"

He kept that same pace until he met his release again, filling the condom. He kissed her deeply before getting up to flush the condom.

"You didn't have to flush it," she said, rolling her eyes as she put her robe on.

"Yeah, I did."

"What are we doing today?"

"We are going zip lining, canoeing, paddle boating, and rock climbing."

"I think I'll just watch from a distance." She exited his room and he shook his head.

6

Kamaria sat on the back patio enjoying the spread that the chefs had prepared. Everyone else was still asleep. Jordan had to tend to some business with his company, and so that left her to eat alone until Jeremiah came out.

"Morning," she said, as he poured himself some coffee.

"Morning." He sat down and fixed his plate with pancakes, fruit, sausage, eggs, and grits.

"How'd you sleep?" she inquired.

"Great," he responded, stuffing his mouth.

"I slept marvelously."

"I bet you did," he mumbled.

"I'm sorry, what's that supposed to mean?"

"If I was fucking someone in a cabana under the moonlight, I'd sleep marvelously too."

"What are you talking about?"

"I saw you fucking Jordan last night in the cabana over there." He pointed to his left.

"That's impossible. My sister, Carter and I had a sleepover." Kamaria thought about what Jordan said last night, that he was going to kick it with Mehki. Who could he have been fucking, or was Jeremiah lying?

"I know what I saw, Kamaria."

"Not that I have to explain shit to you, it wasn't me!" She grabbed her plate and tea before storming off inside the house. On her way to her room, she passed Persia.

"Morning," Persia smirked.

"You know what? Fuck you, you lying scheming ass bitch. You spewed all that bullshit about Jeremiah and then you fucked him. You are a conniving, psychotic…" Before she could finish, her tea and food was flying in the air as Persia attacked her. Kamaria regained her composure and was pounding on Persia to get her off. Persia grabbed Kamaria by her hair and swung her around into a side table in the living room, shattering the glass.

Sharp shards of glass sliced through Kamaria's sides, and that gave her more adrenaline to get up and attempt to kill Persia. Unbeknownst to Persia, Kamaria held a large, sharp shard of glass in her hand. When Persia pulled her to standing, Kamaria swung her arm with the glass in her hand sliced from Persia's right arm, across her chest, and her left arm in one swift move. Persia cried out as blood spewed everywhere. She fell to her knees as everyone else in the house came running.

"What the fuck?!" Bahati demanded. Kamaria dropped the glass and stormed out, Carter and Bahati right behind her. Jeremiah was running in at the same time they were heading up the stairs. Kamaria stopped short and walked towards him, his eyes wide at all the blood all over her. "I pray to God that bitch is dead." She slapped him across his face. He stood there, stoic. She walked away as her sister and best friend shook their heads.

Jeremiah watched as they went up the stairs and he headed into the living room to see one of the housemaids tending to Persia.

"I'm going to sue her for everything she's worth!" she spat. His brothers glared at him, especially Mehki. Mehki walked over to him and stopped shoulder to shoulder.

"If you fucked up this destination wedding for me, I will fuck you up," he whispered. Just then Moriah and Jeremy came in.

"We have arrived!" she announced, then stopped as she laid eyes on the living area. It was as if a tornado had blown through and brought red water with it, there was so much blood. "Oh my God! What the fuck is this?"

"Ask your son," Mehki sneered as he left the house, followed by Jerome. Marlon grabbed Jeremiah's arm and pulled him to the back patio.

"Jeremiah..." he began.

"I know Mar, I know. I have to tell Persia. But how can I now?"

"You don't have a choice. Kamaria is upstairs getting bandaged, an ambulance is on its way to get Persia. You created this shit, and you need to fucking fix it, or Mehki will never forgive you, and neither will Kamaria." He got up and went back in the house as Moriah and Jeremy came out.

"What is that bitch doing here, Jeremiah?" They sat across the table from him, waiting for an answer. He sighed and told them about Valencia.

"Boy, are you fucking stupid?" his dad scolded. "You think that you could get Kamaria to be with you if you showed up here with the woman you introduced her to? Where the hell did we go wrong?" Moriah stared at her son.

"Baby, what were you thinking?" she asked softly.

"I wasn't. I know Kamaria isn't like other women and doesn't respond to moves like that, but I did it anyway. And now I probably lost her for good."

"And fucked up your brother's wedding," his dad added.

"They're already married," Jeremiah reminded.

"Yes, but they wanted to have this wedding, the one they wanted at first," Moriah chimed in. They sat in silence for a while.

The ambulance finally arrived and took Persia to the hospital. Jeremiah knew the right thing would be to go with her, despite not wanting to. But the look he got from Marlon made him realize that he didn't have a choice.

Upstairs, Bahati tended to Kamaria and her injuries, insisting she go to the hospital.

"No, because if I see her, I will kill her," she said through gritted teeth as Bahati poured alcohol on her wounds, and then peroxide.

"The wounds aren't that deep," Carter said as she bandaged her up. She handed Kamaria some pain meds and a glass of water. Kamaria knocked them back.

"I need some time to rest," she mumbled.

"I'll give you your time, but you will tell me what the fuck happened. And you're paying for the damages," Bahati ordered, leaving the room. Carter stayed and looked at Kamaria.

"You're going to need a lawyer."

"Yes, Carter, I want you to represent me."

"Ok, well, get some rest. I'll be available later."

7

At the hospital, Jeremiah waited bedside for Persia to wake up. She had to get stitches to close the gashes that Kamaria had made. He felt like shit. All of this could've been avoided had he just told Kamaria how he felt. She began to stir, and he sat up straight.

"Hey, how are you feeling?"

"How am I feeling?" she muttered. "Look at what that bitch did to me."

"Persia, I'm so sorry. I didn't expect any of this to happen."

"When we get back to the states, I am going to sue her."

"What do you mean "when we get back to the states?""

"Now that we are engaged, I'll be moving to the states with you."

"Persia, I can't ask you to do that."

"You didn't, I offered." The look in her eyes was making it harder to break things off with her.

"Persia, look..."

"It's okay Jeremiah. I get it."

"You do?"

"Yes, it's too soon to talk about moving in together. Why don't I stay in the states for a week, get the legal stuff going, and then come back when it is time for trial."

"Persia, what exactly happened between you and Kamaria?"

"I mean, clearly the bitch is crazy. Look at me."

"Yes, but before this happened. She was cut up and a table was broken. Did you push her into that glass table?"

"I mean she attacked me first. She said all kinds of evil things to me, and then she slapped me." He could tell she was lying, but he let it go for the time being. The doctors came in to check on her. They would be keeping her overnight for observation.

Back at the house, Kamaria awoke to Jordan lying beside her.

"Hello gorgeous," he smiled. That smile used to make her melt, but now, she felt nothing.

"Hey," she said, wincing as she tried to sit up.

"Take it easy."

"Jordan, what happened last night?"

"You're lying here wrapped in bloody bandages, and you're worried about what I was doing last night?" he chuckled

"Well?"

"I was with the boys. We played dominoes, cards, talked shit, drank, and just had a good time." The way the lie flowed smoothly off his delicious lips made her blood boil. "Now about you, what the hell happened?"

"Persia."

"She did this?"

"Yes, but she's in the hospital. Where were you all day?"

"What's with the 21 questions?" he sat up, his expression changing. "Anyway, the festivities for today have been pushed to tomorrow. Everyone is on edge about what happened between you and Persia. I need to go handle some work stuff." He got up and left without so much as a kiss on the forehead.

An hour later, she got up and headed to the kitchen. Mehki was there sitting at the bar alone, snacking on the fruit and cheese plates while the chefs prepared dinner.

"Hey," she mumbled, sitting next to him. He jumped back and put up his index fingers to make a cross.

"There's plenty of food for everyone," he joked. She shoved his arm and winced in pain.

"You're such an ass."

"What's up lil sis?"

"Hey, did y'all have a boys' night last night?"

"Naw. We were supposed to, but the girls were being needy, and I needed to help Bahati with them since we sent the nannies to do whatever it is they wanted to do. Why?"

"It's just, Jordan said that y'all had a boys' night. Y'all played cards, dominoes, drank."

"I mean, he and my brothers could've, but I wasn't there. Actually, come to think of it, after the bonfire, Jordan said he had business to take care of for work."

"He always has business to take care of for work," she mumbled, popping a cube of cheese in her mouth.

"And she's up," Bahati announced, coming into the kitchen, slobbing her husband down.

"Get a room," Kamaria gagged. Mehki and Bahati laughed.

"I see it's sister time, so I'm going to grab my food and go play with the girls." He headed out and Bahati took his place, making a plate of snacks for herself.

"How did you know that Mehki was the one?"

"When I got knocked up," Bahati joked.

"I'm serious."

"You never really know that someone is the one. I just knew that he was who I wanted to spend my life with. I don't know what the future holds, but I'm hoping that he's in it. You don't know what's going to happen tomorrow. You can only worry about what is happening right now." Kamaria nodded her head in agreeance. "Now, tell me what the fuck happened."

"I was out talking to Jeremiah on the patio, and we got into it. I came back in and Persia was coming in my direction. We exchanged words and then she lunged at me."

"So she threw the first punch, so to speak?"

"Yeah, and I got a few in."

"I saw."

"Then she swung me into that table, and Bahati, all I saw was red. Had I gone full force, I would have sliced through major arteries and her heart, but I was weakened by all this," she motioned to her bandages.

"Tell me, is Jeremiah worth all of this?"

"I don't know. I think I was more so pissed that she sat in my face and told me all that shit and then backdoor and fucked him. It's like one minute he wants me, the next he's flaunting a bitch in my face. I'm also pissed at him for introducing me to her, and then bringing her here as his plus one."

"Ok, so now, what about Jordan?"

"I don't know what's going on with him, but I have a suspicious feeling that he's lying and sneaking around, but I can't put my finger on why."

"Well, can I give you some advice?"

"Yes, please."

"I think, at least for right now, let them both go. Kamaria, you are too smart, driven, strong, level headed, and a whole meal to be worrying about these fuckboys and the drama they bring."

"You're right." Bahati kissed her sister and got up to leave.

8

Later that night at dinner, everyone except Persia, gathered around the table. There was a lot of awkward silence, and the tension was so thick, a knife couldn't cut it.

"Well, I will speak first. I don't know what the fuck..."

"Mehki," Moriah warned. Mehki sighed.

"I don't know what the hell is going on around here, but this week is supposed to be about me and Bahati. Y'all need to dead the drama until this week is over. Now, tomorrow, we all will be going zip lining, snorkeling, and rock climbing. If anyone puts a damper on me acting like a big ass kid, you're leaving." No one said a word. They just nodded. "Now, let's eat." The tension fell and they all engaged in conversation, except Kamaria.

"Kamaria, how're you feeling dear?" Moriah asked.

"I'm good, Mrs. Panton."

"Oh honey, how many times have I told you to call me Moriah?" Kamaria smiled at her and then dropped her gaze to her plate.

After dinner, they went to sit by the beach

and watch the fire dancers. Mehki even got up to join, along with Jerome, Marlon, and Jordan. Jeremiah was nowhere to be found. Kamaria looked around and saw him in the distance walking along the beach. She got up without anyone noticing and caught up to him.

"Jeremiah." He turned to her and she embraced him with a kiss, so passionate it made his toes curl. His manhood grew, pressing up against her sex. She knelt down and released him, taking him to the back of her throat. He gasped and looked around, but they were out of sight of everyone.

He ran his hands through her hair as she worked him. His cheeks tightened as he released prematurely. He brought her to her feet and led her closer to the water. He took his shirt off and laid it on the sand, guiding her to her back. He dropped his pants and boxers, crawling between her legs. He moved her bikini bottoms to the side and submerged himself inside her, the waves crashing over them.

She winced as she felt the weight of his body on her cuts.

"I'm sorry. Should we stop?" he asked.

"Don't you fucking dare." He moved in sync with the waves, giving her thrust after thrust. She whispered his name and clawed at his back as he pushed deeper into her ocean. She looked up at the night sky, and saw the moon and the stars.

A wave rushed over them as her core tightened and her pussy quacked, an orgasm evoking expletives and screams from inside her. Jeremiah kept going, not letting up. Another wave crashed over them and he released deep inside her with a grunt and a shutter, but he wasn't done.

He rolled them over to where she was on top, and she rode him through another orgasm. She threw her head back as he sat up to give her breasts some attention. Beneath her, he rocked his hips to give her deeper penetration, he himself releasing again.

As they settled, wrapped in each other's arms, him softening inside her, they didn't say a word.

"Now, when you're fucking her, you'll think of me." Like a savage, Kamaria stood up, adjusted her swim bottoms and breasts, then walked off towards where everyone else was enjoying the bonfire. Jeremiah sat there confused at how she just played him. He threw some sand into the water with frustration.

The next morning, everyone piled into cars to head to the woods to go ziplining. The women rode in one car, the men in the other.

Twenty minutes later, they pulled up to their destination.

"Are you sure you're up for this?" Bahati asked Kamaria.

"Why wouldn't I be? Those pain meds

really work."

They filed out of the car and headed to meet the men at the bottom of the ziplining stand. The instructor went over some rules and protocols with the group. They were doing couples ziplining. Since Marlon was single and Persia was still in the hospital, he and Jeremiah were together. First up were Mehki and Bahati. They climbed to the top of the post where another instructor got them strapped into their harnesses.

Everyone else looked up from below. Mehki jumped them off the ledge and everyone could hear Bahati screaming. They laughed as the two went zipping through the woods until they were no longer in sight. Next up was Jerome and Carter, Moriah and Jeremy, Marlon and Jeremiah, and then Jordan and Kamaria.

When it was Jordan and Kamaria's turn, her heart pounded inside her chest. She was nervous and afraid. They were high up above the trees. After they were all hooked up, the instructor told them they could go when they were ready.

"Ready?" Jordan whispered in her ear. The way he whispered it sounded odd, almost devilish. Before she could respond, he jumped them off the ledge. She held her breath and screamed, kicking and wriggling. Halfway through the woods, she felt their hooks detach and they were falling. She tried to grab on to the rope that was holding them, and barely made it. Jordan was holding on to her and yanking as if he were trying to pull her down.

"Let go, you stupid bitch!" he growled. She tried kicking him off, but he held tighter. She tried to reach her other hand up to grab the rope, but he was so heavy. He yanked again and the rope burned her hand, forcing her to let go. They went falling, almost in slow motion, and then everything was black.

9

"What's taking them so long?" Jeremiah asked impatiently.

"Yeah, they should've been here by now," Bahati agreed. They all looked in the direction of one of the instructors coming on the zipline. In the pit of Jeremiah's stomach, he knew something was wrong. The instructor quickly made his way down the post.

"They fell," he huffed.

"What?!" Bahati shrieked.

"What do you mean they fell?" Jeremiah demanded.

"Typically, we wait a full minute until everyone crosses, and then we come. When I was midway, I saw one of their harnesses hanging." He held up the harness.

"Was it faulty?" Carter asked, putting her lawyer hat on.

"No, it's all still intact."

"So that means…" Jerome started.

"It was intentionally disconnected," the instructor finished. Bahati let out a shrill scream and Mehki held her to his chest. Carter kept it together for her friend. Jeremiah headed towards the woods.

"Where are you going, son?" Jeremy asked.

"To find them, and kill Jordan." Marlon, Jerome, and Mehki took off after him.

Kamaria fluttered her eyes open. Her head was pounding and there was a ringing in her ears. When her vision focused, she looked up into the trees. She looked from side to side, and Jordan was nowhere in sight.

She could hear her name being called in the distance, but she couldn't speak. The impact from hitting the ground had knocked the wind out of her.

She kept hearing her name and saw some figures running towards her. It was Jeremiah and his brothers. Two more men came behind them: paramedics. They got her loaded onto the gurney after putting a brace around her back and her neck. Jeremiah held her hand all the way to the ambulance, saying something that she couldn't make out through the ringing in her ears.

They loaded her into the ambulance and she blacked out again.

"What's going on?" Jeremiah demanded.

"She took a pretty hard fall. We are going to pump her with morphine for the pain, but she more than likely has a concussion and some broken ribs," one of the EMTs said.

Jeremiah's jaw tensed. He had noticed that Jordan was nowhere around her. He knew he tried to kill her.

They arrived at the same hospital that Persia was in. They rushed her inside to get x-rays, and made him stay in the waiting area. The rest of the family came in a few minutes later. Bahati was asked to fill out some medical papers.

"Jeremiah," Persia said, walking over towards them. "What's wrong baby?"

"Uh, Kamaria had a ziplining accident."

"What do you care for? After what she did to me, she got what she deserved." Bahati dropped the clipboard and lunged at Persia.

"You bitch! I can make damn sure you get what you deserve!" Mehki pulled her off, and Jeremiah pulled Persia back.

"You're going to let her attack me like that after what her sister did?"

"Save it you bum ass bitch. Kamaria told me that you swung first, and the shit is on camera," Bahati spat. Jeremiah let Persia go.

"Is that true, Persia?" he asked.

"Does it matter? I ended up in the hospital." He glared at her. She walked off to sign release papers.

"You didn't handle that, now did you?" Marlon asked.

"Handle what?" Moriah asked. Jeremiah sneered at his brother and walked off to find Persia.

A few hours later, Kamaria woke up in the recovery room. It was night time now. She cleared her throat and her sister and Carter woke up. Bahati came over with a cup of water.

"Food," Kamaria whispered after taking a few sips. Carter helped her to sit up and handed her a burger and fries. She scarfed them down as the other two women waited patiently. After washing down the food with some more water, she leaned back and closed her eyes.

"He tried to kill me," she finally spoke.

"Keep going," Carter asked, writing it down.

"He unhooked my harness. As I held on to the rope with one hand, he was yanking me down. He screamed for me to let go, but I couldn't. He yanked again and the rope burned my hand so bad, I let go." She looked at her hand wrapped in bandages.

"Do you know why he would want to kill you?" Carter asked.

"No. I don't know what's going on you guys, but I'm terrified." Tears streamed down her face as Bahati embraced her.

"Well, Bahati jumped Persia," Carter offered.

"He's really going to marry her?" Kamaria asked, sobbing and ignored Carter trying to make light of the situation.

"Looks that way," Bahati responded. They all sat in silence until Kamaria dozed off.

The next two days, Kamaria rested, and did what she could to help prepare for the wedding. Those two days went by without incident. The afternoon of the ceremony, the women got dressed in one of the huge parlors in the house.

When Bahati walked out, Kamaria and Carter shed a tear.

"You look beautiful," Kamaria said. Bahati leaned down to kiss her sister on the cheek. Kamaria was in a wheelchair for the time being.

The ceremony was starting and since Kamaria had been paired with Jordan, who was still missing, she ended up having to be pushed down the aisle by Marlon. The ceremony was beautiful and full of love.

Jeremiah watched as she came down the aisle in the wheelchair and tears streamed down his face. Kamaria smirked at his pain. She knew he was sorry, and he deserved to feel like shit. Looking around, she didn't see Persia, which she wasn't all too surprised.

After the ceremony, the reception was held back at the house. Kamaria was pissed she was in a wheelchair. She had plans for this night to dance and party with her sister and everyone else. She watched as everyone was laughing and dancing. She smiled as she watched Bahati and Mehki. That's what she wanted for herself.

The doorbell rang and Jerome went to answer it. He came back with two officers, the same officers who questioned Kamaria in the hospital. Someone turned the music off as the officers walked over to Kamaria.

"Did you find him?" she asked.

"No," said Officer Santiago.

"Ok, then why are y'all here?" Moriah asked.

"After further investigation, it appears Mr. Blackstone has left the island. His credit card was charged this morning at the airport, and he boarded a flight to Houston," he responded.

"Ok, so what now? The islands are U.S. territory, so I am sure something can be done," Bahati demanded.

"Yes, this is U.S. territory, but they don't have any jurisdiction in the states," Carter responded.

"But can't he be extradited back here?" Jeremiah asked.

"Yes, but that's if he is found. We already put a word in at IAH to hold him, but as for bringing him back here, there is nothing we can do. He will be on American soil. We can send all the information we have on him, but since he fled, our hands are tied."

Jeremiah punched a wall and walked out of the room. Bahati cursed and Kamaria starred in a daze.

10

Two weeks had gone by and Kamaria was walking on her own. After the ceremony, Jeremiah went back to Spain with Persia. She still couldn't believe he was going through with the wedding.

After daily extensive physical therapy, she was up and about. Lucky for her that she had content batched, she didn't have to work as much. It also helped that she worked from home. She focused more on healing from the fall. Bahati came by everyday with Khadija and Lena. It was nice to have girl time, and to see her nieces.

She was walking on the treadmill in the workout room to warm up before her light jog. Her physical therapist was surprised at how quickly she recovered. All those years of working out and eating right had created a strong body that quickly healed itself.

She jogged for five miles on the treadmill, and then went into the yoga studio for an hour of hot yoga. After she showered and threw on a tank and sweatpants, she made an omelet and a smoothie. She sat on her patio and enjoyed her breakfast and the view. She answered some emails, held a few virtual meetings, and wrote a few blog posts.

Opening her archives, she found the photos of the interview with Persia. She shook her head at the fact that she looked up to this woman, and she was nothing but a backstabbing bitch. She went back and forth with the idea of posting the article. Her publicist said despite what had transpired, it was up to her whether or not she would publish it.

If she did, she felt like she'd be lying to her fans and putting out false content. If she didn't post, then that meant that Persia won the war. It was a downhill battle. She sighed and sent the article over to her editor. She tweaked the article a little.

A few hours later, her publicist and editor agreed that her new additions were going to have the fashion industry in an uproar. Kamaria smiled then headed out to link up for dinner at Bahati's house.

Jeremiah was getting dressed when he heard a shrill cry from the bathroom. They had just gotten back in town that morning. He ran in to see what was going on. Persia was standing there hyperventilating.

"What happened?" he asked.

"That bitch!"

"Persia, what?" She shoved the phone at him. There were endless tweets about some articles and videos about Persia. He clicked on one of the links, and it took him to Kamaria's blog. Reading through, it started off great with the photos from their stay in Valencia. As he continued, it took a turn. She included the incident in the Virgin Islands, even going so far as to include pictures of her injuries from when she was pushed into the table, and the video of Persia attacking her.

"She just ruined my career. My stylist, publicist, partnerships, and everyone I've worked with have released statements saying they will no longer work with me." She was pulling at her hair bent over the toilet, dry heaving. Jeremiah had been waiting for the right time to tell her that he wasn't going to go through with the wedding, but it was one thing after another that stood in the way.

He went over and held her hair as vomit was actually coming up now. After she had calmed down and popped a valium, she sat on the edge of the bed.

"I am not going to your brother's house if she's going to be there," she finally said.

"I'm sure she will. My brother is married to her sister."

"Well, I don't want you around her."

"Persia, again, my brother is married to her sister. That's unavoidable."

"Fine, then it's me or your family." She was giving him an ultimatum that, unbeknownst to her, was also an out.

"My family all day every day, Persia," he responded without hesitation. She gasped in disbelief.

"You would seriously choose that woman over me?"

"Persia, I choose my family over you, and like it or not, that includes her. I won't apologize for that." She studied him for a minute.

"I guess this is it then. I think we both knew this wasn't going to work between us, just like it didn't before," she sighed. As much as he was relieved, he didn't want to show it.

"At least we can look back on it and say we tried," he offered. She got up and began packing her suitcase.

"Where are you going?"

"Back to Spain. I'll be gone before you get back home." He walked over to her and hugged her tightly to his chest. After saying their goodbyes, he sped to his brother's house. He couldn't wait to see Kamaria.

Kamaria pulled into the gate at her sister's house and saw everyone was there except for Jeremiah. She parked and walked in to find everyone on the back patio.

"Hey, sis!" Bahati cheered, running to embrace her sister. Carter came over and joined in. They all took a seat around the fire pit.

"Where are my nieces?" Kamaria asked.

"With Genesis and Moriah in the playroom." While they were in the Virgin Islands,

Genesis stayed behind with Jeremy's sister since she wasn't yet cleared to fly.

"Oh, and we read that article you did on Persia. You are a savage," Bahati laughed. They all began laughing. They heard the men howl and turned to see that Jeremiah showed up, sans Persia. She watched as he greeted his brothers and father. He came over to hug Carter and Bahati. He stopped in front of Kamaria.

"Hey, Kamaria. I see physical therapy has done you well." She still glared. "I heard they never found Jordan, and his brothers haven't seen him either." Carter and Bahati looked at each other as if that was their cue to leave. They left Jeremiah and Kamaria alone. Jeremiah sat in the egg chair across from her.

"Listen, Kamaria, I know this has been a struggle between us, going back and forth. I know I've fucked up numerous times, but you have to believe me when I say, I never meant to hurt you."

"Why should I believe shit you say?" she asked, leaning forward.

"I broke things off with Persia. She's getting on a flight now headed back to Spain."

"Let me make this clear for you Jeremiah. You took me to meet her, knowing full well she was an icon that I had been wanting to do a piece on. She tells me all this bullshit about how you want me, and how I should give you a chance. Then, you fuck her that same night."

"In my defense, you went to the grand opening with Jordan."

"Just because you did one nice thing for me does not prove that you have changed, and fucking her proves that you haven't. And that didn't entitle you to take me to the opening. Not only that, you bring her to Mehki and Bahati's wedding week, knowing it was going to cause issues, and don't you dare say you didn't know."

"Kamaria, you were with Jordan! How are you mad at me when you were with another dude?"

"You can't compare us Jeremiah, I didn't pull the shady shit that you did."

"You're right."

"I'm sorry, come again?"

"I said you're right. I'm sorry, Kamaria. I am sorry for everything. All the pain I've caused, the bullshit, what Persia did to you, what happened with Jordan. I'm sorry for it all. I don't care what happens after today, I want you to know that I love you." Kamaria blinked at his confession. She was taken aback because she wasn't expecting him to say that, nor did she think he was capable of loving anyone.

"You what?"

"Food is ready!" Mehki called.

"I love you," Jeremiah repeated. "I'm not expecting you to say it back or even feel the same. I just wanted you to know."

He got up and walked over to the table

where everyone was sitting. Moriah came out of the house with her three granddaughters. After everyone had seated, Jerome stood up.

"I'd like to make a toast to the somewhat newlyweds," he began. Laughter erupted among the group. "I also want to make a toast to my beautiful lady, Carter. We are expecting again." Everyone gasped and cheered, spreading congratulations. Carter had lost their last baby. She had been told by doctors that she'd never get pregnant. When she did the first time, it was a legit miracle. Then she was told she wouldn't be able to carry after losing the first one. But Kamaria knew she was resilient and would keep trying.

"Oh, it's a party and mama wasn't invited?" a woman shouted. Everyone turned to see Rashelle stumbling in.

11

"How the hell did you get in here?" Bahati demanded, jumping up from her seat.

"I'm your mother, I can get in anywhere." She swayed her way over to them. Bahati and Kamaria walked up on her, grabbing each arm. Rashelle yanked her arms away.

"Don't you ungrateful bitches touch me. I heard I had granchiren. Where they at?"

"You don't have grandchildren because you don't have children," Bahati seethed.

"I think it's time for you to leave," Moriah said as she rose.

"Bitch, who are you?" Mehki and his brothers stood, but stopped as their mother raised a hand.

"It's okay boys. I can handle her kind." They sat back down as Moriah glided over to Rashelle. "This is my son and daughter's house. You were not invited. Now I have asked you once to leave. I won't ask again."

"And what are you going to do, you stuck up bourgeoisie bitch?" Moriah took one swift fist to Rashelle's face, knocking her on her ass. Rashelle cried out in pain.

"Leave, now!" Bahati demanded. Rashelle went from crying to laughing.

"You stupid bitch, I ain't the one you need to be worried about." The brothers came over and helped Rashelle to her feet, dragging her out as Kamaria and Bahati followed.

Outside the gate, they let Rashelle go and looked around for a car.

"How'd you get here?" Jeremiah questioned.

"I told you, I'm not the one you have to worry about." Several shots went off in the back of the house as Rashelle cackled like a hyena. The men took off sprinting with Bahati right behind them. Kamaria punched Rashelle in her nose, knocking her unconscious, and then pulled her phone out to call the police. When screams pierced through the air, Kamaria took off towards the house and to the backyard. Jeremy, Moriah, and Carter were laid out, bleeding, but all still alive.

"Where are my babies?" Bahati screamed. Kamaria's heart palpitated at the thought of her nieces being kidnapped. Mehki was tending to Bahati as the men assessed the injuries.

"Genesis is gone too," Jerome wept, pounding a fist through the table as he held onto Carter.

After the ambulance arrived and took Moriah, Jeremy, and Carter, and the police took their statements and arrested Rashelle, they headed to the hospital. Bahati paced back and forth in the waiting area. Everyone was on edge about the missing girls. Kamaria knew somehow that Jordan had something to do with this.

Hours later, an officer came to talk to them. He let them know that they had an APB out on Jordan and Amber Alerts for the three missing girls.

"That's it? Our daughters are missing and that's all you can do?" Bahati screamed. Mehki pulled her to him as tears left his own eyes. Lack of sleep and fear was making everyone delirious.

The next morning, Kamaria went home, taking Bahati with her. She gave Bahati a mild sedative at Mehki's request. She then went into her own room, showered, and passed out. It was 5 that evening when she finally awoke to see Bahati standing over her. She jumped back, frightened.

"I'm sorry," Bahati whispered. "I didn't mean to scare you."

"It's okay," she said, scooting over to allow her sister in the bed. They curled up next to each other.

"Mehki called. Everyone is out of surgery and is doing fine."

"That's good," said Kamaria, relieved.

"Do you think they're still alive?"

"Bahati, don't think like that," she urged. "Yes, they are still alive. They weren't taken just for any reason. Rashelle was a decoy. They took her in cuffs and promised they would get something out of her."

"Do you believe them? Will they believe her? She was obviously high, Kamaria."

"Bahati, please think positively. We need that for the girls." They lay in silence for a while. No matter how she tried to fight it, something kept nagging at Kamaria.

"Bahati, you know the night of the bonfire, when the men were supposed to have a boys' night?"

"Yeah, but Mehki ended up staying with me."

"I know, but, that night, Jeremiah said he saw me having sex with Jordan in one of the cabanas behind the house."

"That's impossible. You were with us."

"That's what I said. I know this is going to sound crazy, but if he's telling the truth, do you think Jordan was screwing Persia?" Bahati sat up and looked at her sister confused.

"You know, it doesn't sound crazy at all. I should've told you, but I saw them getting real cozy earlier that day. I didn't think anything of it, but now that you brought that up, it reminded me of that."

"Do you think they had anything to do with the girls being missing?"

"The thought crossed my mind."

Kamaria's phone buzzed, and she grabbed it off the nightstand. It was from a blocked number.

Bring Jerome to me to get the girls back. Only you and him are to come. No cops or anyone else, or the girls die. I will text you in an hour with the directions

Kamaria gasped at the message. Bahati leaned over and read it, then snatched the phone from her.

"So this has nothing to do with me," Kamaria said.

"What are you talking about?"

"I thought that the girls were taken because of me. I know Jordan attempted to kill me and was unsuccessful, but it was never about me."

"Kamaria, how could you think that it's your fault my girls are gone?"

"That doesn't matter now. We need to get to the hospital and talk to Jerome." They quickly took care of their hygiene and got dressed. Bahati sped to the hospital. After parking, they ran inside, opting for the stairs to the fifth floor. Bursting through the doors of the private waiting area, the men looked up at them.

"We have something," Bahati blurted out. The four men rose as the women came over. Kamaria handed her phone directly to Jerome as the men crowded around.

"The fuck did you do Jerome to get my girls taken?" Mehki asked.

"Need I remind you, brother, my daughter

was taken too. And I haven't done anything, by the way. So pipe the fuck down." He handed the phone back to Kamaria.

"So what now?" Marlon asked.

"We wait."

12

They waited, and waited, and waited. Kamaria stared at her phone like it was a bomb ready to detonate at any moment. When the phone buzzed, everyone jumped.

"It's just my publicist," she apologized. She quickly responded to the text. It buzzed again. This time, it was from the blocked number, with an address.

"They texted," she said. Everyone came over as she laid the phone on the table. They read the address.

"That's my house!"

"So this is Jordan doing this," Kamaria concluded.

"But, why?" Marlon asked.

"I don't know. But we are about to find out," Jerome said, getting up.

"We're coming too," Mehki announced.

"They said just us," Kamaria reminded.

"I don't give a fuck. Those are my daughters and niece they have."

"What about when your parents and Carter wake up?" she asked.

"I'll stay," Bahati offered.

"I'll stay too," Marlon added.

Mehki, Jerome, Jeremiah and Kamaria got in her car and headed to Jerome's house. They parked a half mile down the road and let Mehki and Jeremiah out. Luckily, they stay strapped.

"Now look," Mehki began, "I don't know how this is going to go down, but our first priority is to get the girls out." They all agreed. Mehki and Jeremiah took off to scope the place.

"Turn your phone on vibrate," Kamaria said as she did it to hers.

"Why?"

"Because Rome, if they text us, we don't want the phones going off."

"Right." He turned his phone on vibrate as they pulled up to the house and entered the code to the gate.

"I have to get new security measures if they were able to bypass all of this," he said to himself.

Mehki and Jeremiah jogged up to the back of the house. Jeremiah noticed the electric gate was still hot.

"How the hell did they get in?" he asked.

"Knowing them, they probably found some loophole, or dropped from that helicopter over there." Jeremiah looked in the direction Mehki was pointing.

"I'm going to kill every last one of these muthafuckas," Jeremiah growled as he entered the code to the back gate. Once inside, they split up and crept up each side of the house. The night sky was on their side, as well as their choice of dark clothing and having dark skin.

Jeremiah peeked in through one of the side windows, but it was dark inside. Jerome had such a huge house, there was no way to tell where they were. He shot a text to Jerome to turn the lights on remotely. A few seconds later, the entire house lit up.

Jeremiah crept from window to window. He didn't see anyone until he got to the back of the house. Tobias, Jordan's brother, was making a fucking sandwich in the kitchen. Jeremiah shook his head and pieced his silencer together. He got to the back door which was facing Tobias's back.

He found it was unlocked. He turned the knob and opened it without a sound.

"Tobias!" Jordan called. Jeremiah froze. "Getcho greedy ass in here. The lights coming on automatically means Jerome and that bitch Kamaria are here."

Jeremiah's blood began to boil at Kamaria being referred to as a "bitch." Tobias licked his fingers and took his sandwich, leaving all the fixings on the counter. Jeremiah made his way inside and saw Mehki coming from the underground landing door. They nodded at each other. It was showtime.

13

Jerome and Kamaria were at the front door. He punched in the code to unlock it. When they came inside, they didn't see anyone. They split up and looked around the first floor landing.

"Upstairs," Jordan called.

"Stay behind me," Jerome whispered to Kamaria. She nodded her head vigorously. They went to the stairs, and Jerome drew his gun, pointing in every direction. Once they made it to the second landing, they saw Jordan, Tobias, Dimitri, and Persia.

Kamaria's heart stopped. This bitch just won't quit. She watched as Persia sashayed over to her.

"You thought you could get rid of me, huh?"

"Where's my daughter and my nieces?" he barked. She jumped back at his aggression, and then regained her composure.

"Don't worry about them," Jordan said.

Kamaria kept her eyes on Persia. She was going to finish this bitch once and for all. She picked the right day to wear her Converse.

"What is all of this about?" Kamaria

asked. "Jeremiah? Because you can have him."

"Oh, honey, I know that. I don't need your permission."

"Then why take my nieces? They're innocent."

"Hardly. One of them shit on me."

"Serves you right," Kamaria smirked.

"You killed our sister," Jordan seethed, walking over to Jerome.

"I what?" Jerome asked, genuinely confused.

"You heard him," Tobias chimed in.

"You weren't there. At that moment, it was either me or her who was going to die in my house."

"She had been clean until you tried to take Genesis. The drugs clouded her better judgment. You knew what that would do to her." Jordan's eyes filled. Kamaria could see the hurt and pain in his eyes.

"It's not my fault that Melina had no self-restraint. Jordan, you know I was there while she was in rehab. I even paid for it each and every time. I wanted her to get better, but she didn't want to."

"Bullshit!!" Dimitri interjected. "She would still be alive had you not taken Genesis, and caused her to get high and come try to kill you."

"Correct me if I'm wrong. You all have money just like I do. Where were you all when she was living in a homeless shelter? Where were you all when my daughter was getting treatments? And Jordan, you knew she had a daughter and that she was mine. As often as we hung out, you never said shit to me! You didn't think I wanted to know that I have a child?" Jerome had tears falling from his chin. Jordan stood there, speechless. Kamaria knew that he knew that Jerome was right.

"She asked us not to tell you, and she's my sister, so my loyalties are first and foremost to her," Jordan responded.

"What about Genesis, huh? You didn't think she deserved to have her father in her life?"

Jordan blinked back more tears. Out of Kamaria's peripheral vision, she saw Jeremiah and Mehki coming up the back staircase.

"But I was there before any of your siblings," Mehki called out. "I was your best friend, and you didn't even think to tell me I had a niece." Jordan, Tobias, and Dimitri whirled around.

"Jeremiah, hey baby," Persia smirked. Jeremiah's expression darkened as he fixed his gaze on her.

"You conniving bitch!" he spat. Mehki held him back as he was about to charge at her.

"Not now, Jeremiah," Mehki whispered.

"So if this is about Melina, what the fuck was that when we went ziplining?" Kamaria asked, her attention focused on Jordan. The men's expressions darkened again, especially Jeremiah. He wanted bloodshed, and he wanted it bad.

"The goal was to kidnap you and hold you ransom, but I hadn't expected to break my leg, and captain save a ho and his goons came faster than we could come back to get you," Jordan explained, referring to Jeremiah. Mehki had a death grip on his arm.

"So you played me this whole time? I gave myself to you. I cared for you," Kamaria sobbed.

"Yeah, I know. And I will miss that tight ass pussy and my dick hitting the back of that throat." Jordan smirked and Mehki let Jeremiah go. Jeremiah flew at Jordan, tackling him. They broke through the banister and landed on the first floor marble landing.

Tobias and Dimitri drew their guns at Mehki and Jerome, the brothers drawing theirs back.

"Where are the girls Persia?" Kamaria asked.

"As if I would tell you." Kamaria connected a right hook to Persia's jaw, hearing a loud crack. A baby crying caught all of their attention.

"Kamaria, go!" Jerome said. "We got this." Kamaria looked at Mehki, and he nodded. She ran in the direction of the crying. She checked every room down the hall. The crying became louder and louder. She got to the last room and stopped short.

"How the fuck are you here?" Kamaria asked.

"Oh, you didn't think the cops could hold me long, not with the Blackstone men and their attorney," Rashelle smiled, showing her missing and rotting teeth. She was rocking Lena as Genesis and Khadija played in the corner.

"TiTi Mari," they squealed, running over to her. She squeezed them tight. Gunshots rang through the air. Kamaria prayed her brother-in-laws were okay.

"Genesis, I need you to take Khadija to your room okay. Show her your doll collection. Can you do that for TiTi?"

"Yay!" Genesis took Khadija's hand and they went out the door.

"The little whores are escaping!" Rashelle screamed.

Jerome saw Genesis and Khadija running the same time Dimitri did. Dimitri drew his gun and let off a shot in their direction the same time Jerome let off two hitting Dimitri in the arm and the chest. Dimitri hit the ground with a loud thud. He was still alive, but unconscious.

Mehki had laid Tobias out as well. Both men ran to their daughters.

"Lena's still missing," Jerome said.

"Why hasn't Kamaria come back yet?"

"I don't know."

"Stay here with them," Mehki told his brother. Jerome scooped up both girls and headed for the stairs.

Jordan and Jeremiah were having a standoff downstairs, circling each other. Despite the pain in his back from the fall, Jeremiah's adrenaline was kicking in high gear.

"You must really love that bitch," Jordan smiled.

"Call her another bitch," Jeremiah warned.

"I'm sorry, bitch does not describe what that girl can do on a dick," Jordan threw his head back and laughed, letting his guard down for Jeremiah to catch him in his throat.

Jordan stumbled back, holding his neck, not able to breath. Jeremiah finished him with a roundhouse kick to the jaw. Jordan lay there unconscious. As much as he wanted to kill the man, he wanted him to suffer even more.

Jeremiah looked up to see his brother carrying his nieces down the stairs.

"Where's Mehki, Kamaria and Lena?"

"In the guestroom you usually sleep in," Jerome said as he headed to the kitchen. Jeremiah took stairs two at a time. At the top he went to the right and jogged down the hall. He stopped short at the door as he saw Kamaria and Mehki, standing there.

"What's going..." he began to ask as he got closer and saw Rashelle holding Lena with a gun to the baby's head.

"You know, she looks so much like your

sister when she was first born," Rashelle said, her voice raspy. "I remember the day she was born. It was the best day of my life."

"Rashelle, please, don't hurt her," Kamaria pleaded. Rashelle put her finger on the trigger.

"As much pain as you and your sister have caused me, I want y'all to feel the same."

Bang!

14

Bahati pushed past them to catch her baby before Rashelle hit the floor. Kamaria, Mehki, and Jeremiah stood there stunned.

"You muthafuckas were just going to stand there and let this junky bitch kill my fucking baby?" Bahati barked.

"When the hell did you get here?" Mehki barked.

"Just now. Your mom and dad were asking about you, and Carter told me if I didn't get here, she'd kick my ass."

Mehki walked over and pulled his wife and daughter into an embrace as sirens could be heard in the distance. Mehki took his wife and daughter downstairs to their eldest daughter. Kamaria stood there staring at Rashelle lying in a pool of her own blood, not feeling any type of emotions. Jeremiah couldn't find any words to say.

He walked over to her and pulled her hand, bringing her to him. He hugged her as her body shook from sobbing.

"I thought my nieces were going to die," she said.

"Me too," Jerome whispered. "Kamaria, I fucking love you. I don't want to live this life without you. I know we have been to war over the past year or so, but baby, you're it for me." Kamaria lifted her head to look into his eyes.

"Jeremiah, I love you too. For some reason, we keep coming back to each other, so it must be meant for us to be." He smiled and leaned down to envelop her mouth.

"You still choose that bitch over me!" Persia shrieked. Jeremiah turned and put two bullets in her: one in the chest and one between the eyes, dropping her to the floor.

"Finally," Kamaria said.

They met everyone downstairs as the cops were taking Tobias, Dimitri, and Jordan.

"There's two dead upstairs," Jeremiah told them. The coroners went upstairs with gurneys and body bags. Kamaria watched as Bahati and Mehki were hugging their girls, and Jerome held Genesis.

"I'm going to head to the hospital with Genesis," Jerome said. Jeremiah and Kamaria nodded.

A few months later, Kamaria lay out on the beach in Costa Rica. After everything that had happened, she needed the vacation. Moriah and Jeremy had recovered greatly, so much so that Moriah tried to kick Jeremiah's ass for messing things up with Kamaria. Carter's baby was fine and it looked like she was going to carry the baby to term. Mehki and Bahati left their daughter with Moriah and Jeremy to go on a getaway. Life was great.

Jeremiah came and sat beside Kamaria. He stretched out on the towel and looked at the night sky.

"This is where I want to be Kamaria: with you, forever and for always." Kamaria smiled as he rolled over, parting her legs. Releasing his manhood, he slid her swim bottoms to the side, and plunged deep inside her slick wetness under the moonlight.

LAST CHANCE

1

Marlon watched as she walked into the lecture hall. He was hoping she'd be there. Over the past two years and several financial conferences, he had been eyeing her, but never got up the nerve to talk to her. It was something about her that was daunting. It could be that she was a black woman in finance, and it could also be that she was sexy as hell. It stirred something inside of him every time he saw her, almost like a familiar feeling that he couldn't quite put his finger on.

He watched as she made her way around the room, networking, smiling, genuinely happy to be there. The way she worked the room as if she knew she belonged there was enticing. He wanted to make a move, but was waiting for the right moment.

This weekend was the Money in Business conference that was held every year at the George R. Brown Convention Center in Houston, Texas. And every year, Marlon was one of the panelists. This year, he got a sneak peek at the panel and noticed that she was on: Ms. Cassidy Chase, financial advisor and coach. She owned her own business coaching people on personal finance, and she was making a big name for herself.

Marlon had been following everything she has been doing online, so he knew she was about her business. He also knew she was single, if only from her solo photos on her social media and in magazines.

"Okay, here's your water, and your notes," Maya said, interrupting his thoughts. Maya Greene was his long-time friend. They met back in the sandbox and even went to college at Xavier University. They never dated and nothing ever happened between them, though Maya has attempted many times going unnoticed by Marlon. When Maya got laid off from her previous job six months ago, Marlon offered her a temporary position as his assistant until she was able to find a job of her own. He paid her triple what she was making before.

"Are you nervous?" she asked.

"No, not anymore," he smiled, keeping his eyes on Cassidy.

Maya followed his gaze and frowned. She had hoped that he would eventually just give up on the woman. She was all he talked about when they would hangout, and any time she would go in his office, he would be scrolling her social media or reading an article about some new accomplishment. Maya never knew where the fascination came from aside from the fact that the woman was gorgeous.

Maya looked the woman up and down as she made her way to the stage. She twisted up her lip. She hated the woman, and if Marlon knew why, he'd hate her too. Marlon headed toward the stage as well and to Maya's surprise, the two were seated next to each other.

"Great," she muttered as she went to take her seat in the front row.

The rest of the chairs began to fill as everyone took their seats. The financial panel was always the one thing everyone looked forward to in the entire conference. Most of the audience were newbies into the world of finance and used the panel at the conference to gain insight on how they can succeed in their own businesses and lives.

Marlon smiled as he and Cassidy walked towards each other. She gave him a shy grin.

"I'm Cassidy Chase," she said, extending her hand.

"I am well aware. I'm..."

"Marlon James-Panton, financial management at Panton Scaping."

"She does her research," he chuckled.

"I always research things, or people, that fascinate me." Before he could respond, it was time for them to take their seats.

"Ladies and gentlemen, welcome to the second annual Money in Business conference. I will be the moderator for the evening. My name is Nate Bagsby, and I am the owner and creator of Bagsby Full of Money, LLC. Let's have each of the panelists introduce themselves." Cassidy was first.

"Hi everyone, I am Cassidy Chase, owner and creator of Chase the Bag, Not the Man. I have been in finance for the past ten years. Currently, I am working on several projects, including a charity fundraiser here in Houston." Everyone applauded.

"I'm Marlon James-Panton. I am the finance manager at Panton Scaping. I, too, have been in finance the past few years. My brothers and I are looking for some interns for our new internship program, so if you are interested, see my lovely assistant, Maya Greene, after the panel." He made sure to point to Maya as she stood up and waved her hand.

The rest of the panelists introduced themselves, and the moderator began asking questions. After about an hour of audience questions, one woman stood up and asked a question that threw Marlon off guard.

"I have a question for Mr. Panton," she said with a devilish smile. "You are a very successful black man. You have three successful brothers, and your parents are successful as well. Over the past few years, your brothers have traded in their bachelor pads for marriage and diaper bags. Why are you still single?"

Marlon was taken aback at the question.

It was something he thought about often, but he didn't think he'd have to think about it here. He gave her a smile and cleared his throat.

"You know, I am happy for my brothers and their marriages and kids. That is something I want for myself one day. I just haven't met the right person who makes me want to trade in my bachelor pad, as you put it."

"But you're a black man in finance, which makes you extremely rare and a hot commodity. There isn't a single woman that has caught your eye?" He chuckled at her question.

"The jury is still out on that one," he responded. The crowd let out a light laugh. The woman sat down and another woman raised her hand to ask a question.

"I have a question for Cassidy. As a black woman in finance, which is also rare, how do you deal with dating? Do men find you intimidating because of your career path and success?"

"That's a great question. I will be honest and say that dating is a challenge. As you stated, being a black woman in finance, or any career field that you don't see many black women, is off putting to men. Having such great success and making my own money, and a lot of it might I add, is tough for some men to handle. It puts a dent in their ego, and quite frankly, I don't have the time to stroke a man's ego. That's partially why I created Chase the Bag, Not the Man. I want to inspire women to believe in themselves, work for themselves, get their own money, and don't rely on a man to take care of you. If a man can't handle you being at the top of your game, let him go. There is a man out there who will be cheering for you, lifting you up, and encouraging you to keep being the business woman you are. Trust me, there are men out there who are secure enough in themselves that being with a woman who makes her own money doesn't faze him in the slightest. I just haven't met that man yet. But I say to all you women, keep chasing that bag, because chasing a man will make you lose your bag to another sister who was gunning for your position anyway." The women in the audience erupted with cheers.

2

After the panel was over, Marlon spotted Cassidy surrounded by a crowd of black women, taking pictures and signing autographs.

"Are you ready to go?" Maya asked, hoping he was. She saw him staring at Cassidy and rolled her eyes.

"You go ahead. I'll call you later."

"But we were going to go over the reports at your place."

"We can do that tomorrow. There's no set deadline for those."

"Um, okay. I guess I'll talk to you later then?"

"Yeah," he said, walking off toward Cassidy now that the crowd was dying down. He walked up behind her with his hands in his pockets.

"Can I get an autograph?" he asked.

"Sure. Who can I make..." She stopped as she turned around to meet his gaze. She smiled and his heart stopped, nearly knocking the breath out of him. Gorgeous did not come close to describing the beauty of the woman standing in front of him.

"What do you want me to sign?" she asked.

"You can verbally sign an agreement for a date tomorrow night."

"As tempting as that sounds," she began, closing the gap between them, "I am getting on a plane tonight back to Arlington to pack the rest of my things."

"Well, let me know when you're settled in, and we can grab something to eat."

"How did you know I was moving here?"

"I always research things, or people, that fascinate me." He gave her a wink as he handed her his card and walked off.

Maya threw her purse on the couch and slumped down on it. She couldn't believe Marlon blew her off for Cassidy. Maya Knew Marlon forgot that they and Cassidy grew up together. From preschool all the way to senior year. Cassidy and Maya started off as friends, but fifth grade came around and Cassidy got a new group of friends, leaving Maya by the wayside. Things only got worse in high school when Cassidy developed quickly physically.

Boys started showing her more attention and she let the attention go to her head. She began bullying Maya and others that weren't on her level. It got so bad to the point Maya attempted suicide three times, almost succeeding the third time. She wanted to remind Marlon about Cassidy, but since she began stalking Cassidy on the internet, she knew she was flying back home tonight because she had an event tomorrow.

Her phone buzzed, and it was a reminder to remind Marlon that there was a meeting tomorrow with a new client. She called him, and his phone went straight to voicemail. She hung up and called again. She did this several times before she finally just sent a text.

It was only 9 o'clock, so she decided to call Toni, her best friend, to come over. Toni answered the phone in her usual peppy manner and agreed to come over.

"Hey boo!" Toni practically screamed. Toni Preston was a real estate agent, and she was the best of the best. In fact, she was voted number one three years in a row as the top real estate agent in Houston Homes Magazine, the first and only black woman to make it to the top ten.

"Hey, Toni," Maya said, unenthused.

"Girl I know damn well you didn't call me over her to sulk." Toni closed the door behind them as Maya headed back over to the couch and slumped back down in her same spot.

"She was there," Maya grumbled.

"She who, and where?" Toni grabbed a bottle of wine from the fridge and two wine glasses.

"Cassidy."

"The only Cassidy I know is the bitch from high school who I should've killed."

"Same bitch." Toni poured them each a

glass and sat down on the couch handing a glass to Maya. Maya took a large gulp.

"Oh, uh uh. Tell me everything that happened." Maya started from the beginning of the panel and ended with the fact that his cell was going straight to voicemail.

"Ok, that proves nothing. Doesn't mean they did anything." Maya knew that he didn't do anything, but just the mere thought of Cassidy touching him and him touching her rubbed her the wrong way.

"Still. Toni, why can't I just tell him I love him?" she whined.

"Because you're afraid that it may ruin your friendship if he rejects you, ultimately you'd end up fired, broke, and lose this condo." Toni had a point, and it was something Maya had thought about often.

"So what do I do?"

"You need to be worried about getting a job that is not being Marlon's assistant."

"Ok, until then, what do I do?"

"Nothing. Just be a supportive assistant and friend. You were the one who made all of us promise not to tell him or help him remember what happened. Besides, we all know you're in love with him."

"Really? Am I that obvious?"

"No, you're just that desperate." Maya scolded her, and Toni fell out laughing.

"You're not funny." They stayed up the

rest of the night reminiscing on the hell that Cassidy had put them through growing up. Toni ended up spending the night in the guest room.

3

The next morning, Maya sat at her desk getting some last minute paperwork done before the meeting. She returned some calls, scheduled some meetings, and booked the resort for their upcoming trip to Bali for a team building adventure.

"Good morning, Maya," Marlon said, his deep baritone voice alerting her homegirl between her legs. She didn't even look up at him.

"Good morning. Your messages are on your desk as well as your latte. Mehki is running a few minutes behind, and Jerome and Jeremiah are setting up in the conference room."

"Thanks," he said and went into his office. She finally turned to look in the direction of the place he was standing. His cologne lingered in the air, engulfing her senses in an electrifying hold. She let out a sigh and got back to work.

Two hours later, after the meeting was over, Maya ordered lunch for the whole office. Once it was delivered, she was headed to eat in Marlon's office like she always did, but then changed her mind. She sat at her desk and ate her sandwich.

"Hey, you aren't eating with me today?" she heard him ask.

"Oh, I didn't know if you wanted to be alone." He chuckled the way he always did when someone spoke nonsense. She felt embarrassed that she was being childish and petty.

"Come in my office for a second, will you?"

"I'll be right there," she said, plastering a smile on her face that instantly dropped as he turned his back. She let out a sigh and gave herself a pep talk, getting her emotions in check. She knew all he was going to talk about was Cassidy and what they did, or didn't do, last night. She grabbed the other half of her sandwich and drink, and headed to his office. She sat across from him like she usually did.

She took a few bites of her sandwich as he watched her. She avoided having to ask him about last night at all costs.

"So, about last night. I'll be honest Maya," he began as he leaned forward. "I almost gave her my virginity." Maya choked on the tea that she had just swallowed. As she gagged and coughed, Marlon ran to her side, patting her on the back. As she regained control, she waved him off.

"Are you okay?" he asked, eyeing her. He slowly sat down as she nodded.

"Sorry, it went down the wrong way."

"Are you sure?" he asked again.

"I'm fine Marlon."

"Well, I know we have that trip coming up

to Bali, and I wanted to let you know to book an extra room."

"Oh, are your parents coming?"

"No, I actually invited Cassidy," he smiled. Her stomach twisted and turned at his mentioning of her. "Also, see if you can get conjoining rooms." She nodded with a slight smile.

"Anything else?"

"Are you sure you're okay? You usually have a lot to talk about at lunch, but today you're awfully quiet."

"I'm fine. I just have some things on my mind."

"Well, we can talk about them."

"No thanks. I have to get back to work." She grabbed her things and went back to her desk. Taking a long plane ride on a private jet with Cassidy was not in her plans. She needed to find a new job and fast.

Later that evening, Marlon went over to his parents' house for dinner with his siblings and their wives. As soon as he walked in, his nieces and nephew came running to greet him. He pretended to be knocked over as they squealed and climbed on top of him. More than anything, Marlon had longed to be a father. And his nieces and nephews gave him that fatherly feeling when they were around.

"Alright, now let your uncle up," Moriah said. They got up and ran back to their play area. Marlon got up and hugged his mother.

"How are you dear?"

"I'm well, Mother. And you?"

"Wondering when I'll get another grandbaby. Jeremiah and Kamaria are stubborn, talking about how they want to explore the world and shit." Marlon laughed as Jeremiah walked in with his mouth agape. "And you," she continued, his smile dropping quickly, "I understand you want to wait for the right woman, but son, I am getting too old for you to be waiting. Virginity my ass. Be a hoe like your brothers and bring Mama home a grandbaby." She pinched his cheeks and walked off. He hadn't noticed that all his brothers had walked in until they started howling.

"Man, fuck y'all. You know she just called y'all hoes."

"We know!" they said, still laughing. Marlon shook his head and headed into the dining area. Everyone else gathered in. The kids were set up at the kids' table and served their food by their parents, as the rest of the adults made their own plates.

"So, how was the conference?" Jeremy asked the patriarch.

"It was great. We got a lot of applicants for the internship program," Marlon said. "We start interviews next week. We also got a potential new client who wants an office space built over on Montrose. They were having some financial issues, but it's nothing we couldn't work out."

"That's good news. I'm glad business is doing well," Jeremy said.

"Pops, business is always doing well," Mehki chuckled. The men guffawed as the women shook their heads.

"So, I talked to Maya earlier," Moriah began.

"Ma, not this Maya business again. I told you we are just friends," Marlon groaned.

"Does she know that?" Bahati, Mehki's wife, asked.

"What makes you ask that?"

"Brother, you've known Maya your whole life, and she's been like a sister to us. But we also know she's been in love with you for just as long. Through all the girlfriends, she was there. Through the break ups, she was there," Jerome pointed out.

"Yeah, but so have y'all. That's what friends and family are for," Marlon shot back.

"Listen, don't get all defensive," Jeremiah added. "We just want you to know you may be missing out on a good thing."

"Thanks, but no thanks. Besides, I've met someone and we are set to go out on a date once she moves here. I also invited her on the business trip to Bali," Marlon smiled. Everyone stared at him. It got eerily quiet. "Why are y'all looking at me like that?"

"You invited someone on a business trip that we don't even know?" Mehki asked.

"You do know her, well, you know of her. It's..."

"Please don't say Cassidy Chase," Jerome mumbled.

"Cassidy Chase," Marlon said.

"Cassidy Chase? The chick who runs Chase the Bag, Not the Man, Cassidy Chase?" Carter, Jerome's wife, asked.

"Yes, that Cassidy," he confirmed.

"Boy, are you fucking stupid?" Moriah asked.

"Sweetheart," Jeremy warned.

"Fine, but when shit hits the fan, don't say I didn't try to warn you." Moriah grabbed her plate and glass of wine and left the table.

"What's the issue? Y'all don't even know her," Marlon said.

"No, we know her, you just don't remember her," Jeremiah said.

"Remember her? How would I remember her and we just met?"

"Brother, do you remember in high school when Maya kept missing a lot of days, sometimes months at a time?" Jeremiah asked.

"Yeah, she had family issues," Marlon nodded.

"No, Mar, she didn't have family issues," Jeremy sighed, placing his napkin on the table.

"Yo, just tell me!" Marlon spat.

"Maya tried to commit suicide several times because of Cassidy. Cassidy severely bullied her. She would sneak and take pictures of her in the girls' locker room while she was undressing and she'd send them around. She would lock her in the bathroom and have her friends pick on her while she recorded it."

"Pop, you're lying," Marlon teared up.

"No, Mar, he's not," Jerome said quietly.

"How come I never knew this? Or remember it?"

"During that time, you were really distraught about it," his father began. "Your mother and I put you in therapy, and after a while, somehow, you blocked that out of your memory. I guess when you didn't remember, Maya made up stories to fill in the holes so that you wouldn't. When she slit her wrists and hung herself from the balcony at her house, and you found her, you had a mental breakdown. We had you institutionalized for a while. We all came to see you everyday Marlon. We knew it was hard on you. You were in love with her. But over the years, as everything slipped from your memory, Maya decided to move on from it and we respected her wishes. She wanted to protect you from it all."

The women wiped their tears as Marlon's brothers comforted them, wiping away their own. Marlon sank back in his chair. He really didn't remember any of it. The tears came streaming down his face as he shook violently, bawling. His brothers and father crowded around him. They hadn't even told him the worst part of it all.

4

A couple of hours later, Maya heard a knock at her door. She was in boy shorts and a tank with no bra, and her locs in a messy bun. She opened the door and gasped when she saw Marlon standing there.

"Marlon, it's late. Oh my God! Did I forget to do the reports for the day?" She tried to replay the day in her head as he walked in and closed the door. "Marlon, what are you doing?"

He pulled her to him and embraced her, engulfing them both in a kiss that took her breath away. He felt her relax against him as his hands made their way to her ass, palming each check. He turned them around and pressed her back against the door. He slipped a hand between her legs and found her soaking. He moved the seat of her shorts to the side and found her pearl. With his thumb, he applied a little pressure and made circular motions.

He swallowed her moans and gasps. She moved her hips against his thumb. He moved his lips to her neck as she arched her back.

"Marlon!" she trembled as she had her first ever orgasm. He gripped her waist as she shook and her knees became weak. He met her gaze.

"Let me make love to you," he growled. She nodded her head quickly. He lifted her up as their lips met again. He walked them to her bedroom. Laying her down gently, he removed her shorts and made himself comfortable between her legs, kissing one thigh, nibbling the other. The scent of her sweet nectar traveled up his nostrils and stirred his beast that waited all this time to finally be unleashed.

He slid the tip of his tongue between her pussy lips and against her still pulsating bud. He slid a hand under each cheek and lifted her up as he worked her.

Maya gripped the sheets. She was too entranced to realize that they were about to lose their virginity to each other, consensually this time. She felt her core tighten again. She gripped his locs as she came again, creaming his beard.

"Oh my God, Marlon! Shit!" She pushed his head away and he moved between her legs, taking his shirt off, then his pants and boxers, releasing his manhood. He helped her to a seated position and pulled her tank over her head. He kissed her deeply, guiding her back to her back. She wrapped her arms around his neck.

"Tell me if it hurts," he said against her lips as he gently, and slowly pushed inside her. He was trembling as the warmth and tightness of her canal swallowed him whole. She let out a yelp and he stopped.

"Keep going," she whispered.

"Are you sure?"

"Marlon, please." she begged. He filled her and gazed into her eyes as he rocked his hips back and forth, sliding in and out of her ocean. He leaned in and kissed her. She moaned his name against his lips as he kept the same pace.

He slipped both hands under her waist and wrapped them around her as he pushed deeper inside her, evoking louder moans, screams, and expletives from her. He felt her get even tighter and become sleeker.

"Marlon, I'm coming!" She wrapped her legs around him as he sped up. He felt the heat rushing to his loins as he released for the first time.

"Shit, Maya!" He squeezed her tighter to him as he let off all he had, both of them reaching their peak. He slowed down and looked in her eyes. He kissed her lips, down to her neck, moving to one breast and then the other.

She pushed him over to his back as she straddled him. She moved over his still erect manhood and lowered on him, wincing as she was spread open.

Marlon watched as she relaxed on him and began moving her hips. He gripped her thighs as the sensation made him harder. She was so tight and warm. He never thought that this is what sex would be like. He also never imagined that this is what sex would be like with her. She moved up and down his shaft, the friction causing him to tremble. He didn't want to nut again until she did.

With her hands on his chest, she leaned a little forward and he sucked on her breasts as she rode him. He thrusted his hips up every time she came down, matching her rhythm.

"Marlon, fuck!" She started to shake and he knew she was about to release again. He pulled her to him and thrusted inside her from underneath. She screamed and gushed down his dick, her warm nectar running down his balls.

"I'm coming! Ahhhhh!" she screamed. His cheeks tightened and he thrusted faster and harder as he let off another load inside her.

"Fuuuuuuuuck!" he growled. He slowed as he felt himself soften. He released his hold on her. She moved down him and licked all her cum off his dick. He stiffened at her touch. His shaft was still sensitive. She stroked him hard again and he watched as she swallowed him whole, gagging.

"Got damn, Maya!" he moaned. He lay back as she worked him down her throat. He put one hand on her head and moved his hips to her rhythm. Before long, he was shooting down her throat.

"Ahhhhhh, shit!" He pulled her up to him to meet his lips. He rolled them over and pushed back inside her. They spent the next several hours sharing themselves with each other.

5

Maya stirred as Marlon watched her. She fluttered her eyes open and met his. His gaze was soft, but concern filled his eyes.

"Morning," she said, sitting up, wincing.

"Morning," he said. "You okay?"

"Yeah, just a little sore."

"I'm sorry."

"Don't be. It's a good kind of sore."

"I didn't even have sex on my mind when I came over, but when I got here, I felt compelled to be inside you. I'm sorry if that wasn't what you wanted or how you wanted it to happen."

"Marlon, I've kept my virginity this whole time because I was hoping, praying, and waiting to lose it with you. So trust me, I have no regrets."

"Well, we need to talk."

"About the fact that we didn't use protection?"

"I'm not concerned about that. If you're pregnant, I am well prepared to take care of the both of you."

"Um, okay," she said slowly, thrown off at his response.

"We need to talk about Cassidy." He

watched as she shifted uneasily.

"Do we have to?" she moaned.

"Yes, we do. My father told me." She whipped her head around to him, tears filling their eyes.

"They promised not to ever tell you," she sobbed. He scooted over and pulled her into his lap.

"I'm glad he did. Maya , why didn't you tell me?"

"Because Marlon! When you found me the last time, you ended up in a mental hospital. I didn't want you to relive that."

"Maya, the thing is, I don't remember any of it."

"And that's why I made your family promise me that they wouldn't let you remember. I made my parents promise too."

"But Maya..."

"No Marlon. We aren't going to sit here and help you to remember something that I nearly killed myself over. When you had that breakdown because of me, I literally wanted to die. I had never wanted to die so much in my life."

"But do you know why I had that breakdown?"

"I mean we're best friends. We love each other, like family."

"What I did to you last night is not something I'd ever do with anyone who is family. Maya I do love you."

"What?" she asked, looking up at him in confusion.

"I said, I love you."

"What about Cassidy?"

"Maya, honestly, we're all adults now. I'm not dismissing what she did to you, but I'm sure she feels guilty about it."

"Are you still going to see her?"

He rolled her to her back and climbed between her legs. Massaging her pearl until she was sleek, he pushed and sunk deep inside her.

"Does this answer your question?" he asked, looking her in her eyes as he stroked her speechless.

That afternoon, Marlon was sitting at his desk when he received a text from Cassidy saying how much she was looking forward to meeting up when she got back. He told her likewise.

They went ahead and made plans for Friday night. She was coming back to Houston earlier than she had expected. She had business here that required her to come back sooner. He lay his phone down as soon as Maya walked in. He smiled as he watched her blush.

"We're at work, you can't look at me like that," she said, holding her head down.

"Maya, never put your head down. You're too beautiful to feel ashamed of anything." She lifted her head and met his smoldering gaze. "Besides, I'm the boss. Who can fire me? Now, close and lock the door."

She did as he instructed while he undid his pants and released his bulge. She hiked up her skirt, slid her panties to the side, and walked over, straddling him. Her warmth engulfed him as he undid her shirt and unhooked her bra, letting her breasts fall out. He sucked on one and then the other as she shuddered against him. She let out soft moans as she rolled her hips. Each time they had sex, she came faster and faster.

"Fuck, Marlon! I'm going to come!"

"Then come on your dick baby," he growled. She bounced up and down faster and harder as she came, gripping his dick tighter with her walls. He held her tight as he released too. He stood up and walked her over to the couch, laying her down as he pumped out the rest of his nut.

"Ahhhhhhhh, shit!" He collapsed on top of her. He got up and removed her panties, devouring her sex in his mouth. She gripped the side and back of the couch as he expertly slid his tongue around her bulging bud.

"Oh, God! Oh, God! Marlon! Fuck, I'm coming!" She arched her back and pulled his head closer as she moisturized his beard.

He slurped up her sweet nectar and then pushed back inside her. He couldn't get enough of her. He didn't know if it was because of the guilt or because she was who he was waiting for, but right now, he knew he just needed to be inside her, touch her, please her, love her.

They went another two rounds until their sexual hunger was satiated. They got dressed and kissed before she left his office as his brothers walked in, one by one, each with a devilish smile. Mehki was the last to walk in and closed the door. They stood there in their suits with their hands crossed in front of them.

"I swear I fucking hate y'all," Marlon said, trying to keep a straight face.

"So we have a sister, or nah?" Jeremiah asked. Marlon shook his head and sat behind his desk. His brothers took a seat in the chairs in front of his desk.

"I don't know what y'all are talking about."

"Lil bro lost his virginity, finally," Mehki teased.

"Ok, big deal," Marlon said, a smile still plastered on his face.

"Was it worth it? Are you okay?" Jerome asked.

"I don't think y'all understand. It was fucking perfect. She's perfect."

"What made you do it?" Jeremiah asked.

"I don't know. After dinner with y'all last night, it was like I was on autopilot. I didn't realize what was happening until after I made her come the third time. Once I snapped into reality, it just felt right. It felt like it was right, like she was right."

"This whole time, the woman you've been waiting for has been right there," Mehki chuckled, shaking his head.

"Just know, office sex is frowned upon," Jerome said.

"And how many times have we had to disinfect the conference room after you and Carter's sexcapades?" Marlon reminded. The brothers guffawed.

"So about this trip to Bali," Jeremiah asked, getting serious.

"Well, I am meeting with Cassidy Friday for dinner, and I'm bringing Maya," Marlon stated.

"Nigga are you stupid? You don't think that'll be triggering for Maya?"

"Why would it be?"

"Have you talked to Maya?" Jerome asked.

"Yeah, we talked last night."

"And she told you everything?" Mehki asked.

"Yeah," Marlon said. Jerome, Jeremiah, and Mehki looked at one another.

"What is it now?" Marlon demanded.

"She should be the one to tell you," Mehki said, getting up and his brothers following.

"But y'all are my brothers."

"Yeah, but Maya is a tough chick. She may be tiny, but she throws a mean left hook," Jeremiah said.

"How would you know that?"

"Talk to her," Jerome said. The men left out leaving Marlon more confused than ever.

6

Thursday evening, in the middle of November, Marlon invited his family and Maya over for dinner. He and his brothers barbecued ribs, roasted corn on the cob, made shrimp and vegetable kabobs, and whipped up a few apple pies. His parents had gone out of town for a getaway like they do every month.

The women sat by the fire with the kids, chatting about the men. It didn't usually get cold in Houston, but the weather was surely starting to change.

"So we heard about you and Marlon," Kamaria teased, giving her best seductive look. The women laughed and Maya just smiled.

"Don't mind her. She can be hella annoying," Bahati added.

"It's fine," Maya said, taking a sip of her hot chocolate.

"What's the matter?" Carter asked.

"I'm sure your husbands told you about Cassidy, and about me and Marlon back in the day." The women nodded. "Well, I haven't told Marlon everything, and he invited me to dinner tomorrow with Cassidy. I don't know what to do."

"Honey, you have to tell him," Kamaria said. "I may joke a lot, but something like what she did to you and him, he needs to know, especially if he's going to be doing business with her." Maya looked at her in confusion.

"Dammit, Kamaria," Bahati scolded.

"What do you mean doing business with her?" Maya asked, sitting up straight in her chair. Carter sighed.

"Cassidy proposed a business deal that would actually be really good for the company, though nothing can make them better than they already are. They're looking to expand into new areas, mainly the financial department. Yeah, they are a construction company, and very innovative might I add, but they want to delve into new areas, especially Marlon."

"Why hasn't he told me any of this?" Maya asked, tearing up.

"Maya, don't cry," Kamaria said, walking over to sit by her. "We actually just found this out today. I think Marlon may have been thinking about this for a while."

"But we tell each other everything."

"Apparently not everything," Bahati reminded her. And she was right. She and Marlon needed to talk.

After the food was ready, everyone gathered around in couples by the fire and enjoyed their meal and sharing stories. Marlon noticed how quiet Maya was, and was anxious to sit down and talk to her.

"So this trip to Bali, I am most definitely looking forward to it," Bahati said, dancing in her seat.

"Calm down woman, this ain't no hot girl kind of vacation," Mehki said.

"Maybe not for you, but for me, tuh, I'm ready to be half naked on the beach. Besides, it's a company team-building trip that y'all do every year." Everyone laughed except Mehki.

"Keep it up and make me put another baby in you."

"Boy, shut up," she said, shoving him.

"Well, Maya here has taken care of everything, from the private jet to the resort. I think that this will be the best trip yet," Marlon chided. Everyone nodded in agreement.

A couple of hours later, everyone left and Marlon and Maya cleaned up his patio. They ended up back by the fire.

"Marlon, we need to talk," Maya said.

"I know, I could tell something was bothering you."

"How come you didn't tell me you had other business ventures you wanted to do, especially working with Cassidy?"

"I wanted all the kinks worked out first. I've been speaking with Cassidy the past few days, and I think partnering would be a good idea. That's why I invited you to dinner tomorrow. I want y'all to make amends. I don't want any negative energy looming over this deal."

"Does she know I'm coming?"

"Yes, she does."

"Oh."

"Maya, I feel like there's something you aren't telling me." Marlon looked at her as she sat there staring at her hands, contemplating whether or not to tell him. She didn't want to ruin the business deal, so she made up something.

"I guess I'm just not over what she did to me. The bullying and now she's going to be around. I guess tomorrow we will settle everything."

"I can nix this deal, Maya, just say the word."

"No, Marlon, I can see how much this means to you."

"You sure?"

"I promise." She leaned over and kissed him. He pulled her onto his lap. They quickly shed their clothes and he groaned as she slid down him. He pulled the blanket that was on the back of the bench over them and watched as she pleasured herself on him, the glow from the fire creating a golden aura around her.

He knew she was lying about Cassidy. He knew something happened that she didn't want him to know about, and he was going to find out. He let it rest, for now. They entangled themselves by the fire the rest of the night.

7

Maya stood in front of the mirror obsessing over her reflection. Cassidy had only grown more attractive over the years. Maya almost felt like she was back in high school again. She needed to look more attractive and confident when she was in Cassidy's presence. Despite being adults now, she still had that gnawing, anxious feeling.

Her doorbell rang, and she took a few deep breaths. When she opened it, Marlon looked her up and down slowly, taking every inch of her in. He bit his bottom lip and pulled her to him, taking in her bottom lip, his tongue entangling with hers. He released her and his eyes bore into her.

"Well, I'm glad to see you too," she laughed. He smiled and chuckled.

"I'm sorry, but you look so damn good, I want to rest my head between your legs and make you scream my name." She was taken aback at his bluntness.

"We have time for that later," she said, clearing her throat.

"Or, I can do it on the way," he said, nodding to the awaiting limo. He held his hand out and she took it, locking the door behind her. He opened the limo door for her, and helped her in, climbing in behind her. He nodded to the drive, and the partition went up.

Marlon knelt on the floor between her legs and pulled her soaked panties down.

"Damn, you stay ready for me Maya," he said as he stroked her bulging bud with the tip of his tongue. A chill went up her spine as he made himself well acquainted with her center. In the 20 minutes it took to get to The Grande Luxe Café, she came four times.

Luckily, she was the type to stay ready. She took out a fresh pair of undies and some homemade wet wipes. She handed Marlon a few for his face, and he watched as she freshened up. He licked his lips at her.

"Boy, get out of this limo," she said, hitting him with her clutch bag. He laughed and got out, holding his hand out for her. They walked arm in arm into the restaurant. A waiter guided them to their table where Cassidy was already waiting. Maya's gut clenched and turned as anxiety crept back in.

"Oh my gosh, Maya! Is that you? It's been so long, and my have you gotten more gorgeous over the years." Cassidy stood up to embrace Maya tightly. "And Marlon, nice to see you again." She hugged him as well and kissed both cheeks. They sat down and placed their drink orders. "So, when did you two become a thing? At the conference I specifically remember you saying that you hadn't found the right one yet."

"Well, that was true since the right one was there all along. I didn't have to find her," he said, smiling at Maya sitting next to him.

"Isn't that sweet? So, Maya, what do you do?"

"Right now, I'm his assistant."

"Really? What a cute cliché?" Cassidy grinned widely. Maya knew she was faking. Despite having not seen each other in years, she had known Cassidy far too long. They used to be best friends, and she knew when Cassidy put on a show.

"Are you all ready to order?" the waiter asked as he set their drinks down. They each placed their order. When the waiter left, it was Marlon's turn to ask the questions.

"Cassidy, why at the conference did you act like that was our first time meeting when it wasn't?"

"Well, you acted the same way," she reminded.

"Funny thing is, I don't remember you."

"I'm so hurt," she said, clutching her chest, pretending to be hurt. "No, but seriously, I knew you went through a hard time back then and when you came back to school, you didn't remember me at all. But I didn't stay at the school that long. After the trial, my parents sent me to an all-girls boarding school."

"What trial?" Marlon asked. Cassidy looked at Maya, and Maya slightly shook her head.

"I was a fucked up kid back then. I did a lot of stupid things and hurt a lot of people," Cassidy said, winking at Maya. Maya knew Cassidy was going to hold this over her. Marlon nodded his head, though Maya could tell he didn't believe Cassidy.

"So, tell me about this new deal y'all are working on," Maya said, changing the subject.

"Well, your wonderful beau here is probably the most intelligent man I've ever met. Good thing you snagged him up before I got my claws into him." Maya shifted in her seat, and Marlon took note.

"Well, I thought about our internship program, and since it was more so students interning for finance reasons, I figured that I should make the program separate, and have my own business apart from the business I own with my brothers. My brothers agreed."

"Where does Cassidy come in?" Maya asked.

"Well, since she owns her own business working with black women on building their own finances and businesses, I figured she could mentor the young women. You saw the amount of female applicants we received. As a man, I didn't think it would feel right if I headed them, so we are going to separate the program where she mentors the women, I mentor the men, and you, my beautiful queen, will head the program altogether."

"Me?"

"Her?"

"Yes. Babe you've worked in the financial world almost as long as I have. I've been there through all the projects you oversaw at your first company. I felt this would be the perfect thing for you. You can name it whatever you want."

"Why can't you oversee it?" she asked.

"Yeah, why can't you?" asked an irritated Cassidy.

"The same reasons I don't head the company my brothers and I own. I wasn't a business major. That isn't my forte."

"But you run the financial department," Maya said.

"Yes, because I know money. You know business, and Cassidy knows mentoring, as do I. I mean if you don't want to head it, I can find someone else. I'm sorry if I overstepped my boundaries."

"No, I'll do it. Thank you Marlon." She tongued him down in front of a scolding Cassidy. When they stopped, she quickly changed her expression. They spent the rest of dinner going over plans for the business. After dinner, Marlon took Maya back to his place, and she fucked him like it was their last time.

8

The trip to Bali snuck up on Maya. Over the past three months, she had been working endlessly on the new business. She interviewed interns, scoped out an assistant for herself, and worked on web designing. Most of her time was spent at Marlon's place when they decided to have her move in with him.

Despite the amount of unprotected sex they had been having, Maya got her period right on time except for now. She was a week late. Toni came over to help her pack. Maya invited her on the trip as well. Marlon was still at the office. He was sending a car to pick them up.

"Toni, what if I'm pregnant?"

"Girl, bye. We've known Marlon our whole lives, and his family. Would it be such a bad thing? Besides, you live with him."

"Yeah, but we've only been together a few months."

"But you've loved each other a long time. I'm sure he'd be excited." Toni handed her the pregnancy test and a bottle of water, then shooed her into the bathroom. Maya chugged the water and then peed on the stick. She set a timer and they finished packing. When the timer went off, they stared at each other.

"I can't look," Maya said.

"Shit, I can." Toni walked into the bathroom and screamed. Maya knew what that meant.

An hour later, Marlon and his brothers were walking out of the office and saw Cassidy waiting with her bags at the front door.

"This is going to be an interesting trip," Mehki said, shaking his head as he, Jeremiah, and Jerome ducked off.

"What are you doing here?" he asked.

"I figured since I would be passing by here on the way to the airport, I might as well hitch a ride."

"You should've called first," he said as he loaded her bags into his car. He opened the passenger's side and waited for her to get in.

"You've become quite the gentleman," she quipped.

"I've always been a gentleman," he corrected.

"Not always," she muttered. He rolled his eyes and got in the car. She talked all the way to Bush Airport nonstop about the plans for their new business venture. He could barely get a word in but was thrilled once they reached the landing strip where the jet was.

He saw Maya standing there with Toni, his sisters-in-law, and his brothers. They all wore the same look.

"Shit," he mumbled. Maya walked off onto the jet as he put the car in park. He got out as the crew began unloading their bags.

"How mad is she?" he asked Toni.

"How long have you known Maya?"

"Dammit," he sighed.

"A damn shame," Carter said, then walked off with Kamaria, Bahati, and Toni.

"You might want to stay in the cabin with us tonight brother," Mehki offered.

"Y'all are all on the outs with your wives? At the same time?" Marlon asked.

"Seems that way," Jeremiah sulked.

"The fuck did y'all do?"

"You will soon find out," Jerome said, heading towards the jet. After taking their seats, the pilot let them know they were getting ready for takeoff. Their family jet was on the larger side. It had several cabins fully furnished with a queen sized bed and bathroom with a toilet, bathtub and shower, and a sink. Once in the air and it was safe to move about, he went to the cabin that he was supposed to share with Maya.

She was rummaging around in her bag, ignoring him. She grabbed her toiletries and headed to the bathroom.

"So you're just going to ignore me, Maya?" he asked softly.

"No one said I was ignoring you, Marlon," she retorted.

"Then baby, tell me why you're mad."

She turned on the faucet to the tub and ran a bath. She put in some bubbles and began to undress. He watched her slip out her clothes. She took the scrunchie out of her locs and let them fall to her shoulders. His eyes roamed over her curves and lady lumps. His dick was rock hard, but he knew she wasn't about to give it up.

She slid into the tub and lay back against the opposite end of the faucet. He walked over and sat on the side of the tub. Reaching in, he parted her thighs and then her pussy lips. She moaned as he massaged her clit. He watched her face distort at the electrifying pleasure it gave her.

She guided his movements with her right hand. He heard a knock at the cabin door, but he ignored it. The knocks grew more rapid and impatient. Maya squeezed his wrist and trembled from her orgasm, the water sloshing everywhere. She moved his hand, and lay back against the tub, closing her eyes, ignoring him again.

"You are something else," he said, shaking his head.

"I know," she said, smiling. He went to answer the door, and it was Cassidy. She jumped back and gasped. He followed her gaze to his manhood still standing at attention.

"Sorry, about that," he apologized. "Do you need help with something?"

"I, uh, uh, um, never mind," she said, and

quickly walked off. He shook his head, smiling. He shut the door and turned around to an upset Maya standing there, naked with her arms crossed over her breasts.

9

"Come on Maya, what now?"

"Do you still like her? Or was fucking me pity sex?"

"What?"

"Negro you heard me, I didn't stutter."

"Baby..."

"Don't 'baby' me, Marlon. Answer the damn question."

"Maya, listen and listen good. I don't have eyes for anyone but you. I don't get hard for anyone but you. I don't love anyone in a romantic way, but you."

"You're just trying to get some," she smirked.

"Is it working?"

"No, now get out." She stood there glaring at him.

"Are you serious?"

She said nothing. He took that as a yes and left the room. He headed towards the main cabin where his brothers sat at the bar pouring drinks. Mehki saw him coming and poured him one too.

"How is it that your woman lets you get her off, but won't get you off?" Marlon asked. His brothers looked at him.

"Oh, you in dog shit, fuck the doghouse," Jerome said.

"What did I do?" Marlon asked.

"You rolled up to the jet with Cassidy in your car. You couldn't possibly think Maya would've been okay with that," Jeremiah said.

"But she Ubered to the office."

"And she could've Ubered her ass from the office to the tarmac," Jeremiah added. "That's your problem little bro, you always have to be a gentleman and a nice guy. Women like Maya, that works for. Women like Cassidy, they take advantage of that shit, especially since…" Jeremiah trailed off.

"Especially since what?" Marlon asked. His brothers said nothing. "Look, I'm fucking tired of y'all walking around here on fucking eggshells like I'm going to have a breakdown."

"Like when you had a breakdown after you raped Maya and she tried to kill herself?" Cassidy asked, waltzing in. Jeremiah, Jerome, and Mehki glared at her.

"What?" Marlon asked.

"You are a dirty ass bitch, Cassidy," Jeremiah growled, jumping up from his seat. Jerome held him back.

"He was bound to find out anyway," she shrugged.

"What are you talking about? Maya and I were virgins up until a few months ago, and I never raped anyone."

"You seriously don't remember?" she asked.

"You're making shit up. I knew this was a mistake to do business with you. When we land, find your own way home." Marlon got up to leave.

"It was homecoming, sophomore year in high school," she began.

"Cassidy, don't," Mehki warned through gritted teeth.

"No, he needs to hear this. He needs to know what he did. I threw a party at my house. You came in with all the football players. Maya was already drunk and passed out. So, I made my move on you. You wouldn't even give me the time of day. It was always Maya, Maya, Maya."

"Cassidy stop!" Maya yelled, coming into the cabin.

"I gave you a drink, and I laced it with a bunch of different shit. I didn't know the effect it would have, but I wanted to have a little fun. Some of my friends and I got you in the room with Maya. Part of the drug made you aggressive, part made you horny, and part clouded your judgment. We all backed out of sight and watched as you tore Maya's clothes off."

"Shut up Cassidy!" Maya screamed, tears streaming down her face.

"Maya woke up to you pinning her down and forcing your dick in her. She screamed and begged for you to stop, but you wouldn't. There was blood everywhere. The thing is, while everyone else felt sorry for her, I felt a sense of power. No man had ever rejected me before, and especially not for someone that looked like her."

"You're lying!" he growled, running to her and wrapping his hands around her throat. His brothers tried to pull him off, but not before she cracked a bottle over his head from the bar and knocked him out.

10

Homecoming, Sophomore year

"You're coming to my party right, Marlon?" Cassidy asked. Their team had just won the homecoming game with Marlon making the winning touchdown.

"Hell yeah, we all coming!" The entire team barked and hooted. Marlon went home, showered, and dressed. Jeremiah and Jerome were going too. Jeremiah was a junior, and Jerome was a senior.

They pulled up to Cassidy's parents' mansion and the place was packed. They parked and got out. Once inside, they headed their separate ways to their own group of friends.

Cassidy sauntered over to Marlon and sat in his lap. He gently pushed her off.

"What are you doing Cassidy?"

"Just wanted to give a thank you to the reason we won tonight."

" A simple 'thank you' will suffice."

"Oh come on, live a little."

"Have you seen Maya?" he asked. She instantly became annoyed.

"No, I haven't seen her. What's the deal with you two anyway? Are y'all like, together?"

"Not that it's any of your business, but no, we aren't."

"Fuck buddies?"

"What's with the questions?"

"I'm just trying to understand how you have all of this in front of you, yet you are sitting here wondering about someone who isn't even your girlfriend, nor does she look half as good as me."

"Cassidy, I'm not trying to be rude, but I'm not interested and never have been, nor will I ever be. Now, I'm thirsty, please point me towards the drinks." A smile crept across her face.

"You know what, I'll get you that drink," she offered, walking away. The rest of the team laughed as she went into the kitchen. A few minutes later she came back with his drink in a red cup.

"Thank you, Cassidy," he said.

"You're welcome." She walked away. Thirty minutes later, Marlon all of a sudden felt rage and his dick was so hard it hurt. His vision was blurred and he couldn't walk straight. He leaned against a wall until a few people came over and helped him. He assumed they were his teammates.

"Ya I fi funny," he slurred. No one said anything. They helped him up the stairs and into a dark room. He stumbled onto the bed.

"I bet his virgin ass wouldn't know what to do with that hard dick," a voice said.

"What?" he asked. His head was spinning and so was the room. His hand landed on something and he squeezed it. It was a breast.

"You like how my breast feels?" a voice asked.

"Umhm," he nodded.

"You want to see how this pussy feels?" the voice asked.

"Ya," he mumbled. He felt hands on him and he was then naked.

"Shove that hard dick in my pussy," the voice came again. He followed the direction of which the voice came. It was dark and he couldn't see anything anyway. He felt around and there was a naked woman lying in the bed next to him.

"That's right, show me what that dick can do."

He climbed on top of where the voice was coming from. Little did he know, it was one of Cassidy's friends who was kneeling beside a passed out Maya, giving Marlon a false sense of consensual sex. Marlon felt around and found the woman's pussy.

He shoved himself in and the woman screamed. He couldn't decipher if it was screams of pain or pleasure. Cassidy's friend put a hand over Maya's mouth to muffle the screams until Maya bit her.

"No! Stop! Stop!" Maya repeatedly screamed. Marlon felt rage in him and kept going. The woman he thought had been talking all the shit couldn't handle him, so he thought.

"Get off of me! Stop! You're hurting me!" He felt a sharp pain in his jaw and tasted blood. The lights came on, but his vision was still skewed.

"Marlon, what the fuck?!" Jeremiah said.

"Jeremiah, oo see I uckin dis bih?" Marlon slurred. His eyes then rolled back and he began foaming at the mouth and convulsing. He rolled off Maya and fell on the floor.

Maya rolled over and vomited. There was blood all over the bed. She looked up to see Cassidy smirking at her. Maya quickly grabbed her clothes and ran out the room. She didn't even notice Marlon.

11

Over the next week, Maya avoided everyone, and skipped school when it became too overwhelming. She even avoided Marlon. She didn't say a word to anyone about what happened, not even to Toni who wasn't there that night.

At lunch, she got her food and went into the bathroom. She heard some girls come in and the lock clicking. She stopped chewing.

"Come on out Maya," Cassidy chided. Maya didn't move. "We know you're in here." Tears started streaming down her face. She was trapped. Suddenly, the door to the stall flew open, and she dropped her tray. Two girls grabbed her and pulled her out the stall.

"Aww little Maya finally got her cherry popped, and by her best friend," Cassidy teased.

"What are you talking about?" Maya whispered. Cassidy held her phone out. There was a video playing. At first Maya was confused until she recognized Marlon. Then she heard her own voice screaming for him to stop, and he didn't.

Horror, disbelief, and embarrassment had Maya frozen in place. Bile crept up and she vomited all over the floor. She remembered being raped but not that it was Marlon. She ran out the bathroom and down the hall. Marlon tried to stop her but she kept going. She didn't stop until she reached her house.

Marlon hadn't talked to Maya since the day of the party. She didn't return his calls or messages. When he would go to her house, her mom always said she was busy, which was unlike her.

After school, he headed to her house. He was going to make her talk to him. He pulled up in the driveway and shut the engine off. He walked to the door and noticed it was cracked. He looked around to see if anyone was looking before he entered.

Marlon walked in and saw a pool of blood on the floor of the foyer. He took his gaze up, in utter fear of what he was going to see. His eyes were fixed on Maya's which were bulging out of her head. Her wrists were slit and she was hanging from a rope, still jumping and moving.

He couldn't move. He couldn't think. All feeling left his body. He felt people rushing in passed him and loud screams. Everything else went black after that.

Present Day

Marlon woke up with a raging headache and to bright, white lights. He looked around and realized he was in a hospital. He tried to move his arms, but they were restrained.

"Easy, baby," he heard his mother say.

"Ma? Where am I?" he croaked. She grabbed the cup off the tray next to his bed and held the straw to his mouth. He drank for a while until his throat no longer felt like sandpaper. “Where am I, and why am I restrained?”

“You’re at Kingwood Pines Hospital,” she said softly.

“I’m at a mental hospital?! Ma, please tell me what happened. Where’s Maya?” She sighed as she looked into his pleading eyes.

“You had a mental breakdown sweetheart. Over the past couple of months, you have been having episodes like you did back then when you found Maya, and after you found out why she tried to kill herself.”

“Ma, please. Tell me everything.”

“Alright,” she said, bringing her chair closer. “After it happened, your brothers took you to the hospital and called me and your father. We rushed over, and the doctors said you were lucky that Cassidy didn’t give you even a sliver more of that drug cocktail than she did. They said they had never seen anyone be able to regain full function of everything after experiencing a seizure like you did.

So, your brothers then told us what happened when they walked in. That’s also when the video surfaced of you raping Maya. What Cassidy forgot was that her parents set up hidden cameras around the house, and she was caught slipping something in your drink. That’s why she was arrested. “

“Maya, Ma.”

"Baby, I'm getting there. Maya stayed in a mental hospital about as long as you did. When she found out that you had been drugged, she didn't want to press charges, and her parents didn't either. They knew you could ever do anything like that, willingly. As time went on, you kept having these episodes of nightmares that caused really bad seizures. Baby, we tried everything to help you. We finally settled on shock therapy. That was the last resort. We knew the risks, which included a certain extent of memory loss.

And it worked. For many years. Once we realized you had no recollection of that night, Maya made us promise to never bring it up, and that if you did somehow get that memory back, she would be the one to explain it to you."

"Where is she?" he sobbed.

"Maya, decided it was best that she remove herself from the situation."

"Tell me she didn't..."

"No, Marlon, no. She's fine. She just moved to the east coast."

"How long have I been here?"

"Two months."

His shoulders shook as he cried. Moriah held him in her arms and cried with him.

12

Just then, his brothers came in to relieve Moriah. They all pulled up a chair around him.

"Why didn't y'all tell me?" Marlon asked.

"Mar, like we said, it wasn't our story to tell," Mehki began. "Maya didn't want your friendship to be ruined, so she made us promise that she would tell you when the time came. We never thought that Cassidy would come back around and do what she did. And we banked on you never remembering."

"Well, I do remember. Every single detail. Her screams, the blood, the rage, the pain. Everything. I guess in between episodes, I've been having flashbacks in the form of dreams. How could I do that to her?"

"It wasn't you," Jeremiah explained. "It was the drugs. Cassidy really fucked you up."

"How is it that I've gone all these years without an episode?"

"I guess she was a trigger," Jerome said. "It could also explain why you felt drawn to her and then felt drawn to have sex with Maya."

"She must hate me."

"No, she doesn't. Marlon, that woman is so

in love with you that she moved away so as to not keep triggering you. Believe us Brother, she does not blame you for any of it," Mehki assured.

They all sat there in silence. Marlon felt sick to his stomach that he could even do that. And now she's gone.

"How long do I have to stay here?" he asked.

"Well, since it is the longest you have been coherent since you've been here, and the longest you haven't been belligerent, the counselor wants to do an evaluation today," Jeremiah said.

"We'll let you get some rest," Jerome said as they stood up.

"Can y'all stay? Please?" His brothers nodded in agreement and sat back down.

A couple of hours later, the restraints were removed and he was able to take a shower and put on his own clothes. He went down to the counselor's office for his evaluation.

"Good afternoon, Marlon," Dr. Wisp said.

"Morning Doc," he responded as he sat down.

"I hear you started to remember what happened."

"Yeah, but I wish I hadn't. I feel like such a horrible person.

"I get that you may feel that way, but just know, none of it was your fault. They didn't even take you to trial because they knew the side effects of the drugs and as much as you had in your system, no one held you at fault. When I evaluated you..."

"You were my doc back then?"

"I was." Marlon put his face in the palm of his hands.

"Why don't I remember?"

"One of the side effects of shock therapy is to erase certain memories. I guess due to the extensiveness of it, it erased other parts."

"Will I ever get all of my memories back?"

"Seeing as how you've regained the most tragic memories, I'd say, over time, other memories will come back."

"Doc, I need to go. I have to get to Maya."

"Marlon, be patient with the process. We need to focus on getting you better."

Over the next couple of weeks, Marlon saw Dr. Wisp every day. He progressed rapidly and cooperated with all of the doctor's exercises. He was released the following week and was scheduled to see Dr. Wisp once a week for now.

Marlon walked into his house and saw no remnants of Maya. She had truly gone. He called her several times and texted, but she didn't respond. He wasn't cleared to fly just yet, so he went to the office to get some work done, to try to get his life back to normal.

In his office he found flowers, balloons, cards, stuffed animals, and all sorts of get well gifts. He sat at his desk and went through them he teared up at how much he was missed.

The last card he opened smelled of Maya. He tore open the envelope and pulled out the card.

Dear Marlon,

By the time you're reading this, I will already be in Boston. After your third episode, I had to leave. I knew I was triggering them. I felt it was best if I moved and let you heal. Marlon, I don't hate you nor do I blame you for anything. I love you with all that I have, and I'm sure our daughter will too.

When you found me, after I tried to kill myself, I didn't realize it would affect you like it did. When Cassidy showed me the video, I was hurt. I couldn't believe you would do that to me. After spending months in the psych ward, my mom came in and explained what Cassidy had done to you.

Baby, I swear I didn't know. That's why I didn't press charges. I knew deep down that you would never hurt me, but in that moment, in that bathroom, I thought the worst of you. You were the last person I ever thought that would hurt me.

I hope you forgive me for leaving. When I give birth, I will be sure to call you prior to. You can see our daughter whenever you like. I won't keep her from you. Marlon, I love you. Always have, and always will.

Love always,

Maya

Marlon stared at the card. Maya was pregnant. He hadn't noticed that Jeremiah had walked in.

"Hey, brother. We weren't expecting you to be back so soon."

"She's pregnant," Marlon whispered in disbelief.

"Maya?"

"Yes, and I'm going to have a daughter."

"Congrats bro!"

"I need to get to Boston." Marlon stood up and rushed out of the office.

"Marlon, but you aren't cleared to fly!" Jeremiah yelled, running after him.

"Then come with me!" Marlon yelled back.

"Kamaria is going to kick my ass!" Jeremiah groaned as they got in the car.

"Tell her that it's my fault." They sped to the airport. Marlon had called the pilot on the way there to have the small private jet ready. Once they boarded, Marlon called his counselor.

"Doc, I know I'm not cleared to fly, but I just found out I have a daughter on the way."

"Marlon, where are you? Are you alone?"

"I'm on our private jet. No, I am not alone. Jeremiah is with me." He heard the doctor let out a breath of relief.

"I wouldn't typically advise this, but since you have one of your brothers with you, I will accept it, but only this once."

"Thanks Doc." Marlon hung up and looked at Jeremiah who was shaking his head.

"You think I'm crazy?"

"Not at all."

"Then why are you shaking your head?"

"Because never did we think it would take this long and through these extremities for you to finally be with Maya. I'm just glad I'm here to witness it."

13

Maya stood in the mirror and looked at her reflection. She had a small bump, but it was definitely noticeable. She never thought she'd end up being a single parent, or that she would have a baby by the man she has always loved, yet they couldn't be together. She put on her little black dress and some heels.

Toni was in town visiting and wanted to go to some fancy, expensive restaurant.

"Ready?" Toni asked, coming in.

"Yep." They headed out to the awaiting limo. Toni kept looking at her phone and smiling, sending texts back and forth.

"Who has your attention?" Maya asked.

"Oh, no one."

"That isn't a "no one" type of smile."

"In due time, I will tell you."

"Sneaky hoe," Maya teased.

They pulled up to the restaurant and the driver opened their door.

"I don't know why we spent money on a limo when we could've just drove my car," Maya said. Toni rolled her eyes and took her friend's hand. They walked to the door where a man in a suit stood.

"Good evening, Ms. Maya Green and Ms. Toni Harte." He opened the door as Maya stood there confused.

"How does he know our names?" she asked. "Toni, what's going on?" Toni ignored her and walked inside. She stopped short. "Why did you stop?" Maya saw the smile on Toni's face and then followed her gaze. She gasped at the sight before her. Her parents were there along with Marlon's parents, brothers, and their wives. There was a banner that read, "Be my wife." Toni moved to the side as Marlon came up behind Maya on bended knee.

"Baby, turn around." Maya slowly turned and started shaking from crying.

"Marlon," she sobbed.

"Maya, I love you, and I wouldn't want anything more than to make you my wife and raise our daughter and future children together. I know we went through hell to get here, but I am not letting this chance of true happiness escape me, again. I'm not saying it's going to be perfect, and I may still have some episodes, but I remember everything now. I know I can control it. You protected me from ever knowing any of what happened, and I know that's nothing but love. All these years you stood by me, through failed relationship after failed relationship, and you knew we were meant to be together. You knew I loved you, but you couldn't risk me rehashing those memories for fear of what would happen.

I have loved you since we first met in the sandbox. And I will love you until we are in a fancy casket box. I am not leaving here until you are my wife."

"Marlon," she whispered, looking into his tear filled eyes. "Yes, baby. I will be your wife." He put the ring on her finger and pulled her into a hug as everyone cheered.

They enjoyed the party with their friends and family. Maya's parents welcomed Marlon with open arms, and reassured him how much they loved him.

Back at Maya's condo, they lay in bed.

"How did you pull this off?" she asked.

"Well, on the flight here, I called your dad and asked for his permission. He agreed and I had him and your mother board a jet with my family. Trust, it wasn't easy to have everyone drop everything last minute, but we have a lot of people who love us and have been waiting on us." He rubbed her baby bump with his hand and then leaned down to kiss it.

"Marlon, are you sure about this?"

"Maya, please stop asking me that. I am positive. I don't think we will get any more chances at this than now." He parted her legs and watched her eyes roll back and her lips part as he slid deep inside her.

"Marlon!"

He sucked on her neck and gave her deep

stroke after deep stroke. She dug her nails into his back, and they made love the rest of the night.

A MESSAGE FROM THE AUTHOR

Thank you for rocking with me through this series. I can't believe how well it was received. When I first thought about writing this series and releasing each book in October of 2020, I thought I was crazy, but apparently it was my calling. Stay on the lookout for more reads from me in the very near future. Follow me on all social media platforms to stay up-to-date on new releases.

Made in the USA
Middletown, DE
28 March 2022

63286063R00199